Elementary, She Read

Also Available by Vicki Delany

Year Round Christmas Mysteries

We Wish You a Murderous Christmas
Rest Ye Murdered Gentlemen

Lighthouse Library Mysteries (as Eva Gates)

Reading Up a Storm
Booked for Trouble
By Book or By Crook

Constable Molly Smith Mysteries

Unreasonable Doubt
Under Cold Stone
A Cold White Sun
Among the Departed
Negative Image
Winter of Secrets
Valley of the Lost
In the Shadow of the Glacier

Klondike Gold Rush Mysteries

Gold Web
Gold Mountain
Gold Fever
Gold Digger

Fiction

More than Sorrow
Burden of Memory
Scare the Light Away

Elementary, She Read

A SHERLOCK HOLMES BOOKSHOP MYSTERY

Vicki Delany

CROOKED
LANE

NEW YORK

Published in the United States by Crooked Lane Books, an imprint of The Quick Brown Fox & Company LLC.

Crooked Lane Books and its logo are trademarks of The Quick Brown Fox & Company LLC.

Library of Congress Catalog-in-Publication data available upon request.

ISBN (hardcover): 978-1-68331-096-9
ISBN (ePub): 978-1-68331-097-6
ISBN (Kindle): 978-1-68331-098-3
ISBN (ePDF): 978-1-68331-099-0

Cover design by Louis Malcangi.
Cover illustration by Joe Burleson.
Book design by Jennifer Canzone.

Printed in the United States.

www.crookedlanebooks.com

Crooked Lane Books
34 West 27th St., 10th Floor
New York, NY 10001

First Edition: March 2017

10 9 8 7 6 5 4 3 2 1

To Mom

Chapter 1

The Great Detective eyed me.

I eyed him back. "Don't give me any of your cheek, you." I gave him a swipe across his exceedingly prominent nose with the feather duster.

"Talking to him again, Gemma?" said a voice behind me. "You know what they say about conversing with inanimate objects."

"He does give me the creeps, this one," I said. "He always seems to be watching me. And not in an approving way." The clay bust of Christopher Lee as Sherlock Holmes got another pass with the duster before I turned to greet the new arrival.

Jayne Wilson struggled to get through the shop door carrying a large box. With a grateful sigh, she dropped the box onto the table in the center of the room. "Scored! Big time."

My sigh wasn't so grateful. "Not more junk."

"How many times do I have to tell you, Gemma? This is not junk. This is valuable memorabilia."

I put down the feather duster and approached the table. Jayne carefully unfolded the cardboard flaps. Out of a mound of bubble wrap, she extracted a teapot. She shoved aside a stack of books waiting to be shelved and put the pot down. Next came a matching cream pitcher and sugar bowl. She stepped back to admire the new purchases. "Isn't it perfect?"

"Perfect." I refrained from adding, "In its hideousness."

The teapot and accessories were made of quality bone china and in excellent condition. Not so much as a crack or chip that I could see on a quick inspection. The decoration on the pot was of a hook-nosed man in a deerstalker hat peering through a magnifying glass, a pipe clenched firmly in his teeth. The accompanying cream pitcher and sugar bowl were adorned with smaller versions of the hat, pipe, and magnifying glass.

Jayne beamed. "Marg McKenzie found it when she was on vacation in Halifax and got it for us. I paid her back, of course, because I'd asked her to be on the lookout for this sort of thing. It's for the tea room, not for sale, so hands off, Gemma."

"How much did it cost?" I ventured to ask.

"Price is no object."

"Price is always an object," I replied. "And an excessively large one."

She didn't bother to answer the question, thus confirming my suspicions. "My customers adore using this sort of thing. If I can get a few more of them, I'm thinking of putting specialized cream teas on the menu. 'The Sherlock Special.' 'Irene Adler's Tea Party.' That sort of thing."

"Holmes never had a cream tea," I said.

"A minor point. If he wasn't so busy dashing around London or heading off to the 'smiling and beautiful countryside,' he would have. I bet Watson's wife made him a proper after-noon tea all the time. When he wasn't helping Sherlock, that is." She began repacking the items. "Haven't you got dusting to do or something?"

"I always have dusting to do. I never seem to stop dusting."

"Cheerio!" she said, heading for the door connecting my shop to the tea room next door. I watched her go with a smile. The word that best describes my friend is petite. The second best would be pretty. She has shiny blonde hair, bright-blue eyes, a wide mouth containing perfect teeth, a pointed chin, and a heart-shaped face. She is short and fine-boned and works hard at keeping herself in good shape. She comes up to my shoulder. I am not small, blonde, or delicate, and I have always felt like an awkward lump standing next to Jayne. I love her dearly.

Jayne also likes to pretend she's English. I am English, but after more than five years in Massachusetts, even I don't say things like "Cheerio!" anymore. Not that I ever did.

I went back to my dusting. There's always a lot of dust-ing in a shop like this one. I am the half owner, manager, head shop clerk, and chief duster of the Sherlock Holmes Bookshop and Emporium in the Cape Cod town of West London, Massachusetts. As well as reprints of the original Sir Arthur Conan Doyle books, we carry new books representing anything and everything in the pastiche or vaguely derived from the Holmes legend. From Laurie R. King's Mary Russell (a.k.a. Mrs. Holmes) mystery series to *The Curious Incident of the Dog in the Nighttime* to *Holmes for the Holidays* and all the myriad short story collections inspired by the canon. At the moment, I have a first edition of *The Sign of the Four* for sale, but it's not worth much because of its condition. I suspect that at one time a mouse attempted to use some of the pages for her nest. I bought it for a pittance, carefully wrapped it in plastic, and stuck on a tag showing a minimal price as well as one explaining its condition. Someday, someone will buy it. I can still be surprised at what a dedicated follower of Sherlock will consider a treasure. Once in a while my uncle Arthur will locate original books in reasonable condition, as well as copies of the *Strand Magazine*, in which many of the stories first appeared, but we don't deal in rare and valuable editions. That's not our business.

Because not everyone (certainly not me!) wants to read about Holmes all the time, one wall of shelves is labeled "gaslight" and features novels or anthologies, mysteries mostly, set in the late Victorian or early Edwardian period. Another shelf is for nonfiction, including biographies of writers of the age, anyone and everyone Sir Arthur Conan Doyle might have bumped into in his travels, as well as histories of the times in which Sir Arthur lived.

Books are my first (and, I sometimes think, my only) love, and my intention when I came to America to take over Great Uncle Arthur's business was to continue to run this place as a bookstore featuring Conan Doyle, his contemporaries, and modern books influenced by them. But I quickly came to realize that these days, as everyone knows, Sherlock Holmes is far more than books, so we branched out into all forms of Sherlockania. I have tried to keep our stock dignified, but what I call "junk" and Jayne calls "memorabilia" began creeping onto the shelves as of day one.

The shop now sells movie posters; DVDs of the movies; collectables, such as the aforementioned bust of Christopher Lee; and even mugs, towels, and dishcloths. First thing this morning, only a few minutes before I started dusting, I unloaded—I mean, *sold*—a life-sized stand-up cutout of Benedict Cumberbatch as Sherlock along with a full-color illustrated book on the making of the contemporary BBC series.

As well as the Bookshop and Emporium, Uncle Arthur and I own half of the business next door. Jayne owns the other half and runs the place. We call it Mrs. Hudson's Tea Room.

The bell over the door tinkled, and I glanced toward it. Then I glanced again.

The man standing there was definitely worth a second look. He was tall and lean, with deep-brown eyes, a strong jaw showing a hint of stubble, chiseled cheekbones, and a mass of brown hair curling around his ears in the damp sea air. He wore Italian loafers, khaki Dockers, and a blue-checked shirt with the top two buttons undone. His clothes were clean but not new, and the trousers could have done with the touch of an iron. He gave me a smile that practically lit up the room.

"Hi," I croaked. "I mean, welcome. If I can help you with anything, let me know."

"Thanks," he said. "Nice cat."

The creature to which he was referring was Moriarty, the shop cat. Moriarty had roused himself from his morning nap and was rubbing himself against the man's legs.

"Uh," I said.

The man gave Moriarty a pat on the head and then straightened up again. The cat meowed for more attention. "Quite the place you have here."

"We're all Sherlock, all the time."

"You're from England, right?"

I nodded.

"The heart of London, I detect."

"You have a good ear." Most Americans can't distinguish one regional English accent from another. Or even Scottish from Irish or Welsh from English.

"I've spent quite a lot of time in the UK," he said. I smiled, but I didn't reply that I could tell. I also have a good ear. His accent told me he was from Boston, educated at a private school or a very good public one, and his education had been completed in England. He wandered around the shop, followed closely by Moriarty. When the man stopped to examine the shelf containing games and puzzles, the cat jumped up. Moriarty almost smiled; I didn't know he could do that. The man scratched behind the feline's ear. Moriarty purred. He was small and thin, despite the prodigious quantities of kibble he consumed, and pure black except for his amber eyes. "Friendly little guy. What's his name?"

"Moriarty."

He laughed. That is, the man laughed, not the cat.

"Let me know if I can help you with anything." I returned to my dusting. The man spent a couple of minutes idly looking at the Holmes and Watson chamber pot (which I suggest using as a planter), leafing through the movie posters, and examining the DVD collection. It was obvious by the way he barely looked at the objects he was pretending to be interested in that tasteless chamber pots and movie memorabilia were not the reason for his visit. His eyes wandered constantly to the bookshelves. The Holmes shelves, not the gaslight or nonfiction.

Eventually, he oh-so-casually drifted over.

"Are you looking for anything in particular?" I asked.

"Nope. Just browsing." He picked up the first-edition *The Sign of the Four*. "Too bad this is damaged."

"It's a tragedy. But I get new stock in all the time. Occasionally, I have some second edition books in moderately good condition."

"Is that so," he said, moving on to the bound collections of the *Strand Magazine*.

"I can take your name if you like. Keep you posted if I hear of anything."

He turned to face me. That smile again. "Good idea."

"I do a mail-order business, too," I said. I wasn't digging to find out where he lived. Really, I wasn't. I didn't know anything about him other than he was a native New Englander, had enjoyed a comfortable childhood, was educated at an Ivy League college, had spent several years in the UK (probably around Oxford, as either a postgraduate student or junior professor), and was not here as a casual tourist. He was not wealthy but not struggling either. And unlikely to be married.

"I've recently moved to West London," he said.

"Welcome," I said. It was a mild spring day, and earlier a strong breeze had been blowing in from the ocean. But the temperature in the shop was climbing rapidly.

"What came first?" he asked. "The store or the address?"

"They do go together, don't they? This was formerly a hardware store, but my great uncle bought it for the address. 222 Baker Street, West London, New England."

He smiled. I felt myself smiling back. I momentarily forgot myself and extended my hand to stroke Moriarty.

In return the cat hissed and scratched my left arm. It hurt.

Uncle Arthur had found the starving, abandoned kitten in the alley behind the shop two years ago and lured him in with a dish of cream and sweet words. Moriarty's lived here ever since. He's a great shop cat; everyone loves him, and he loves everyone in return.

Everyone except me. I try not to take it personally. Other animals seem to like me just fine. Maybe he misses Uncle Arthur and blames me for taking his place. Still, I keep trying to make nice.

"I'm Grant, by the way. Grant Thompson." He held out his hand.

I took it in mine and we shook. "Gemma Doyle."

"Doyle?"

"A distant relation, or so my family says."

"There's a story there," he said with a grin. "And I'm going to hear it one day. But for now, here's my card." He handed me a small square of stiff cream paper. "Is the place next door strictly a tea room? I haven't had lunch yet, but I'm not much of a tea person."

"Surely at Oxford you got accustomed to tea?" I said. Was I flirting? Why, I think I might have been.

"How did you know I went to Oxford?"

I waved my hand in the air. "You picked up a trace of an accent." That, plus an educated guess on my part; he might have gone to Cambridge.

"You're very observant, Gemma Doyle."

"Am I? I don't think so."

"I did my PhD at Oxford, yes. Never did care for tea, but I learned to love a good British pub."

"Mrs. Hudson's specializes in cream teas and afternoon teas," I said. "But we do sandwiches and salads for lunch, and good old American muffins and bagels in the morning. Coffee, lattes, and cappuccinos too."

"I might give it a try then. Catch you later, Gemma."

Moriarty jumped off the counter. Tail high, he followed Grant to the door that led to the tea room. He was, of course, forbidden from going where food was served, and so he sat by the door gazing wistfully inside. He was small in size but gigantic in personality.

I wiped a drop of blood off the cat scratch on my arm. Then I flipped the card over. "Grant Thompson. Rare book collector." No street address, just an e-mail and phone number.

A hiss caught my attention. Jayne, dressed in a long white apron over a black T-shirt and denim capris, stood in the doorway. She pointed behind her to the restaurant, opened her eyes and mouth wide, and waved her hand as though it were on fire. Trust Jayne to notice every handsome man that came into her tea room.

Business was brisk for most of the day. It was the beginning of the tourist season on Cape Cod, and we'd placed ads in the visitors' brochures. Many of the mugs and toys moved, mostly the cheap stuff that appealed to laughing groups of college kids or parents with small children. In season, I always keep a good stock of paperbacks for beach and pool reading, and as the forecast for tomorrow said it would rain, the DVDs sold well too.

I kept half an eye on the tea room, and although Grant Thompson didn't appear again, I was pleased to see a steady stream of customers coming in for lunch and, later, to enjoy afternoon tea.

At twenty-two minutes to four every day, I go to Mrs. Hudson's for a much-needed tea break. Today, as I was alone in the shop, I hung a "Back in 15 Minutes" sign on the front door. The phone underneath the sales counter began to ring, but I didn't go back for it; voice mail would pick it up.

The tea room closes at four, and by this time it's normally almost empty. Jayne had done a great job decorating the place. The walls were papered in soft shades of sage green and peach, with white wainscoting. A portrait of Queen Elizabeth II was prominently hung on the back wall, among paintings of castles and thatched-roof cottages nestled in verdant pastoral landscapes. The wall adjoining the Emporium consisted of open shelves displaying row upon row of bone china teacups and teapots, while a multitude of jars of loose teas and locally made jams and preserves filled the space next to the swinging half door leading into the kitchen area.

I settled myself at my favorite table, a small one tucked into the window alcove. A bench seat was under the window, padded in soft fabric that matched the color of the walls, with two white-painted chairs opposite. A tiny white vase, containing a sprig of greenery and a single fresh flower, sat in the middle of the table. Fiona appeared, dressed in the tea room's waitress uniform: a knee-length black dress, black stockings, and a white apron with the Mrs. Hudson's Tea Room logo on it—a steaming teacup next to a pipe. She brought my drink in the new Sherlock Holmes pot.

As someone who owns the Sherlock Holmes Bookshop and Emporium, you'd think I'd be a Sherlock fanatic. I am not. I leave that to Jayne and Great Uncle Arthur.

I might not admire the decoration on the pot, but it was a proper china tea service and so would suffice. I let the tea steep for a few minutes and then poured it carefully. The rich, full scent of Darjeeling rose up to caress my nose. I breathed it in and then added a splash of milk to the golden liquid. Perhaps the hardest part of my entire job has been to teach Americans to make a proper cup of tea. I take great pride in the fact that I have succeeded, here at least.

I was enjoying my first welcome sip when Jayne dropped a plate in front of me and sat on the window bench. I selected a warm scone, sliced it open, and spread butter, clotted cream, and strawberry jam. "Good day?"

"Excellent." She took a salmon sandwich for herself. At twenty to four every day, we have our afternoon tea (consisting of whatever's left over) and discuss the day's business.

"I see Fiona had another fight with her husband," I said.

"She didn't tell me that. How do you know?"

"Wedding ring's off again."

Jayne leaned out and peered into the room. Fiona was sweeping the floor. "So it is," Jayne said. She turned back to me with a smile. "That big group's coming tomorrow."

"What big group?" I asked.

"I told you about them. Twenty-four ladies on a bridge group holiday, plus their guide."

I vaguely remembered something about it. I vaguely remembered promising something . . .

"You're helping in the kitchen."

Oh, right. That was it. "Why am I doing that?"

"Because they're coming at four, our usual closing time, and Fiona had committed to picking up her sister's kids at play group at four fifteen. I'm taking Jocelyn out of the kitchen and having her serve, with my help."

"Can't you prepare the food ahead of time?"

"Gemma! We discussed this. I will do all the prep I can, but I have a restaurant and tea room to run the rest of the day, remember?"

"Why don't I wait tables? That way you'll be able to stay in the kitchen."

"Because you'll drop one of the three-tiered glass trays, scattering my precious baking all over the floor, or you'll spill tea down an elderly lady's new silk shirt. The one she bought specifically for this holiday."

"That only happened once."

"Twice."

"Once each."

She rolled her eyes. Okay, so I'm not a very good waitress. I'm not much of a cook either, but I can slap a couple of pieces of bread together to make a sandwich. Provided, that is, Jayne tells me what to put in the middle.

I popped the last piece of scone into my mouth. Then I stuck my finger in the small pot of clotted cream, scooped out the remains, and sucked cream off my finger while Jayne rolled her eyes again. "Business meeting over?" I asked.

"Not yet. I'm about to run into a problem with one of my suppliers."

"What sort of problem?"

"Ellie McNamara's handing her farm over to her daughter, and I'm worried about that. I get most of my berries from them. I need to find a new supplier, and fast. You know I try to source everything as locally as possible."

"Leave it to me. I heard something the other day about a new operation out near Sandwich."

"Thanks. Before you go, you did ask Ruby to work tomorrow afternoon, didn't you?"

"I did." *I think.*

"Then we're all set." Jayne leaned back in her chair, signaling that we were now moving from business-partner to friend mode. "Did you notice that dream of a guy who came in around noon?"

"No," I said.

"Liar. What was he looking for?"

"Books. First edition, good condition. And very interested too, although he pretended not to be."

"You don't stock books like that."

"No, but Uncle Arthur does sometimes come across something rare. I took his card and said I'd let him know if I found something."

"You have contact info. Good work, Gemma."

"It's a business transaction."

"That can change."

Time to change the subject. "Do you have plans for tonight?"

"I'm going to hit the gym when I finish up here, and later Robbie and I are going to McGillivray's Pub to hear some live music."

I tried not to let my disapproval show. Fortunately, Jayne was finishing the last of her tea and not looking at me.

Jayne was my best friend as well as my business partner, but she had the world's worst taste in men. Every time she found a new boyfriend, I figured it couldn't get any worse. And every time, it did. Not that her boyfriends were violent or of the criminal element. Nothing like that. But they seemed to have problems finding—and keeping—regular employment. In a thriving tourist town in season, that was a difficult thing to accomplish. Robbie was an artist, as Jayne's boyfriends usually were. The sensitive, creative sort. The sort, Jayne always patiently explained to me, who couldn't be lumbered with the tedious monotony of a regular job, as they had to be ready to leap into the act of creating art whenever the muse happened to strike. I might have mentioned once that Picasso was said to have remarked that inspiration comes when you are working. Jayne reminded me that Picasso hadn't *always* been famous.

"What about you?" she said. "Want to come with us? We're going to have dinner before the show."

I got to my feet. "No thanks. I have a wild night planned in the company of Violet and a good book." Violet is Uncle Arthur's dog. "I better get back at it. See you tomorrow."

"Be here at three o'clock. I need you in the kitchen, Gemma. Don't forget."

"As if I ever forget."

"Did you call Ruby to remind her of the extra shift?"

"Why? Oh right."

Jayne dug in the pocket of her apron. "Never mind. I'll do it."

Chapter 2

A kitchen is not my natural environment, but the following afternoon found me in the back of the tea room as ordered, ready to help out.

"It would look more appealing if you mixed the offerings up a little," I said.

"No, Gemma, it would not."

"We can tuck the circular sandwiches around the scones, and the square sandwiches in with these small brownies, that way you'd have consistency of shape."

"I don't want consistency of shape. I want sandwiches on the bottom tier, scones in the middle, and the tarts and cookies on the top. That's the way afternoon tea has been served since time immemorial."

"Actually, afternoon tea isn't a long-standing tradition. It's generally considered to have begun around 1840 when Anna, Duchess of Bedford . . ."

"Gemma, stop talking. Butter that bread. The smoked salmon spread and the chicken salad are already prepared. The cucumbers, watercress, and herbs are sliced. All you have to do is put the sandwiches together. Follow the assembly instructions I prepared, and cut them according to the design I printed out for you. When they're ready, cover them in plastic wrap. Got it?"

"I am capable of making sandwiches." I glanced around the busy kitchen. "Do you have a ruler?"

"What do you need a ruler for?"

"It says here that the cucumber sandwiches are to be two inches long by three quarters of an inch wide. A ruler would ensure accuracy."

"Roughly, Gemma. Roughly is good enough."

"Very well." I set about cutting the crusts off the white sandwich bread slices laid out before me. Jayne began rolling out the dough for another batch of strawberry tarts. The tea room had been exceptionally busy all day, she said, meaning they'd had to serve some of the food she'd prepared for the big group due to arrive at four. At the moment, Jocelyn was washing dishes and Fiona was arranging pots of tea for a table of six who'd just come in.

I, of course, had neglected to ask my shop assistant, Ruby, to work today. Mondays and Tuesdays were her days off. She told Jayne she couldn't possibly come in at the last minute. So Jayne had offered her double time and a half. Jayne was not happy with me.

I was rather enjoying this making of sandwiches. Like a well-oiled machine, I went down the row buttering the crustless slices of bread (lightly), back up the row adding an ice-cream scoop of chicken salad, down the row sprinkling on pretty green herbs, back up the row putting the tops on, and finally slicing them into triangles.

"Those have got to be the neatest sandwiches I've ever seen," Fiona said.

"Thank you," I said. Next up: the smoked salmon spread, which would be rolled into pinwheel shapes.

At five minutes to four, I had assembled and sliced one hundred sandwiches, the scones were warming in the oven, and the last of the tiny lemon tarts were cooling on the counter. The dishes were washed, the pots of clotted cream and strawberry jam laid out on the tray, the huge kettles boiling.

"Got any plans for tonight, Gemma?" Jocelyn leaned against the counter, enjoying a brief moment of quiet before the tea-loving hordes descended. Jocelyn was in her midtwenties but already had three school-aged kids. She adored those children (if not her husband, a regular—or so I've been told—at many of our town's drinking establishments), but she noticeably pined for her lost youth and all the fun times she thought we single women were having without her. This time, I didn't have to make up a story about planning a wild night on the town.

"Uncle Arthur's leaving tomorrow for who knows where, and I'd like to spend some time with him before he goes. I never know how long it will be before he comes home again. That reminds me. I said I'd treat him to dinner out. I'd better take care of that now . . ."

"Dinner in a nice restaurant," Jocelyn said dreamily. "With an adult. How wonderful that must be."

I took out my phone and texted my friend Andy White-hall to make a reservation for dinner. Andy owned the Blue Water Café, one of the most popular places in town. It sat at the edge of the boardwalk and extended out over the water. The fresh seafood and traditional New England cooking were as fabulous as the view. "Now," I said, putting the phone away again, "where were we?"

Before Jocelyn could answer, my phone beeped with an incoming text. Out it came once more.

Andy: *Gemma! Not again. You have to call earlier. We're full to the rafters tonight.*

Me: *Sorry. I'll be with U. Arthur. He's leaving town tomorrow. Pls?*

Andy: *This is positively, absolutely the last time. Come at seven thirty. We'll find you a table.*

Me: *Thx.*

Fiona's head popped around the kitchen door. "A tour bus is coming down the street."

Jocelyn wiggled her shoulders and straightened her uniform skirt. Jayne took off her baking apron and put on the waitress one. Earlier, she'd slipped into the washroom to replace her jeans and T-shirt with a plain black knee-length dress cut into severe lines. "Show time. Now, Gemma, you remember what you have to do?"

"Sandwiches on the bottom, scones in the middle, pastries on the top. Sir! Yes, sir!" I saluted.

She did not smile. "Keep the kettle hot and the tea flowing."

"Good luck," Fiona said, heading out the back exit.

At that moment, the front door opened and an explosion of laughter and excited chatter filled the tea room.

Now that the guests had arrived, I didn't have all that much to do. The tour company had arranged for everyone to have the full afternoon tea, so there wouldn't be any individual orders, other than the tea itself. We offered a full menu of loose-leaf teas, and I had been given the heady responsibility of ensuring that the right blend got into the correct pot.

Once everyone had been served, my duties were over. I took off my apron and returned to the Emporium to prepare for the rush of customers when the women finished their tea. A couple of people were browsing, and Ruby was ringing up purchases. I gave the shop a quick glance before slipping behind the counter to help pop items into paper bags with our store logo on them.

"I'm going to have to reorder *The Beekeeper's Apprentice*," I said to Ruby. "I see you had a rush on it. As well as four of the boxed sets of the complete canon. And that hideous Robert Downey Jr. puzzle moved at long last. Nice to see the Jeremy Brett poster was sold, and three sets of playing cards and two of that Scotland Yard game." The game didn't actually have anything to do with Sherlock, but we pretended it did.

"The puzzle didn't sell," Ruby said. "I put the mugs on top of it."

I was horrified. "How many times have I told you, don't do that. How am I supposed to keep inventory if things are always moving around?"

"Most people these days keep their inventory on the computer," Ruby said.

"The computer is a functioning backup," I admitted. "The large group about to come in are bridge players. This once only, you can rearrange the displays so the playing cards and bridge sets are front and center."

"Got it," Ruby said. She flicked a lock of purplish-colored hair out of her eyes. She had intended the color to be deep red—ruby—but something had gone badly wrong. She'd only been working for me for two weeks, and I wasn't entirely comfortable with her yet. She seemed to always be watching me, more than I liked. Then again, maybe I just wasn't comfortable with having someone else working in my bookshop. In the winter, when business was slow, I enjoyed being in the shop by myself, watching the snow fall, tending to the occasional customer, and sometimes having time to settle into the reading chair by the window with the newest Laurie R. King or Rhys Bowen and a cup of tea. But summer hours are longer, and we're much busier, so it isn't possible for me to do everything on my own. Finding good temporary staff can be difficult, and I've heard some real horror stories from my fellow shop owners. At least Ruby always showed up on time and could count change. At her interview, she'd told me her father was a huge Sherlock fan and she'd grown up with the canon. I'd tested her with a few easy questions (Where had Dr. Watson served as an army doctor? The answer—Afghanistan) and she'd passed with flying colors. I'd hired her on the spot.

The women finished their tea and poured into the Emporium. They all looked much the same: five foot four to six, either thin but not excessively so or chubby but not fat, iron-gray or dyed-blonde hair, dressed in ugly but sensible shoes, beige shorts or capris, and T-shirts adorned with some sort of flower pattern. Their jewelry was subdued and tasteful. Several of them made a big fuss of the preening Moriarty, who'd emerged from his bed under the center table to accept the praise he thought of as his due. They smiled broadly and laughed heartily at each other's jokes. At a guess, this was one of the highlights of their trip: I couldn't imagine they were able to maintain this level of excitement all the time. Even

I had trouble keeping track of my stock the moment they hit the floor. They picked up everything, turned boxes over, put them back in the wrong place, showed their finds to their friends, exchanged items with each other.

But most of all, they bought. And oh, how they bought.

It was quite delightful.

I was wrapping up the Christopher Lee bust for a lady whose own bust could have stood on a pedestal when a woman came in off the street. She was in the same age range as the bridge players but clearly not part of this group. She was in her mid- to late sixties, about five foot two and very thin, with a prominent chin and a nose like a hawk. Her dark trousers and jumper looked to be too hot for the day, and a brown cotton scarf with tattered ends was tied loosely around her neck. Her gray hair was pulled back into an unkempt bun; her nails were chewed and the cuticles ripped. The jumper had a layer of dust on the shoulders and the right hem of the slacks was unraveling. The laces on her trainers (what Americans call "sneakers") dragged behind her. But for some reason, I didn't think she was a street person. Just a woman who was too tired to go through the motions anymore. Perhaps she'd been on a long, difficult journey or had suffered an emotional trauma.

She carried no handbag, only a generic white plastic bag with little in it.

"That high tea was great," the customer with the grand bust said to me. "I'll be telling all my friends about this place."

"What high tea?" I said. "Oh, you mean afternoon tea. You really shouldn't get those mixed up. High tea, sometimes just called tea, is what the working man calls his dinner, and afternoon tea is what you had."

She took her bag of purchases and whispered something to a friend that I didn't catch. I waved good-bye to Christopher Lee. Now that he was leaving, I might miss him.

Like many of the buildings on Baker Street, this one had started life as a home. Later, most of the interior walls on the main floor had been removed to make one big room. A set of steep stairs at the back leads to the second level, which contains my small office, an excessively crowded storage area, and an overflow storage room that also serves as the staff restroom. A sliding glass door has been cut in the east wall, leading directly into the tea room at 220 Baker Street.

The shop space is crammed full with bookshelves, display racks, and tables. A comfortable reading nook nestles by the front windows, with its cracked and worn brown leather wingback chair, a small pie-crust table, and a good lamp.

With the twenty-four women on the tour, their guide in her neat blue uniform shorts and matching T-shirt, and assorted other customers, I lost sight of the small woman almost immediately.

Ruby took the floor, walking through the crowd and asking if anyone needed help, while I staffed the cash register. The sets of playing cards ranged from reproductions of the original Strand illustrations to Benedict Cumberbatch as Sherlock and, as expected, we sold a lot of them. The Holmes and gaslight bookshelves were thoroughly picked over, the salt and pepper shakers decimated, the bone china thimbles gone. Only one of the women didn't seem to be having a marvelous time. She kept to herself, idly flipping through the books. Eventually, she selected a copy of *How to Think like Sherlock* by Daniel Smith and handed me her credit card. Her face was pinched, and I suspected her shoes were too tight.

Jayne had left Jocelyn to finish cleaning up the tea room and came in to give us a hand. "Do you have any more of volume two of *The Complete Sherlock Holmes*? I don't see it with the others and a customer wants to get both volumes."

"There are none upstairs," I said. "I saw one on the shelf when I came in from helping you with the tea. Ask Ruby if she moved it. She tends to do that."

"Where is Ruby? I don't see her around."

"Probably on what she thinks of as her break. What I call 'hiding out at the busiest time.'"

"That's a bit harsh, isn't it, Gemma? She did come in on her day off."

"For double time and a half. But I take your point. The perfect employee is unlikely to exist."

"Not in retail," Jayne said.

A woman placed a DVD of *Game of Shadows* on the counter. Jayne busted off to search for Volume II, and I asked the customer, "Have you seen this? A different interpretation of Sherlock, to be sure."

"I have seen it, and I didn't like it. It's a gift for my daughter who loves Robert Downey Jr."

Over the heads of the eager shoppers, I caught sight of Donald Morris, one of my regular customers. He pushed his way toward the counter, not looking at all happy. It took a lot to get Donald to discard his habitual houndstooth-check wool cape and deerstalker hat, but today he was dressed almost like a normal person. His black T-shirt proclaimed, "The Game's Afoot," and a gold-framed pin showing a silhouette of the Great Detective with his pipe was fastened to his chest. Donald was the president of the West London chapter of the Baker Street Irregulars. At the moment, Donald was the only member of that branch of the illustrious organization, as his dictatorial attitude and strict attention to the minutiae of the canon tended to discourage those with a more casual interest.

"You're busy today, Gemma," he said.

"Bus tour," I replied.

He sniffed in disapproval. "Has anything of interest come to your attention lately?"

"Donald, you know I'd contact you if it had." Donald had no interest in playing cards or teapots, but he was always on the lookout for Sir Arthur Conan Doyle books or the magazines in which the stories had originally appeared.

He glanced to one side and then to the other. A few of the contented shoppers were beginning to drift away. Jayne had located Volume II on a side table, and the customer left, happy with her purchase. Ruby had reappeared, and I made a mental note to talk to her about leaving the shop floor without permission.

At the moment, no one was in hearing range or paying us any attention. Donald leaned over the counter and dropped his voice. "Word's getting around that a particularly important edition of a *Strand Magazine* original is about to be released onto the market."

"Important in what way?" I asked.

"Signed by Sir Arthur."

"That would be worth locating." Original copies of the *Strand Magazine* in which the Holmes stories first appeared weren't rare, and for that reason, they weren't valuable. Not unless something, such as a signature or notation by Sir Arthur Conan Doyle, distinguished one from the rest. If that was the case, neither Donald nor I were likely to be able to afford it. I didn't mind—I wasn't a collector—but it would eat Donald alive to know that if a rare magazine did manage to come in range of his grasp, he didn't have the funds to buy it.

"Rumor has it a private collection of some significance is in the process of being disbursed. If you or Arthur hear something, Gemma," he said, tapping the side of his nose, "I'd appreciate a heads-up."

"Sure," I said. I didn't buy collectors' editions or sell them, but Uncle Arthur kept his ear to the ground, and he'd once or twice found a reasonably priced item for Donald.

"Ladies! Ladies!" The tour group leader clapped her hands and shouted to be heard above the chatter. "The bus is leaving in fifteen minutes. Please finish your purchases and make your way to the parking lot."

The rush to the checkout counter was on, and I didn't see Donald leave, nor did I see the small woman again.

"Wow!" Ruby said a few minutes later as we surveyed the decimated shop. "That was one bunch of determined shoppers."

"And eaters," Jayne said. "There wasn't so much as a crumb left for the resident mice." She rubbed Moriarty's head. "Not that we have any mice, do we, old fellow?"

Moriarty purred. I tentatively extended my own hand in a gesture of friendship. He narrowed his piercing amber eyes and hissed. I hastily withdrew my hand. I never learn.

"A good day, Gemma," Jayne said. "If you don't need me anymore, I'm off home."

"See you tomorrow."

She gave us a wiggle of her fingers and left.

"Let's try to get this stuff straightened up," I said to Ruby. "Some people have no respect for the proper placement of goods. I see we sold the entire collection of Jeremy Brett DVDs. Excellent. I'll order more tomorrow."

"Everyone says he was the best Sherlock," Ruby said, heading for the center table to attempt to restore some sort of order to the display.

I glanced around the shop, trying to make sense out of the chaos. As well as the Brett DVDs, I'd need to order more of *Mr. Holmes*, starring Ian McKellen, the playing card sets, thimbles, *The Mind Palace* coloring book, some of the Laurie R. King books, and *Echoes of Sherlock Holmes*, a recently published pastiche anthology.

As usual, customers had picked up books to read the inside cover or the first page and, finding it not to their liking, retuned them to the shelves in the incorrect place so that many were now out of alphabetical order. That would never do. Shaking my head, I set about organizing them. A book with fading red leather binding had been shoved in the middle of the bottom shelf. I could tell instantly it didn't belong there. That sort of leather binding should be with the historic books and magazines, not the current ones. I pulled it out. It had been slipped into a clear plastic wrapping. The binding was Morocco leather, adorned with gilt flourishes. *A Study in Scarlet* was embossed in ornate gold cursive on the cover. Judging by the thickness, it was probably not a book but a bound magazine. A common practice for preserving magazines of value—financial or otherwise—early in the twentieth century. It was old but at first glance seemed to be in good condition, with no obvious stains, discolorations, or tears. It certainly didn't belong to me. I pulled it out of the wrapping and flipped it open. A cold sweat ran down the back of my neck.

Beeton's Christmas Annual. 1887. The illustration on the original cover was of a man rising from a desk chair to switch on a lamp. The large headline read, *"A Study in Scarlet."* Smaller print said, "by A. Conan Doyle."

I was so shocked, I might have yelped.

Ruby came over to see what I was holding. "What's up?"

"I . . ." I leapt out of my skin as the door flew open.

"Sorry," Jayne said, "I forgot my . . . Are you okay, Gemma? You look like you've seen a ghost."

"I . . ."

"What have you got there?" Jayne said. "Did someone dare to file the second editions in with the modern books?" She plucked *Beeton's Christmas Annual* out of my hand. "Wow, this one is really old. It cost one shilling. I wonder how much that was."

"Ruby," I said, "lock the door."

"But it's only quarter to six."

"We're closing early today."

"You're the boss." She crossed the room, flipped the sign on the door, and turned the lock.

"You can take the rest of the day off," I said.

"Fifteen whole minutes? Thanks, but I can stay longer. Won't even charge you for my time." She leaned close to Jayne, attempting to get a good look at what she was holding.

I snatched the magazine back and snapped it shut. "Good night, Ruby."

She looked for a moment as though she might argue. But instead she said, "Okay, okay. I'm leaving. Night, Jayne."

"Good night, Ruby." Jayne gave me a questioning look. I touched my finger to my lips and held it there while we listened to Ruby's footsteps on the creaking old wooden floor, and then heard the back door open and close.

"Check the door's locked," I said.

"Gemma, are you going to tell me what's going on?"

"After you check the door."

"Okay, okay." She dashed off and was back a couple of seconds later. "All present and accounted for. My lady's castle is secured for the night."

"This isn't ours," I said, showing her the bound magazine.

"Are you sure? Sorry, foolish question. What do you suppose it's doing here?"

"That is the question." I opened it, slowly this time. "This looks like an original. The magazine, I mean. The leather binding would have been added later. If it is, and if it's in as good condition in the inside as appears from the cover, it might be quite valuable. *A Study in Scarlet* is the first Holmes story published, and it was first published in *Beeton's Christmas Annual* in December of 1887."

"Didn't you once tell me these magazines were so common they aren't of any monetary value?"

"This one is different."

"How valuable is it?"

"If it's intact and in good condition, it might be exceedingly valuable. Virtually priceless."

"Can you take a guess?"

"I never guess." I hurried to the computer. Jayne followed. I quickly found what I was looking for. "This is the most expensive magazine in the world. Only thirty-one copies are known to exist and many of them don't even have the front cover. In 2010, a copy signed by Sir Arthur Conan Doyle was offered for auction by Sotheby's London at four hundred thousand pounds. The highest price offered was two hundred and forty thousand, so it went unsold."

"How much is four hundred thousand pounds?"

As was my habit, I'd checked the business news over my breakfast. I calculated. "At the exchange rate as of this morning, that amounts to approximately six hundred twenty-eight thousand and forty-six dollars."

"Approximately," Jayne said.

"The rate of exchange varies throughout the day," I pointed out.

"For a magazine?"

"It didn't get that price," I said. "I'll investigate further to see if it sold at a later time, and for how much. In 2007, however, a copy that was not in excellent condition, having some minor repairs, sold for one hundred and fifty-six thousand dollars."

"Do you think this one is also signed?" Jayne said.

I'd placed the bound magazine on the counter while typing at the computer. We leaned over it. Moriarty jumped up and studied it also. I was prepared to put him on the floor, but he made no move to touch the precious object. "I don't dare turn the pages to find out," I said. "Judging by the thickness, it might be fully intact. Even having all the original pages of advertising will increase the value, although the Holmes story itself is the most important thing. We can see that it has the original cover, and it seems to be in good condition. A signature or some sort of writing by Conan Doyle would up the price considerably. We need to take this to a rare book dealer."

"Aren't you a rare book dealer?" Jayne asked.

"Not in the least," I said. "We carry what's generally available on the market. Second and later editions, reprints, occasionally some damaged firsts. I've never seen anything remotely of this quality. Or potential price."

"How did it come to be here?"

"That's the question, isn't it?" I said again.

I opened a drawer and pulled out a magnifying glass. I bent over the magazine and studied it in closer detail. As far as I could see, the paper didn't have a single flaw apart from natural aging. My quick reading of the web page that discussed sales of the magazine mentioned that even copies with missing or torn pages were worth a small fortune.

"What are we going to do?" Jayne asked.

"First, we're going to move it. It's far too valuable to leave lying around. The bank will be closed by now, so I'll put it in Uncle Arthur's safe overnight." I closed the binding and slipped the magazine back into its plastic wrapping.

"Arthur has a safe?"

"It came with the house. Next, we have to locate the owner. I find it impossible to believe she left it here by accident."

"Why do you say 'she'?"

I remembered the woman who'd come in while the bus group was here. She'd been carrying a plain white plastic bag, the type you get at any store to carry your purchases home. The object the bag contained had been about the size and weight of this magazine. She'd been swallowed by the crowd, and I had not seen her browsing, nor had I noticed her leave. Had she come here wanting to sell me the magazine and changed her mind for some reason? Perhaps she hadn't expected the shop to be so crowded and us to be so busy. In that case, why on earth would she leave the magazine behind and not just come back another time?

"I believe I saw her," I said.

"Do you know her?"

"Never seen her before."

"Then how can we possibly find her?"

I closed my eyes and mentally pulled up the scene. The woman, badly dressed, appearing down on her luck, not smiling, eyes darting around the room. I focused on the bag in her hand. It was made of thin opaque plastic, with no decoration or store logo printed on it. The contents, the magazine with the red binding, were a faint outline. But something else had been in the bag. A piece of paper of some sort, either small or folded over.

"Search for a bag," I said. "An ordinary store bag. White plastic. She took the magazine out of the bag it was in and slipped it onto the book rack in an attempt to conceal it. She might not have bothered to take the almost-empty bag away with her."

It didn't take us long to find what we were looking for. The bag had been shoved into the small trash container next to the sales counter.

While Jayne peered over my shoulder, I reached into the bag and pulled out a postcard. It showed a view of boats in West London Harbor, bobbing happily on the water on a sunny summer's day. I flipped the card over. Nothing was written on it, but it had been stamped "West London Hotel" with a phone number and address. I knew the place. Not one of the finer tourist accommodations in the area, but clean and inexpensive.

"I suggest," I said, "we pay a visit to the West London Hotel."

"Elementary, my dear Gemma," Jayne said.

"Sherlock Holmes never said that," I replied.

"Perhaps not, but Jayne Wilson did."

Chapter 3

Great Uncle Arthur is a wandering soul. He loves ships and the sea and all the places they take him to. He'd been desperate to join the Royal Navy during World War II, but to his intense disappointment, the war ended before he'd been old enough to enlist. He joined up as soon as he could and had a long and honorable career, eventually becoming captain of one of HRH's battleships. Arthur was my father's uncle, and although he rarely visited us over all the years I was growing up, I received a steady stream of postcards with colorful stamps from exotic and exciting places.

Arthur's passions in life were the sea and Sherlock Holmes. He was, so he maintained (although my father had his doubts), a distant cousin of Sir Arthur Conan Doyle himself. When he retired from the navy, he bought himself a sailboat and spent years wandering from one port to another. Eventually, in 2008, he found himself in West London, Massachusetts, looking at a "For Sale" sign blowing in near-hurricane winds next to a pretty little yellow two-story building at 222 Baker Street. He bought the building as well as a house by the harbor to live in and opened the Sherlock Holmes Book-shop. Great Uncle Arthur is a wonderful sailor, but not much of a businessman; 2008 wasn't a good year for independent bookstores, so the business didn't do very well. But he'd never married and had no children; he had his navy pension and life savings to provide a comfortable income. He'd been content for three years, spending as much time on his sloop, the *Irregular*, as at the shop. Then the wanderlust returned, and it returned with a vengeance. Uncle Arthur decided it was time to sell the store and move on, but he couldn't find a buyer.

At the time, I was living in London, where my husband and I owned a mystery bookstore near Trafalgar Square. People tell me I'm highly observant, but I wasn't observant enough to notice that my husband was having an affair with one of the part-time sales clerks—willful blindness perhaps. Until the day the other part-time clerk took me aside and told me I was being made a fool of.

My husband got the store and the clerk (good luck to her, and good riddance to him) and I got the value of my share of the business as well as half of our house. And a row house in central London isn't inexpensive. Uncle Arthur suggested I come to America to get a fresh start, and I jumped at the chance. I bought half the bookstore, keeping him as a silent partner. I meant to run it as a bookstore, the way Arthur intended, but I soon came to realize that books about Sherlock Holmes weren't enough to keep the store profitable. I changed the name to the Sherlock Holmes Bookshop and Emporium and started stocking Holmes-related knickknacks and collectables as well as books and magazines. I bought half of Uncle Arthur's house, too, and he kept rooms to use whenever he happened to be passing through. He's almost ninety now, and although his steps are getting slower and his hearing is fading, he can still be counted on to wake up one morning and decide he's off to Africa for a couple of months.

"Not a word to Uncle Arthur," I said to Jayne as we walked toward the harbor and my house. I'd put the magazine into an Emporium tote bag and clutched it firmly.

"Why not? He might be able to help." Jayne had lived in West London all of her life except for the years in which she'd owned a bakery in Boston. But she'd missed her beloved Cape Cod—waking up every morning to a view of the sea—and she'd missed living in a small town. She came home a year ago, just as the drugstore at 220 Baker Street was closing. It had been Arthur who'd introduced the two of us as well as the idea of Mrs. Hudson's Tea Room. Fortunately, the two buildings shared a wall, and it was an easy job to break through.

"I want to find out what we're dealing with first," I said.

"What do you think we're dealing with, Gemma?"

We came to the end of Baker Street and turned north to take the road that runs beside the small harbor. West London sits on the eastern shore of Cape Cod, with the Atlantic Ocean to the east and Nantucket Sound to the southwest, not far from the better-known town of Chatham. Restaurants overlooking the water spread out onto spacious patios, lined with pots of brilliant flowers and protected by colorful umbrellas. Lineups waiting for tables stretched down the sidewalk. The boardwalk on the far side of the road was crowded with people licking ice cream while they strolled and watched boats bobbing in the calm waters of the harbor and fisherman trying their luck from the pier. More tourists took pictures of the West London lighthouse, painted white with three thick red bands, built in 1821.

As we passed the Fish Market, which at this time of day displayed little more than crushed ice, I said, "I'm acting on the assumption that the woman, we will call her 'The Small Woman' for lack of a name, is aware of its value. Otherwise why attempt to hide it? She must be intending to come back for it at a later time."

"Isn't she taking a heck of a risk? Suppose someone wanted to buy it."

I suppressed a shudder. "And suppose I hadn't been there, and Ruby sold it for a dollar ninety-five? The need to hide the magazine must have been so vital, she was prepared to take that chance."

"But why there? Why the book rack of the Emporium?"

"Where would you hide a tree?" I asked.

"In a forest?"

"Precisely."

"You know the exact location of every tree in your forest, Gemma. If The Small Woman doesn't know you, she wouldn't know that. She must have thought it would be safely hidden. I wonder when she planned to come back and get it."

We left the row of restaurants and shops and headed up the gentle hill of Blue Water Place toward my house. The houses here are a mixture of old and new, most of them expensive but not ostentatious. Many of the houses serve as B and Bs, and they all have some mixture of immaculately maintained lawns, precisely cropped hedges, tall old pines or wide Japanese red maples, lush flowers, and coats of fresh paint on doors and window frames. It was late spring, and the peonies were in bloom, perfuming the air and a providing delight to the eye.

My tote bag contained nothing but an old magazine, but in my imagination, it weighed six hundred twenty-eight thousand and forty-six dollars' worth of solid gold. I'd caught Jayne more than once looking over her shoulder and peering into alleys. I had to fight down the urge to do so myself.

"We have to go to the police, Gemma."

"Not yet," I said.

"Something funny's going on here. You can't deny that. The magazine might be stolen."

"It well might," I said. "If it is, we'll take it to the authorities. If it wasn't stolen, the rightful owner, whoever that might be, must have a reason not to go to the police if she's in trouble."

"I don't agree, Gemma. This isn't any of our business."

"The Small Woman made it my business," I said. For reasons I did not confess to Jayne, I maintained a healthy distrust of the West London police. I'd find out what I needed to know and call upon them when I had sufficient facts. Not before.

We reached my house. I opened the front gate in the freshly painted white picket fence, and we walked around the house to the back entrance. Our yard is small, but the garden was a riot of spring color. I'm not much of a gardener, but one of Uncle Arthur's lady friends (he seems to have a lot of lady friends) loves puttering about in our yard, and I'm very happy to let her. The house is a perfect saltbox, meaning two stories in the front and one in the back with a steeply sloping roof. It was built in 1756 from traditional Cape gray wooden siding with a red roof and a red brick chimney. Through renovation, a small second-floor balcony was added that affords a view over the neighboring roofs to the ocean. When Uncle Arthur is home, we often begin our mornings there together with a pot of tea, toast and marmalade, and the international papers online. The house is enormous, with five bedrooms, six bathrooms, a formal dining room, a thoroughly modern kitchen, and a den as well as an upstairs study. It's obviously far too big for the two of us, never mind for Uncle Arthur when he lived here alone. But as well as being a wandering soul, he's a spontaneous one, and when he saw the house with its uninterrupted view overlooking the harbor and out to sea, he loved it and bought it on the spot. Some of the bedrooms don't have any furniture, and we never use the dining room. When I arrived, Uncle Arthur moved into the rooms on the second level, giving us both some much-needed privacy when he's at home.

Fortunately, he did not seem to be at home at the moment. His prized blue 1977 Triumph Spitfire 1500 was not in its place—my red Mazda Miata was the only car in the parking area at the back of the house. Another one of Uncle Arthur's passions in life is grand opera. He is hard of hearing. Sometimes those two things don't go well together, and the music of *Carmen* or *La Traviata* can often be heard in the farthest reaches of the house. But now, all was quiet. Just in case he'd put the Triumph in the garage, once I'd unlocked the door, I put my fingers to my lips, slipped off my shoes, and gestured for Jayne to do the same.

We needn't have bothered trying to be quiet. Violet greeted us with a single joyous bark. I told her to shush.

Because he traveled so much throughout his life, Uncle Arthur had never had a pet. Neither had I, as my mother was highly allergic to animals, and once I'd grown up and moved away from my parents' home, the idea never occurred to me. A few years after I arrived in West London, Arthur came home one day with a happy smile and a cocker spaniel puppy. I'd looked at the man, and then I'd looked at the animal. "What is that?"

"This is a dog. She's coming to live with us."

"Why?"

"My friend Janet's dog had puppies, and I promised to give one of them a good home. You'll enjoy the company when I'm away."

"I don't need company."

"Perhaps not, but you'll love Violet."

The dog was light brown with big floppy ears, giant paws, and enormous liquid-brown eyes. She gazed adoringly up at me, and in that instant she wiggled her way, stubby tail wagging and tongue drooling, into my heart. I crouched down, and she crawled into my arms.

"Why's her name Violet?" I asked.

"Violet Hunter."

"*The Adventure of the Copper Beeches.*"

"Good girl. You know your Holmes."

Two years later, the dog was bigger, and she'd finally stopped chewing my shoes, but she was still an important part of my life.

We tiptoed across the black-and-white tiled mudroom, through the kitchen, and along the wide-planked wooden floor of the hallway toward the front of the house to what was once a TV room and is now my den.

The den is my favorite room in the house, the place I sit on cold winter nights in front of a blazing fire, curled up in a soft wingback chair with a good book while the dog snoozes on the rug and chases rabbits in her dreams. The room is decorated purely for relaxation, with comfortable furniture and a wall of floor-to-ceiling built-in bookshelves. A rarely used modern entertainment center is fitted into another wall next to a collection of DVDs (also rarely used now that I have an iPad), Bose speakers, and music-streaming equipment. When not being used, the iPad is kept in a reproduction Chippendale secretary desk Uncle Arthur picked up cheap at an estate sale. Most of the art was nothing special, just colorful paintings that had caught my eye. A modern watercolor showing people with umbrellas dashing though the rain at Trafalgar Square provided me with a touch of nostalgia on the rare occasion I found myself missing home.

The focus of the room hung next to the wood-burning fireplace: a large oil painting of a gorgeous woman with blazing black eyes, thick black hair adorned with black feathers, and pure alabaster-white shoulders trimmed with a touch of red lace. The lady, so the family story goes, was Uncle Arthur's one true love, a soprano on the cusp of great fame, cruelly struck down in her prime by tuberculosis. That Uncle Arthur, who loved nothing more than to talk about his salad days, had never said a single word to me about her made me believe the stories were true.

Taking great care, I removed the portrait of the diva from the wall.

Jayne let out a low whistle. "Wow! Just like in the movies."

A safe was set into the solid, eighteenth-century brick wall. I spun the dial and pulled open the steel door. As expected, it contained nothing but our passports and a few legal papers.

Uncle Arthur and I don't have anything that needs that degree of protection. Before putting the magazine inside, I took it out of the tote bag and laid it on a table. I quickly snapped several pictures with my phone. First of the binding, and then of the magazine cover. I didn't take it out of its plastic protection. A closer examination needed to be done in the right environment. "This might all be for naught," I said. "It could be a reproduction, or have most of the pages torn out. If the Holmes story isn't there, the cover will still be worth something, but not a great deal."

I put it in the safe after taking one last long look and shut the door. I spun the dial and replaced the painting.

"Next stop, the hotel. But I have one thing to do first." I punched numbers into my phone.

"Morris," snapped the reply.

"Donald, it's Gemma."

"Good afternoon, Gemma. Did you find the magazine I'm looking for?" If anyone else said that, I'd suspect they knew what was in my possession, but Donald could always be counted on to get directly to the point.

"I was thinking about it earlier. You said a copy of the *Strand Magazine*'s on the market. What issue?"

"It's all very hush-hush, Gemma. Just whispers, you understand. Something about an estate being liquidated and the magazine possibly among the effects. One of my contacts said 'A Scandal in Bohemia' is in it."

Jayne pulled out her own phone to check for messages and punched in her password. I grabbed it out of her hand. "Goodness," I said, typing as I talked. "That might be worth . . . a hundred dollars."

"Depending on condition," he said.

"I'll keep you posted." I hung up.

"What's worth a hundred dollars?" Jayne asked.

"Probably not even that much. Earlier today, Donald came in asking me to let him know if I heard about a copy of the *Strand Magazine* that's for sale. According to the web page I checked, those are worth a hundred bucks or so. Makes me wonder why, if Donald wanted one, he didn't just go to an online retailer and buy it."

"You think he knows that's not the one that's in town? A bluff to find out if you know anything?"

"I don't know what he knows. Of course, even the *Strand* could have something in it that increases the price dramatically. A Conan Doyle signature, maybe some notes he made on the page."

"Why would the one you have"—Jayne nodded at the safe—"be worth so much more than this *Strand* magazine if it printed original Holmes stories as well?"

"Rarity for one thing. There are plenty of *Strands* floating around, but the *Beeton's* is exceedingly rare. There are many Holmes stories, but *Study in Scarlet* was the first time Sherlock Holmes appeared in print. Collecting doesn't have to make sense, Jayne. The only value objects have is what people are willing to pay to own them."

"Like my cousin's collection of Beanie Babies. The one her mom thought would pay her way through college. Last seen they were being passed over at garage sales."

"Because, I imagine, the market for them collapsed. Whatever a Beanie Baby might be, I do not care enough to ask."

"I still think you should contact the police, Gemma."

"All in good time. I want to have it evaluated first. Then I can tell the authorities precisely what it's worth. I can't chance them picking it up in their fat fingers and getting donut crumbs and powdered sugar all over it."

I headed for the back door and swiped my car keys off the hook as I passed. Jayne trotted along behind. "You don't have to come," I said.

"As if I'd miss this. Are we bringing Violet?"

"She'd love a ride in the car, but there's no room for the both of you." I spoke to the dog. "Guard the house, Violet. We'll be right back."

She's wasn't too happy at that and whined plaintively as I shut and locked the mudroom door.

Jayne and I hopped into the Miata. The trip would only take about ten minutes, so although the evening air was clear and fresh and full of the scent of the sea, I didn't bother putting the top down. The streets were busy with meandering tourist traffic and locals heading home after work. My across-the-street neighbor, Mr. Gibbons, waved his pruning shears at me as we drove past, and I tooted the horn lightly.

"What's your plan?" Jayne asked.

"Plan?"

"What are you going to say if we find this woman at the hotel? Are you going to casually let it drop that you have her half-a-million-dollar magazine?"

"I'll say she left something in my shop. We can judge by her reaction if she's aware of the value."

"Going to the trouble of hiding the magazine rather than tossing it onto the seat of her car or her bedside table tells me she's perfectly aware of what it's worth. How are you going to explain tracking her down?"

"Explain? Unlikely she'll ask, but if she does, I'll tell the truth."

"Perhaps you should let me handle that part. I can say I saw her with the magazine, but thought it was store stock at the time. Then we found out it wasn't."

"Okay," I said. Although I didn't know what was wrong with telling the truth.

The West London Hotel is situated on the edge of town, in an area of gas stations and fast-food restaurants. They advertise sea views, but I suspect that in order to get a glimpse of the ocean, you have to climb onto the roof with a pair of binoculars and lean very far out. It probably helps if you take a ladder. A tall ladder.

We pulled into the almost-full parking lot.

"I'll do the talking," Jayne said.

"Why?"

"Because you sometimes say inappropriate things."

"Me? I only ever tell the truth."

"My point exactly."

I parked at the front doors, beside the fifteen-minute sign, and we got out of the Miata. I grabbed my red leather bag, scarcely big enough for a mobile phone, keys, and a change purse, and tossed the strap of the bag over my head so it fell across my chest. I was still pondering Jayne's cryptic statement as we went into the hotel and got hit by the overpowering scent of chlorine and cleaning products. Jayne took her place behind a family—Mum, Dad, two whining toddlers, and a screaming baby—while I looked around. The lobby was decorated in twentieth-century industrial. The carpet was badly worn, the two armchairs tattered and stained, and cracks were appearing in the ceiling. But the place was clean, without a speck of dust on anything. A separate alcove was set up for breakfast, the lights switched off. I flicked idly through the brochures neatly stacked in a display rack. The usual touristy things.

"You're on the second floor. Elevator's to your right," the clerk said. The unhappy family accepted their room keys and dragged enough luggage to see them through an expedition to the South Pole. Jayne stepped up to the desk with a smile, and I joined her. I also smiled. A stack of postcards, the same as the one that led us here, were on the counter.

"Hi," Jayne said. "We're not checking in, but we're looking for a possible guest of yours and hope you can help us."

The clerk—overweight, with overdyed hair and overplucked eyebrows—said, "I'll try."

"I own a store in West London, and earlier today a woman left her bag behind. A shopping bag, I mean, not her purse. It had one of these postcards in it." Jayne tapped the stack on the counter. "So we thought she might be staying here. She's short and . . . uh . . ."

"Five foot two, seven-and-a-half stone—I mean, a hundred and five pounds—in her midsixties. She has gray hair, which she wears tied into a bun, a pointed chin, and a large nose that bends slightly to her left. When last seen, she was dressed inappropriately for the weather in black trousers and a black fleece jumper."

"That's a sweater," Jayne translated.

I ignored the interruption. "The laces on her trainers were ragged and untied and the shoes had the remnants of dried mud on them."

"Gee," the clerk said, "I'm surprised you didn't notice her teeth."

"She didn't smile," I said. "Her lips were thin, and I believe the look of disapproval on her face was more habitual than aimed specifically at her surroundings. But I could be wrong about that."

"Unlikely," Jayne muttered.

"I might have seen her," the clerk said. "A woman like that's staying here. I think she's on her own. She checked in a few hours ago and then went out."

"Did she return?" I asked.

The clerk's eyes flicked to the door to one side of the reception desk, which doubtless led to an office. Obviously, The Small Woman had returned, and the clerk was unsure if she should tell us so.

"We only want to give her back her shopping," Jayne said. "You can leave it with me."

"I'd rather not do that," I said.

"Leave me your number then, and I'll have her call you."

I longed for the days when hotels kept guest keys hung on a rack behind the desk. I had no doubt, if that was the case, I could get the clerk to glance toward the appropriate number. I couldn't see how I could unobtrusively climb over the desk and have a look at the computer. "Why don't you phone the room and tell her we're here?"

"I suppose I can do that." The clerk reached for the desk phone and placed the call. She hung up after a couple of seconds passed. "No answer. Sorry."

"But . . ." Jayne said.

"We'll come back later," I said. "By the way, do you have a swimming pool?"

"Yes."

A large mirror hung on the wall facing us. I could see the back of the clerk's head, and Jayne's and my smiling faces. I could also see a two-car convoy of overloaded SUVs with New York license plates pulling up out front. "How nice. My brother's coming over from England for a vacation, and he's insistent on staying at a place that has a pool. I'd like to have a look at it before I make a booking."

"I don't think . . ." At that moment, the new arrivals spilled through the doors. I headed for the corridor leading to the pool.

"Thanks for your help," Jayne said as she ran to catch up. She then asked me, "What brother?"

The elevator was opposite the enclosed pool area. Parents watched as children splashed. I punched the up button and the elevator doors slid open. "Room two-four-five."

"How on earth do you know that?"

"I watched her push the buttons on the phone, of course. You should be more observant, Jayne."

"What are we going to do? She's not in."

"That she didn't answer her hotel room phone is no indication of absence," I said. "She might be in the shower or asleep. Or, more likely, hiding."

"Hiding from who?"

"From whom, and that is the question we are here to have answered."

We arrived at the second floor, and the doors slid open. Jayne emerged first. She read the signs directing us to the rooms incorrectly and headed in the wrong direction. I called for her to come back.

Room 245 was at the end of the corridor, next to the stairs. No one else was around. The door by the staircase squeaked, and children's laughter drifted up from the pool below. The slightest crack showed us that the door to the room in question was not fully closed. I glanced at Jayne, and then I knocked loudly. "Hello! Anyone at home? It's Gemma and Jayne from the Sherlock Holmes Emporium. You left something earlier today. Hello?"

I pushed on the door. It swung open.

"We can't just walk in," Jayne whispered.

"Of course we can," I said. I gave the door one more solid knock and shoved it fully open.

It was a typical budget hotel room. Two double beds, a desk and chair, a dresser with a large-screen TV on top of it, factory-produced prints on the walls, and thick red-striped curtains. Those curtains were closed, and all the lights were switched off.

"She's asleep," Jayne said. "We can't go in."

"If she's sleeping, she'll thank us for alerting her to the fact that she forgot to check the lock on the door." I turned on the light. I blinked and froze in my tracks.

Behind me, Jayne gasped.

I recognized her instantly. The Small Woman who'd been in the Emporium earlier. She lay on the bed closest to the window, on top of the covers, fully dressed, even down to the dirty trainers. But she was not asleep. Her arms were thrown out, her head lolled over the side of the bed. Her wide eyes were staring directly at us, but she did not see us. She was dead.

Chapter 4

Jayne and I backed slowly out of the hotel room. Or rather, I backed slowly; Jayne tripped over a loose edge of carpet and tumbled across the hallway to hit the far wall. There she stood, hands on her knees, gasping for breath.

"Breathe deeply but slowly." I moved my arms up and down in a rhythm to help time her. "Deep breath in. Deep breath out."

She looked up at me. "I'll breathe any way I want."

"Now that you're back to normal, go to the lobby and call the police. Try not to run. We don't want to create a panic."

"Gemma, a woman's dead in there. How can you be so calm?"

"Panic helps no one," I replied. I was, in fact, not calm in the least. My heart was pounding, my temperature was elevated by at least half a degree Celsius, and drops of sweat were running down the back of my neck. But I knew that running through the hotel corridors, screaming and waving my arms in the air, would be of no use to anyone.

The elevator tinged and the doors whooshed open. A man emerged and turned in the opposite direction from us. He was talking on his phone and paid us no attention whatsoever. Cell phone technology truly has made it possible to move unnoticed through public spaces. Sherlock Holmes would have loved it.

Jayne took one more deep breath and then straightened up. "Okay. Let's go."

"You alert the authorities. I'll remain here."

"Why?"

"So no one else, a hotel maid perhaps, goes into the room inadvertently and is overcome by shock."

"The room's been cleaned already."

"Go, Jayne."

She turned and dashed down the corridor. She pounded at the elevator buttons. It was still on our floor, and the doors opened immediately. As soon as she was inside, I slipped back into the room.

I pulled out my phone and snapped photographs quickly. First, a full view of the room. The Small Woman lay on the bed. The scarf she'd worn earlier was still around her neck but now wrapped so tightly, I suspected that was what killed her. Her sightless eyes bulged, her tongue protruded, and her fingers were dug into the scarf, as if trying to release it. I took more pictures, closer up. I didn't touch anything.

Fortunately, I was also wearing a scarf. A pretty blue-and-white silk one that went nicely with my white capris and blue-and-white-striped T-shirt. I pulled the scarf off and wrapped it around the fingers of my right hand. A tattered backpack lay on the bed nearest the door. I lifted it up. Empty. Then, somewhat awkwardly, I opened doors and drawers. At first glance, the woman didn't seem to have much. A pair of beige trousers hung in the closet along with a baggy sweater and a raincoat that had seen better days. Black flats with drying mud on the toes had been tossed on the floor. The drawer beneath the TV proved more fruitful: two pairs of pants, one pair of socks, a many-times-washed black T-shirt . . . and a small blue box.

I opened the box. A pair of earrings that, if they weren't made of pure gold and real diamonds, were a darn good imitation. A necklace of interlinked gold rings and a large brooch consisting of a circle of diamonds around a brilliant sapphire. The overhead lights caught the jewels and threw beams around the room. I took a picture of them and then replaced the lid on the box, closed the drawer, and continued searching the room. Sirens were approaching, and I knew it wouldn't be long before I was interrupted.

I found the woman's handbag on the floor, half-kicked under the bed. I picked it up, put it on the desk, and opened it as quickly as possible, taking care that my fingers didn't emerge from the protection of my scarf. The contents were typical of a woman's bag: a jumble of tissues, a key ring, scraps of paper, a couple of pens, some lip balm. I pulled out the wallet and flipped it open. The Massachusetts driver's license was in the name of Mary Ellen Longton, with an address in Boston, and a date of birth that put her at age sixty-seven. The picture was definitely the woman who'd been in the Emporium earlier and now lay dead a couple of feet from my probing fingers. As well as the license, the wallet contained one credit card, also in the name of Mary Ellen Longton, five twenty-dollar bills, and a handful of coins. A plain, white, letter-sized envelope lay at the bottom of the purse. My luck was in, and the envelope was unsealed. I slipped the flap open and pulled out a collection of newspaper clippings. They were, judging by the color of the ink and stiffness of the paper, fairly recent. I didn't have time to read them, so I laid them out on the desk and snapped a series of pictures.

Then I put everything back where I'd found it, tied my own scarf jauntily around my neck, and went to wait for the officers of the law in the corridor.

I was thinking that it was time the faded and dated wallpaper was refreshed when the elevator doors slid open to emit Jayne, surrounded by men and women in blue, and a man in a badly fitting cheap suit, flapping his hands.

That must have been one crowded elevator.

"Let's not make a fuss here," the suited man was saying. "No need to disturb anyone, is there, officers?" He could only be the hotel's duty manager.

I indicated the room in question, and after giving me suspicious glances, the police went in. Radios crackled, and outside, more sirens sounded.

None of the police had said a word to me, which suited me fine. I was about to suggest that Jayne and I take ourselves out of their way when one of the cops emerged from the room. He was balding, with a bad comb-over (why do men insist on doing that?) and a red-veined nose. He was substantially overweight and sweating profusely. Considering that the hotel was not too hot, that he had come up in the elevator rather than the stairs, and that the scene of the crime wasn't gory or disturbing to an experienced cop, I gave him about a month before he had his next heart attack. "Perhaps you should sit down. Your color isn't good," I said, trying to be helpful.

Jayne hissed at me.

"Who are you?" he snapped.

"Gemma Doyle."

"On vacation, are you?"

"Not at all. I'm a resident of West London and the proprietor of the Sherlock Holmes Bookshop and Emporium on Baker Street. Ms. Wilson here is my business partner and colleague."

"Oh yeah," he said, "my . . . wife loves that store."

"I'm sorry to hear she left you," I said.

His beady black eyes made me think of a mouse. They studied me. "How'd you know that?"

I shrugged. The hesitation in his voice had shouted it loud and clear. He almost said ex-wife but caught himself. Therefore, he had regrets, even if she did not. He did not appear to be on the verge of tears, so she was likely not deceased.

"What brings you here then, if you live nearby?" he asked. "Are you friends with the dead woman?"

"I'd never seen her before today. She came into my store this afternoon and left something behind. My friend and I wanted to return it." I glanced at his name tag. "Constable Richter."

"Officer," Jayne whispered to me.

"Sorry. Officer Richter. Now if you don't need us anymore, we'll be on our way."

"Not so fast." He pulled a handkerchief out of his pocket and wiped sweat off his brow. I moved my estimate of the arrival of his heart attack up by two weeks.

"Why don't we discuss this in my office?" the hotel manager said. "No need to stand around where everyone can see us." He flapped his hands again, indicating that he'd escort us. It had as much effect as if he were attempting to corral Moriarty and a pack of feral cats.

"What did she forget?" Officer Richter asked.

"A magazine."

"A magazine?"

"Yes, a magazine."

"You came all the way out here to return a magazine?"

"Whyever would I not?"

"Where's she from? Why's she in a hotel in West London?"

"Of that, I have no idea."

"She told you she was staying here. She must have told you why."

"She didn't tell me anything. We never exchanged so much as a single word. I . . . deduced . . . that she was at this hotel."

"You deduced?"

I was about to explain my reasoning when a shout from the room had Officer Richter pointing his stubby pink finger at me. "Stay here. I'll be right back."

Another officer, a young woman, began stringing yellow police tape across our end of the hallway.

"Hey!" the manager cried. "Don't do that. You'll upset the guests." He rushed away to argue his point.

"Are you going to tell him what the magazine's worth?" Jayne whispered once we were alone.

"It's *estimated* worth. I don't think that's wise. Not at this time."

"It looks suspicious. Us coming out here to return a magazine to someone we don't even know. Anyone else would assume she'd finished with it, or, if she'd dropped it, she'd come back another time."

"I am not anyone else."

"You don't have to tell me that, Gemma. But the receptionist is going to tell the police she called up and the woman didn't answer. We snuck in under false pretenses. That looks suspicious."

"Before I reveal the potential significance of the magazine, I want to gather more information. I don't trust Officer Heart-Attack-Looking-For-A-Place-To-Happen to handle this situation with delicacy."

Richter had left the door partially open. I stuck my head in. Two cops stood over the body. Another was peering in closets. I wondered if I should point out to them the handbag on the floor. Judging by the position of the boots of the observing officers, one of them had kicked it further under the bed. Richter was standing by the window, talking on his phone.

The elevator pinged again, and I withdrew my head and resumed my expression of complete innocence.

My foolish heart betrayed me.

"What's the matter?" Jayne whirled around to see what had caught my attention.

A man had stopped to talk to the hotel manager. ". . . begin moving people off this corridor."

"But we're completely full. It's the beginning of the season."

The newcomer didn't bother to stand and argue and resumed walking toward us. He was in his thirties, tall and solidly built, with chiseled cheekbones, cropped black hair, large expressive blue eyes, and a strong jaw thick with five o'clock shadow.

"Nice," Jayne said.

He wore black boots; faded, but not torn, jeans; and a blue button-down shirt under a black leather jacket. The jacket was open, revealing a gun belt and a badge. I was standing slightly behind Jayne. I might have ducked.

He saw Jayne and was about to say something, but the words stuck in his throat.

I stepped out from behind my friend. My pounding heart threatened to burst out of my chest. "Ryan, hello. I didn't know you were back in town."

"Gemma. This is a surprise. It's only been a week. I uh . . . haven't had time to pop around and say hi."

Jayne's head was moving back and forth as though she were at a tennis match, her eyes wide with interest.

"Did you call this in?" he said.

"Yes," I said. "That is, my friend did, while I waited here—outside the room, I mean, not inside, of course—to protect the integrity of the scene pending your arrival. I don't mean your arrival, as in you in particular, but the police in general. I thought it my duty to . . ."

"My friend babbles when she's uncomfortable," Jayne said.

I forced my mouth shut. I have been told that before.

"I'm Jayne Wilson and this, as you seem to already know, is Gemma Doyle."

"Ryan Ashburton." He gave her a nod, but he scarcely even looked at her. "Gemma and I are old friends. How you doing, Gemma?"

"Well, thank you, Ryan. Except for discovering a dead body, that is. Most upsetting."

"I'm going to have a look at the scene, and then I want to talk to you. Why don't you two go downstairs and take a seat in the hotel office? I'll be as quick as I can."

"Brilliant idea." I grabbed Jayne's arm. Now, to get the heck out of here while no one was watching. Ryan could hunt me down if he wanted to. He knew where I lived.

"Officer Johnson," Ryan called to the young woman who'd been stringing crime scene tape while the hotel manager yelled at her, "See that these women have a private place to sit down and stay with them until I can question them. No talking among yourselves, please. No phone calls."

He went into room 245, and Jayne and I meekly followed the policewoman.

"Okay," Jayne said the minute we were in the elevator. "Spill. Who is that?"

"No talking," Officer Johnson said.

"Ryan Ashburton," I said. "Detective Ashburton. I didn't know he was back in West London."

"I know who he is," Jayne said. "I don't know if he remembers me, but he used to hang with my older brother Jeff back in school. What I mean is, who is he to you, and why, I might ask, would you need to know he's back in town?"

"No talking!" Johnson barked. "Except to say, he's sizzling hot, isn't he?"

"Is he?" I said. "I hadn't noticed."

*   *   *

A few short minutes before, the lobby of the West London Hotel had been almost deserted. By the time we returned, it was packed to overflowing. A police officer guarded the elevator, guests milled around, chatting in excitement, and more people were arriving every moment. Irene Talbot, a reporter with the *West London Star*, was trying to get a statement from the receptionist. The news had traveled mighty fast, even by West London standards.

The receptionist saw us heading her way. She pointed a red talon in our direction. "You! You said you were checking out the swimming pool. I told you not to go upstairs."

Irene whirled around. She saw Jayne and me and hesitated for a fraction of a moment before her professional façade dropped into place. "Ms. Doyle, is that true? Do you have a statement for the press? Did you know the deceased?"

"No comment," Officer Johnson snapped. "Don't you say a word to the media. Either of you."

"Wouldn't dream of it," I said.

"Of course not," Jayne said.

"You got here fast," I said to Irene.

"I was passing by when word came from the guy who monitors the police scanner," Irene said.

"No talking," Johnson repeated.

To the great interest of the assembled guests in general, and the *Star* reporter in particular, we were hustled behind the reception desk and into an office. Johnson shut the door firmly behind us.

The room was barely large enough for the three of us. Jayne and I nabbed the two chairs, leaving Johnson to glare at us from a standing position.

"What's this about you two being told not to go upstairs?" Officer Johnson said. "I'm sure the detectives will find that very interesting."

"We didn't . . ." Jayne began.

"No talking," I said. "I'll explain everything in due course."

I'd taken the seat behind the desk and began idly flipping through papers. Most of them were accounts payable, some long overdue.

"You shouldn't be looking at those," Johnson said.

"I get bored quickly without something to read," I replied. The screensaver on the computer showed the hotel chain logo. I wiggled the mouse to clear it, and a password request came up. Drat, unlikely I'd have the time and privacy to hack in.

My phone rang, and I pulled it out of my bag.

"Leave it," Johnson snapped.

"I have to get this. It's my great uncle. He's ninety years old, frail, and in ill health." Okay, so I lied to the police. Not my first offense of the evening. "Hi, Uncle Arthur. Is everything all right? Do you need me to come immediately?"

"Why would I want that?" Arthur's deep raspy voice is still full of the alleys of the east end of London, even seventy years after he left. I could hear the roar of the engine of his car in the background. "I'm calling to let you know dinner's off. I decided to get a jump on my little holiday and left this afternoon rather than tomorrow. I'll be home when I'm home." If he'd been going to the airport, he'd have taken a cab, so I suspected he was planning to drive up or down the coast for a few days. He never told me where he was going or when he'd be back. He usually didn't know himself until he, like Bilbo Baggins, walked out his front door.

"Should you be going out at night?" I said. "The streets can be dangerous."

"On Cape Cod?"

"Where are you going?"

"Ask me no secrets, my darlin', and I'll tell you no lies." He hung up.

"Very well," I said to no one. "If I must. I'm on my way. Try not to move." I put the phone away.

"You're going nowhere," Johnson said. "Arthur Doyle plays euchre with my grandmother on Tuesdays. He's fitter than I am. So fit and frisky, I sometimes wonder what Grandma and Arthur get up to after those card games."

Jayne laughed. I did not.

I wasn't left to stew in boredom for too long. Ryan Ashburton came in, accompanied by a woman dressed as a female version of him—jeans, shirt, leather jacket, gun and badge. He told Johnson she could leave, and she marched out. I gave Ryan a strained smile, but it was not returned. He'd been flustered to see me for a moment, but now he was all business.

"This is Detective Louise Estrada. She'll be giving me a hand with this." He glanced at Jayne. "Jayne Wilson. Are you Jeff's little sister?"

"Yup."

"I heard you'd moved to Boston. We all come back eventually, don't we? How's Jeff doing?"

"Good. He doesn't visit much though."

I've lived in West London for five years, and I like to believe I've made a home for myself here, but every once in a while, I'm reminded of how much of an outsider I still am.

Pleasantries over, Ryan turned to me. "Tell us what brings you here today, Gemma."

And so I did. I told him the whole story, most of it anyway. The magazine left behind, the hotel postcard in the shopping bag, coming here, finding the body, sending Jayne for help. I left out my estimation of the potential value of the magazine and my snoop around the dead woman's room.

"You expect us to believe that?" Estrada snapped. She was as tall and as lean as a racehorse, well-muscled, with thick black hair, dark eyes, and a flawless olive complexion that only added to the racehorse image. But there was nothing at all horsey about her perfectly sculpted face. She glared at me, clearly having decided within seconds of meeting me that I needed to be clapped in irons. Jumping to conclusions, I thought, was not a good trait in a police detective.

"Why wouldn't you believe me?" I asked, in all innocence.

She snorted. "You traced someone you'd never met halfway across town because of a discarded postcard, went to her room even though the receptionist tells us she didn't tell you what room the woman was in? And all to return a *magazine*?"

I glanced at Ryan.

"Ms. Doyle and I have met before," he said.

"Is that so," she said.

"In light of past experience," he said, "I don't find her behavior out of character. How'd you get the room number, Gemma?"

"It was perfectly simple. I watched as the receptionist made the call to the room."

"You expect us to believe that?" Estrada said again.

"It's not just any old magazine," Jayne said.

I threw her a look. Unfortunately, Ryan was watching me, not Jayne. "I thought as much. Go ahead, Jayne."

"We have to tell them, Gemma," Jayne said. "This whole case probably hangs on the magazine."

"Very well," I said. "The magazine was not simply left behind or forgotten, but rather deliberately hidden this afternoon in the Emporium bookshelves."

"If it was hidden," Estrada said, "then how'd you find it so quickly?"

Ryan lifted a hand. "Let her finish. We can come back to that."

"It might be of some value, but only if it's found to be authentic and in as good condition on the inside as would appear from a quick examination of the outside by a nonexpert."

"Give us an estimate, Gemma," Ryan said.

"Half a million to three quarters of a million dollars."

Estrada snorted, but Ryan, who knew me, let out a low whistle. "Worth killing for then. Where's this magazine now?"

"At my house."

"Let's go get it."

"It's perfectly safe where it is."

"Gemma, let's go," he said, and I gave in.

Estrada led the way out of the office and across the lobby. Jayne and I followed her, and Ryan brought up the rear. I tried not to look as though I was being marched out under arrest. "Gemma?" Irene Talbot fell into step beside me. "What's going on?"

"Nothing to do with us," I said. "I'm going home."

"If it's got nothing to do with you, why are the detectives escorting you?"

A flashbulb went off in my face. "What's happening here?" a man yelled. "Louise! You can tell us."

Estrada didn't bother to answer.

"Did you come in your own car?" Ryan asked once we were outside and standing under the portico.

"Yes."

"Still have the Miata?"

"Yes."

"You'll have to leave it here. We'll take my car."

"I'm not going to drive off," I said, thinking that if I could get rid of them, I'd snatch the magazine and go to ground while I figured out what to do with it.

"Detective Estrada and I will be there to ensure you're not tempted," Ryan replied.

A group of cruisers were parked in a confused jumble all over the hotel lot. Ryan held the back door of one car for Jayne and me. We climbed in while onlookers whispered and pointed. I did not like the view from back here, peering through the screen that separated us from the front seats. I noticed that the doors did not have handles on the inside.

Ryan drove, and Estrada twisted in her seat to talk to me. "What's this magazine anyway?"

"Beeton's Christmas Annual, December of 1887."

"Does it have something to do with Sherlock Holmes? I know you own that store on Baker Street."

"Yes," I replied. "The first Sherlock Holmes story was published in that edition."

"And you just happen to be in the Sherlock business," she muttered.

"I hope you're not implying . . ."

"I never imply, Ms. Doyle. If I have something to say, I'll come out and say it."

"Then we understand each other." If Estrada thought it interesting that Ryan knew the way to my house without asking, she didn't say so. We arrived at Blue Water Place, and Ryan pulled to a stop on the road.

Estrada opened the door, and Jayne and I climbed out. The trip had taken no more than ten minutes, but that was enough for me to decide that I did not want to sit in the back seat of a patrol car ever again.

I led the way up the sidewalk to the front door. I put my key in the lock and swung the door open. The house was dark and quiet except for the clatter of Violet's toenails on the wooden floors as she hurried to greet us.

"Hi, Violet." Ryan gave her a hearty pat. "How's my girl? All grown-up now, are you?"

She wagged her stubby tail.

The house was quiet, the dog happy, but I knew immediately something was wrong. The familiar scents were stronger; something was out of place. "Someone's been in the house."

"How the heck do you know that?" Estrada said. "I can't see a thing. Turn on the lights."

I did so.

We rarely come in via the front door, so it has none of the clutter of shoes, boots, coats, umbrellas, hats, discarded winter scarves, and long-forgotten mittens found in the mudroom off the kitchen. The wide oak paneling of the floors gleamed, and the curving staircase rose up into the darkness of the second floor.

"It's not okay," I said. "Someone has been here."

"I don't see . . ."

"Shush." Ryan pulled out his gun. He gave me a look and a slight nod. "We'll go first. You and Jayne wait here."

He moved cautiously into the house. Estrada followed, her weapon also drawn. Violet trotted after him, her tail still wagging. I followed them.

"Gemma," Jayne whispered. "Stay here."

"He's gone," I said. The front hall opens into our living room on one side and the den on the other before proceeding to the formal dining room and then to the kitchen at the back of the house.

Ryan stepped into the living room, gun at the ready, and Estrada threw open the door to the den. I took one look at the living room—pillows tossed, ornaments overturned— and ran past Estrada.

"Hey!" she called.

The den was a picture of chaos. All the drawers of the reproduction Chippendale secretary had been pulled open and the contents scattered across the floor. The books had been pulled off the shelves; Uncle Arthur's neatly arranged stack of CDs lay in a muddled heap. Everything had been disturbed, but this was no act of random violence. The cushions were not slashed, the books not torn, and the pictures not taken down from the walls. My iPad had been pulled out of the secretary and tossed onto the floor, but not stolen, and the TV was still in place.

"Upstairs," Ryan said to Estrada.

"They've gone," I said.

"How do you know?" she asked.

"I know."

"Because you had something to do with it, maybe?" The look she gave me was not friendly.

Mine was not friendly in return.

"Louise," Ryan snapped, "I said check upstairs. Gemma's probably right, but it's worth a look anyway. I'll call this in."

The black-haired diva stared at us from her place on the wall. She didn't appear to have been disturbed. I shuddered when I thought of Uncle Arthur's reaction if she'd been damaged. We had no other art of any particular value, and none of it appeared to have been touched. Presumably our visitor was not a reader of classic mysteries, and thus didn't know to check behind the paintings for a safe. Assuming, that is, they were after the magazine. And there could be no other reason for this.

I walked across the room.

"Gemma!" Ryan called. "Don't touch anything."

I took the painting down from its place and stood Uncle Arthur's diva carefully on the floor. Ryan sucked in a breath. He and Jayne stood behind me, peering over my shoulder as I spun the dial on the safe and swung it open.

"Someone's been upstairs." Estrada came back in. "Dressers and closets were searched, the mattress tossed." She saw what we were looking at and let out a low whistle.

Nothing in the safe appeared to have been disturbed. The magazine, wrapped in its binding and protective plastic, lay on top of my passport. I took it out. Ryan's gun had been returned to its holster. He dug in his pocket and pulled out a clear plastic bag, which he held out to me.

"This is potentially rare and extremely valuable," I said. "You can take a picture of it for your investigation. But I'll take care of it."

"Gemma, it's evidence in a murder case. Not to mention that if your visitor had a bit more time, he would have found this hidden safe."

"He, or maybe she, wouldn't have been able to get into it if so," I replied. "Only Uncle Arthur and I know the combination."

"I'm sure they would have asked you nicely to open it," Estrada said.

I didn't dignify that with a retort.

Ryan shook the bag. With a martyred sigh, I placed *Beeton's Christmas Annual* into it.

"I want a receipt," I said.

"I'm not going to steal it," he said.

"That magazine is potentially worth an enormous amount of money. I didn't open it myself once I saw the cover. A bit of mishandling, a knocked over coffee cup, or a cigarette burn would reduce the value substantially if not eliminate it completely."

"I don't smoke," Ryan said. "And I'm not a clumsy oaf either."

"I need you to promise me you'll not allow this magazine to be opened or handled any more than necessary until a rare book dealer can be contacted to do it for you."

"I don't know any rare book dealers," Ryan said.

"Fortunately, I do." I was still wearing my small handbag, and I dug out Grant Thompson's business card with my free hand. I handed the card to Ryan with a flourish.

"I'll see that it's protected," he said.

I dropped the magazine into the outstretched bag.

"I'm going to take this down to the station and put it under protection," Ryan said. "And then go back to the hotel to see what the forensic guys have turned up. I might need to talk to you later."

"I'll be here," I said. "I appear to have a lot of cleaning to do. I'd better start with the kitchen."

"How'd you know the kitchen's been ransacked?" Estrada said. "I didn't tell you that, and you can't see into the kitchen from the entrance."

"Do you doubt everything you're told, Detective Estrada? Must be a very difficult way to go through life."

She bristled.

"It was perfectly obvious," I said. "I smelled flour, tea, and sugar the moment we came in. Those are normal scents in anyone's house, but tonight they're of a strength that indicates they've been recently dumped from their containers. Overlaid with the odor of rotting vegetables, by which I assume the fridge door has been left open. I keep meaning to eat that kale because it's supposed to be healthy, but I really don't care for it.

"We can also assume that our intruder is a nonsmoker and doesn't apply perfume or aftershave regularly. Unfortunately, it hasn't rained for several days, although the forecast did call for some, so he or she didn't track mud into the house. The flour! An unforgiveable oversight on my part. You will, of course, want to take casts of footprints that have tracked through the spilled flour and sugar."

"It didn't get on the floor," Estrada said. "But it's all over the counter."

"As the front door appears to be untampered with, and I don't hand spare keys for my house to all and sundry, I'll assume our intruder came in through the back door. Therefore the kitchen would be the logical first place to search."

"Enough, Gemma," Jayne whispered to me.

"I only want to point out the obvious facts." I've been told on more than one occasion that some people don't understand my attention to detail and thus misunderstand the conclusions I draw from it. I have tried to stop, but I might as well stop thinking. And this didn't seem like a suitable time in which to stop thinking.

"The back door's been forced open, yes," Estrada said. "I'll admit, that was a good guess."

I was about to inform her that I never guess, but Jayne elbowed me in the ribs.

"I still think," Estrada continued, "you know way too much about what went on here when you were supposedly not at home. Never mind the dog. She doesn't seem to have done much to frighten off an intruder. She didn't have to be locked up or restrained while this person broke in and searched your house."

"That was no curious incident," I said. "She's a pet, not a guard dog. What does she care if someone tosses my living room as long as that person doesn't attempt to abscond with all the dog biscuits?"

"I've asked the fingerprint techs to come over right away," Ryan said. "This is your home after all. In the meantime, I need you and Jayne to remain in this room."

"It scarcely matters," I said. "My fingerprints are everywhere. This is, as you pointed out, my house."

Ryan's phone rang. He lifted one hand, telling us all to stay in place, and answered. As he listened, his eyes opened wide. He let out a low whistle, turned, and walked to the window, so his back was to us. The sneak! He didn't want me reading his face. "Is that so? Looks genuine? Very interesting. Take them into custody. I'm coming back." At last, the police searching the hotel room must have found the jewelry. Took them long enough.

He put the phone away. "We're done here, Estrada. For now."

"Sir," she said, with a glance at me that I didn't care for one little bit. "If I might have a word."

They went into the hall. Estrada closed the door behind her. I righted the overturned desk chair and took a seat. Violet settled onto the floor beside me. Jayne tiptoed across the room and stood with her ear pressed to the door. Fortunately, she heard them returning and leapt out of the way in time to avoid being knocked senseless.

"You two are not to leave town without my permission," Ryan said.

I nodded.

"Don't talk to the press," Estrada said. "Or anyone else about this."

"We won't," Jayne said.

"We'll see ourselves out." At that moment the doorbell rang. Ryan opened it to admit a man and a woman with badges pinned to their shirts. They carried bags of equipment.

"Do this room first," Ryan said, "then the kitchen and the upstairs bedroom."

"You got it, Detective."

"What about my car?" I said.

"Take a cab," Estrada said.

"I'll put the dog outside," Ryan said. "Otherwise, she'll be in the way. Come on, girl. Gemma, get that lock on the back door fixed tonight."

Estrada left by the front door, and Violet trotted happily behind Ryan out the back.

Jayne and I watched the forensics people go about their business. I have to admit, I find it a fascinating procedure. Absolute proof to one's identity and presence can be so small it can't be seen by the unaided eye.

"If you don't mind, ma'am, can you step back, please. Give us some room to work."

"You've missed that spot there."

"Thank you so much for pointing that out."

"Why don't we let these people work and go and pick up your car in the meantime?" Jayne said. "I'll call a cab."

"Might as well."

We waited outside while I tried to ignore Violet's plaintive cries to be allowed back in. Fortunately, the taxi arrived promptly, and a few minutes later, Jayne and I were settling into the Miata. I drove out of the hotel parking lot at a calm, stately pace. Too many cops around to risk getting a speeding ticket.

To the west, the sky was streaked gray and pink in the last dregs of sunset. We crested the hill, and the harbor and town lay spread out before us. The fourth-order Fresnel lens at the top of the lighthouse by the harbor flashed its pattern of three seconds on, three seconds off, three seconds on, and twenty seconds off. Smaller lights bobbed from boats moored in the harbor, street lamps threw soft golden puddles onto the boardwalk, and the Atlantic Ocean stretched out in the distance, black and silent.

Jayne let out a long sigh. "This isn't good, Gemma."

"All I can say is I'm thankful Uncle Arthur left town today and he wasn't home when our visitor played a call." As Officer Johnson had said, my great uncle was a feisty old guy. He was also stubborn and argumentative. If the intruders had found him at home and demanded to know where the magazine was hidden . . . I pushed away the thought.

"She wants to have you arrested," Jayne said.

"Who? Estrada? That's ridiculous."

"I know it is, but she's trying to convince Ryan to do it."

"On what possible grounds?"

"She doesn't believe our story of how we found out where the woman was staying or why we tracked her down. She thinks you . . . we . . . killed her and stole her magazine."

"Even she must be able to see that's impossible. The magazine was in the house. We were elsewhere. At the hotel."

"To keep it secret then. She thinks you . . . we . . . trashed the house to make it look like someone had been searching. She doesn't believe you knew someone had been in there before you even turned on the lights."

I was so shocked I almost missed the next turning. Good thing the Miata's a small, fast car. It was obvious that Estrada had taken an instant dislike to me, but she wasn't in the likeability business. She was suspicious about some of my observations, but I was used to that from pretty much everyone I met. The possibility that anyone might think I was guilty of theft and murder hadn't so much as crossed my mind.

"Ryan told her he knows you. He said that you might appear uh . . . strange."

"Strange? What do you mean strange? I have an English accent, but that's not exactly grounds for arrest. Does the woman never watch Masterpiece Theater?"

"Gemma, be serious. He pointed out that you sometimes notice more than other people do."

"It's hardly my fault if others are too lazy to use their powers of observation. Present company excluded of course."

"Thanks. I think. Anyway, the point is that he's convinced her not to arrest you *at this time.*"

"In that case," I said slowly, "it might be up to you and me to find out who's behind this."

Chapter 5

I'd put my phone on vibrate after photographing the hotel room and stuffed it in my bag. When I checked it again, I had a string of texts from Andy at the Blue Water Café. The latest said:

Gemma, where are you! I've held your table for over an hour! Oops.

I replied, *Dramatic events. All are fine. Check local news Twitter feed. Cancel table.*

Better than telling him I'd forgotten.

We'd arrived back at my house. I had parked in the street and answered my text while Jayne trotted down the driveway to free Violet from confinement in the backyard. Only once I'd climbed out of the car did I notice an unusual amount of activity in my street for eight thirty in the evening. Neighbors were watering their lawns, sitting on their front porches, or standing at their windows. All of which might have had something to do with the police vehicles parked outside my house. I went in through the front door. I still hadn't seen the condition of the rest of the house and wanted to take my time to examine everything properly.

I found the forensic people packing up their things. They repeated Ryan's advice to have the back door fixed and then gave me tight nods and told me they were finished. They left, not bothering to sweep up the trail of black dust they'd left on every visible surface.

When Jayne and Violet joined me in the den, I said, "I'm going to have a look around the house, before we get to work."

"What sort of work?"

"Finding out what we can about the recently deceased." I put my iPad on the coffee table and turned it on. I was afraid it might have been damaged when thrown around, but it came to life instantly. "Good. No harm appears to have been done. You wait here. Try to find out if the police have taken anyone into custody. With luck, this murder will have nothing to do with us or the magazine, and the police will have found some weeping boyfriend hiding in the hotel shrubbery saying he didn't mean to do it."

"You think that's possible?"

"Not for a single moment."

I first ventured upstairs to Uncle Arthur's apartment, which comprises the entirety of the second story. Violet trotted after me. She didn't seem to be at all disturbed by the drama. Not that it had been any sort of an ordeal, for which I was very thankful. Our intruder, whoever it was, had enough common sense to know that a house pet was not trained to protect property. As long as the intruder walked through the door (even if only after breaking it down first), Violet would let them do whatever he or she wanted. I didn't know if she'd make any effort to protect Arthur's or my person, and I hoped I'd never have to find out.

In his bedroom, as Estrada had said, the drawers had been upturned, the closets rifled, the mattress dragged half off the bed. After a lifetime in the Royal Navy, Arthur made his bed to military precision every day and kept his rooms as tidy as though the Queen might to drop by at any moment to inspect them, and it gave me a pang to see his things in such a mess. Uncle Arthur had eclectic tastes and an avid curiosity about everyone and everything. The paintings on the bedroom walls were a mix of framed tourist posters of castles in Scotland, modern art from Haiti, and red-and-black limited-edition prints of eagles and totem poles from the Pacific Northwest. The pictures had not been disturbed. I went through to his study. The walls were lined with shelves where he displayed all the evidence of a lifetime of travel. Graceful statues from East Africa, coffee cups from Saudi Arabia, carved elephant tusks (collected when that was still legal) from South Africa, multiarmed goddesses from India, a conical hat from Vietnam, a tiny red Buddha from Cambodia. Great Uncle Arthur loved to collect souvenirs of his travels, but he didn't care about value. Most of it was standard tourist stuff, and all of it was now on the floor. I picked up two halves of a plate marking the wedding of Prince Charles to Lady Diana Spencer and placed them on a table. I crouched down beside a shattered Japanese tea set and studied it. Violet came to check it out, and I pushed her away from the shards. I was hoping the intruder had stepped on the fragile china and made an imprint, but that didn't seem to be the case. The police had dusted for fingerprints but I had little hope they'd find anything other than Arthur's and mine. This wasn't an impromptu or random act. Anyone who trashed a house these days without wearing gloves would be so stupid they'd post something on Facebook tonight: *Lookin for half-million buck mag. Real old. Call Bill. Don't tell the cops.*

The cut-glass decanter of brandy and matching glass were still in their places on the small table by Uncle Arthur's favorite leather chair. His nighttime indulgence had not been disturbed because it was obvious the magazine wasn't under them. His book lay beside them, and I smiled when I saw that he was reading *The House of Silk* by Anthony Horowitz. Even this, the first Holmes book not written by Sir Arthur to be officially authorized by the Conan Doyle estate, had originally been greeted by Uncle Arthur with a sneer. He might sell books of the pastiche in the bookstore, but he himself had always refused to read anything he considered a "knock-off."

Downstairs, the scene in the kitchen was as Detective Estrada had described. Drawers had been pulled open and rummaged through, the contents of the larger canisters dumped onto the counters. Everything in the walk-in pantry had been swept off the shelves. A bottle of pickles had smashed, adding to the scents I'd noticed earlier. A bottle of Australian Shiraz rolled around the floor, and I scooped it up. Proof, not that I needed any more, that this wasn't an act of vandalism. No teenager on a rampage would leave a bottle of booze behind.

A glass pane in the window next to the mudroom door had been smashed, giving the intruder access to the lock. We didn't worry about home security much in West London. I made a mental note to start worrying about it from now on.

I examined the shards of glass on the black-and-white ceramic tiles but found no clues there. I swept up the glass and tossed the fragments into the trash.

I continued down the hall, past the guest rooms, to my own bedroom. The door was shut, and I opened it cautiously. But no one was hiding within, ready to leap out at me. This room had not been violated. I hadn't served in the Royal Navy, and I am not exactly neat. Everything was as I had left it: bed unmade, around-the-house clothes tossed over a chair, jewelry and hand lotions tumbled about on the dresser. A stack of books waiting to be read teetered precariously on the nightstand, and a couple of pairs of shoes lay on the carpet where they'd been kicked off. Unlike in the shop, where everything must be in its assigned place so I can keep track of it, no one ever comes into my bedroom to disturb things.

And today, as always, no one had.

A quick check in the guest rooms revealed the same thing. I could only assume the intruder didn't have time to finish searching the house—it is a very big house. One room off this hallway had been converted into my home office, as I sometimes do the business accounts at home. It would have been a logical place to look for the magazine. Did failure to complete the task mean the possibility of a return visit?

Probably not. Not if he or she had been watching the house and knew the police had been in. This person or persons might have been standing in the shadows between the street lamps and seen Ryan leave with an evidence bag tucked under his arm.

Violet and I returned to the den. Jayne was bent over my iPad, her fingers flying.

"Find anything?" I said.

Jayne leapt completely out of her chair and half out of her skin. She sank back with a relieved sigh. "Can't you knock?"

"In my own house?"

"Walk noisier then."

"I'll try. What have you found out?" I peered over her shoulder. The screen showed the menu of the Golden Dragon Chinese Restaurant. "You've discovered that our intruder works at the Golden Dragon? Good work, Jayne!"

"No, I discovered that I'm starving. I was about to order delivery. What do you want? I'm having General Tso's chicken with mushroom fried rice and vegetables in black bean sauce."

"We have work to do here."

"So? We can eat and work. Multitasking."

"Sticky ribs and noodles."

"What do you want for vegetables?"

"I'll have some of yours."

"I'll get two orders then. Is the rest of the house okay?"

I told her what I'd discovered and what I thought it all meant. "As long as you're on there, will you find me the number of a locksmith? I want to get someone out tonight." She did, and I made the call. They said they'd be around in an hour.

That task completed, Jayne said, "The magazine must be genuine if someone's going to this much trouble to get it."

"Perhaps. Did you find anything? If the threat of immanent starvation didn't get in your way, that is."

"Don't give me that," she said. "A girl's gotta eat. I found nothing, but that in itself, as you sometimes say, is significant."

"Do I say that?"

"Yes. Anyway, I searched for any mention of the *Beeton's Christmas Annual* of 1887. I got a lot of hits, but when I added 'on the market' or 'for sale,' I got much fewer. I then narrowed the time frame down to a month and got nothing."

"Meaning the magazine is not currently for sale on the open market or through the reputable book dealers or auction houses."

"I then added words such as 'stolen,' 'steal,' and 'police report,' and got nothing."

"It's possible, likely even, that the magazine has been stolen but not reported to the authorities."

"Why would the owner not tell the police?"

"Such is the question, isn't it? To which I might have an answer." I pulled out my phone, entered my password, and called up the photo app. Jayne got to her feet and stood on her tiptoes to see the screen. She sucked in a breath. "I can't believe you took pictures of the dead woman."

"Even I don't have a fully photographic memory."

"You're lucky the police didn't tell you to hand over your phone. That detective Estrada would think you had an unhealthy prurient interest."

I flicked through the pictures of the body and the contents of the drawer as Jayne gasped, "Are those real diamonds?" I stopped at the newspaper cuttings. We peered closer.

"I can't make out what it says," Jayne said.

"I'll print them out." I sent the photos to the printer in my office and ran to get them. I returned with a stack of papers and spread them across the coffee table.

They were newspaper clippings, mostly from the Boston papers, though a couple were from the back pages of the *New York Times*.

A knock sounded at the front door, and Jayne screamed.

"You are jumpy tonight," I said. "Relax, it's the Golden Dragon."

"How can you know that without opening the door?"

"I saw the delivery van drive past the window. We should probably draw the curtains. I'll do that while you answer the door. We'll call this a business meeting and take the funds out of petty cash tomorrow."

"Come with me."

"Why?"

"Suppose the killer is waiting out there, wanting to get back into the house, and he has a knife to the throat of the delivery person?"

"Then he'll kill us both when we tell him we don't have what he's after. He or she, I should say. Answer the door, Jayne. And then get some plates and things."

Grumbling, Jayne answered the door, and the scent of hot, spicy food drifted into the room. She clattered about in the kitchen for plates and cutlery while I skimmed the newspaper articles.

Two of them were obituaries, both of the same man. Kurt Frederick Kent Jr., age ninety-four, passed away three weeks ago after a long illness, leaving three children and three grandchildren. His wife, Juliette Elizabeth Reynard Kent, died in 1975, and he had never remarried. Jayne handed me a plate, and I handed her a copy of the *Times* obituary while I continued reading the one from the *Boston Globe*. A long list of companies of which Mr. Kent was the chief executive followed. Most of them appeared to manufacture car and truck components. His father, Kurt Kent Sr., had made his fortune in the automotive business, rising from car salesman to owner of the company, which he then sold for a considerable profit, switching to the parts business just in time to cash in on the industrial demands of World War II. Kurt Jr. had been educated at Harvard, spent his career working for his father, and when his father retired, he took over the business empire. He continued to control it until illness forced him into reclusion. His eldest son, Colin Kent, now managed the family businesses.

"Why do you suppose our Small Woman has these?" Jayne asked. "She must know this man."

"Kurt Kent. There's something familiar about that name. Let me think." I leaned back in my chair, intertwined my fingers, and closed my eyes.

"Clark Kent," Jayne said. "That's why it's familiar."

"Not Clark, but Kurt. You know someone by that name?"

"Not him. The other one. Clark Kent. Superman."

"Who?"

"Superman's real name is Clark Kent."

"Isn't Superman's name 'Superman'?"

"He's called Superman, but that's like a nickname. His name is Clark Kent. When he was a kid, his mother didn't stand on the back porch calling, 'Superman, time for dinner.'"

"I hate to be the one to tell you this, Jayne, but Superman, like Sherlock Holmes and Santa Claus, was never real, thus never was a child nor did he have a mother. Regardless, I don't see the significance. We aren't trying to locate the owner of a comic book. Although I understand they can be collectors' items and thus of some value."

"I'm telling you why the name's familiar."

"As I have never heard of Clark Kent, a.k.a. Superman, that can't be the reason, Jayne." I let my mind sort through the thousands, maybe hundreds of thousands, of names I'd come across in my life. And then I had it. "Kurt Kent of Boston is a reclusive Sherlockian. He's said to have a substantial private collection, but no one knows for sure because he doesn't allow visitors to view his collection. Donald told me about him some time ago. Donald wanted to invite the man to join the Baker Street Irregulars but he couldn't get past the outer phalanx of secretaries and personal assistants."

"Now that he's dead, what do you suppose will happen to his collection?"

"The heirs might keep it intact. They might sell it off in bits and pieces or as a group. He must have some marvelous books."

"What about Sherlock's possessions? Wouldn't something genuine be valuable?"

"As Sherlock Holmes was not a real person, Jayne, there's no such thing as his possessions."

"You know what I mean. Of the author. Sir Arthur Conan Doyle."

"Quite possibly there are letters to and from him. Something from his publisher to do with the books would bring a handsome price at auction, particularly if it discussed a previously unknown matter. Photographs of him are not rare, but as always, if there's anything significant or unusual about it, it might be worth something. This is all speculation." I discarded the obituaries and found a news article. Mr. Kent's estate was currently in the courts. His children were fighting the terms of his will. "Excellent," I said. "Now we're getting somewhere."

"Where precisely are we getting?"

"Pass me the iPad, will you?" Jayne handed it over, and I did a Google search for Kurt Frederick Kent. The screen filled with hits. All the photographs of the man himself were at least twenty years old. In his later years, Mr. Kent had been somewhat like Howard Hughes. A millionaire recluse. Shots of his house showed nothing but a high fence, sturdy gates, thick hedges, and angry guards.

News articles reported that Mr. Kent's daughter and two sons were fighting the terms of his will. Said will had apparently left items of considerable value to his private nurse, a woman by the name of Mary Ellen Longton. Bingo! The name on The Small Woman's driver's license. The Kent children claimed that the nurse had exerted undue influence on the elderly, confused, dying man and tricked him into mentioning her in his will. She had been in his employ for eight months before his death. I handed the iPad to Jayne. "Read this."

"'Items of considerable value,'" she said. "I'm thinking a magazine."

"As am I. I'm also thinking jewelry that didn't match the woman's apparent means." I picked up a sticky rib with my fingers and nibbled on it. Violet stared intently at me through her deep liquid eyes, attempting to mesmerize me into dropping a bone.

It didn't work.

"Are we going to take this information to the police?" Jayne asked.

"No. They have their own resources, and Ryan is no fool."

"What's the story there, anyway?" She dug into her plate of orange-colored chicken with her chopsticks while I twirled a noodle on my fork. Jayne always eats Chinese food with chopsticks. I have never been able to manage anything smaller than a dumpling. A large dumpling.

"No story."

"Don't give me that. I wish I'd taken a picture of the look on your face when you saw him in the hotel. You were shocked, and he looked surprised to see you too. He kept saying things about knowing you."

"We were friends once, and then he moved away. Now it would appear he's back."

"Friends?"

"More than friends, if you must know. We were in a relationship for a while. We both thought it might turn out to be something significant." I swallowed and turned away from Jayne's questioning eyes. "It didn't work out, and we went our separate ways. That's all."

"How do you feel about that? About him being back in West London?"

"Feel? It's none of my business what he does. I presume he found the world of big city policing not to his liking." I stood up and began gathering dishes. "It's late. I'm going to bed. I'll approach this all fresh in the morning."

Jayne remained in her chair. She glanced nervously around, as though checking the shadows.

"What's the matter?"

"I don't feel entirely comfortable walking home alone. Suppose he's out there?"

"Suppose who's out there?" I asked.

"The killer, of course."

"The killer will have no further interest in us. We don't have the magazine. But if you're worried, I'll take you home. Violet would enjoy the walk."

"No! Then you'll be out at night all alone, and he's more likely to come after you than me. Violet's no protection. I'll call Robbie to come and get me."

I refrained from making a comment while Jayne placed the call to her knight-in-rusted-armor.

Robbie can't have been far away, because he arrived mere moments later. I could hear his rusty Dodge Neon, long overdue for an oil change, the moment it turned into our street.

"Bummer, Gemma," he said, coming into the kitchen. "News is all over town that you found a dead woman. For the record, I don't think you did it."

"Thank you so much for that vote of confidence," I said.

"You're welcome." He put his arm around Jayne and pulled her close. "You're safe now, babe."

She smiled up at him. I refrained from gagging. He was lightly built and shorter than I am, although taller than Jayne, with intense dark eyes. He might even be good-looking, I thought, if he shaved off the goatee and washed his hair regularly. But that was all part of the starving-artist persona he liked to put on.

Speaking of a starving artist. "You don't mind if I take the leftovers, do you, Gemma?" Jayne said. "Robbie can always eat."

I swallowed my disappointment. Nothing I like better than reheated Chinese food for breakfast. Considering Jayne had earlier packed the containers back into their bag and was now swooping them up off the kitchen counter, it was too late to object.

"Do you know your door's broken?" Robbie said.

"I did notice that, thank you."

"I've a great idea," Jayne said. "Why not hire Robbie to fix it? He's done some construction work, haven't you, honey?"

"Uh, yeah. I guess," he said with his usual level of enthusiasm when talk of work was directed his way.

"I'd love to throw the job your way, Robbie," I lied. Conveniently, at that moment a van rattled to a stop in the driveway. "But here's the locksmith now."

Jayne and Robbie left, and the locksmith got to work after explaining that I would be charged extra for the emergency callout. I told him to go ahead and stayed in the mudroom to watch him work. He installed a new lock and fitted a section of plywood into the broken window frame. Then, after giving me a quote for a new door with security features, such as not having a pane of ordinary glass within reaching distance of the door handle, he left.

I was giving my brand new lock a satisfying twist when my phone rang. I was dead beat and considered not answering, but the display showed Irene Talbot. I'd have to talk to her sometime, or she'd hunt me down. Might as well get it over with.

She didn't bother with greetings. "Gemma, what can you tell me about the dead woman found at the West London Hotel?"

Clearly, this was not a social call. Irene had been born and raised on Cape Cod and had eagerly left its shores as soon as she finished high school for the rarified world of journalism college and then a beat at a national newspaper. But newspapers were not exactly thriving these days, and Irene had consistently been laid off when the papers she worked for either went out of business or made cutbacks after merging with another. Eventually, the only job she could get was at the *West London Star*, and home she came.

She put on a brave face and talked to anyone who would listen about her love of the Cape and needing to breathe the free air of a small town again. But she didn't want to be here, and her crushed ambition was plain. She was Jayne's and my friend, but I couldn't allow myself to forget that she might view a sensational murder case as a springboard back to the limelight.

"I can tell you nothing," I said. "Police orders."

"You can hint, give me something off the record. Why were you there? Did you know the woman?"

The hotel receptionist would have been more than happy to tell the members of the press that I'd asked specifically to speak to the dead woman and that I'd been turned away. It couldn't hurt, I thought, to verify what would by now be common knowledge. "She left something at the Emporium this afternoon. I was returning it, that's all."

"The police haven't released her name yet, pending notification of next of kin. But you can tell me, Gemma. I won't tell anyone where I heard it."

"I don't know her name, Irene," I said. Okay, that was a lie, but *officially* I didn't know it. Neither the hotel nor the police had told me. "They ordered me not to talk about this to anyone, certainly not you or your colleagues. Sorry, but I have to go."

"You'll give me the scoop, right? When this is over and you're free to talk."

"Sure," I said.

"I knew Ryan Ashburton in high school. He always was a sharp one. He'll get to the bottom of it soon."

"Speaking of Detective Ashburton," I said. "Do you know what brings him back to West London?"

"Something's happening. The elevator just pinged. Gotta run. Talk to you later, Gemma. Remember, I expect an exclusive."

Chapter 6

I don't know if I dreamt of Ryan Ashburton or not, but my first thought on waking was of him.

Which might be because he was on the phone to tell me the police would be paying a call on me shortly. I fell out of bed and let Violet outside before scrambling into the shower. My hair needed a wash, but I didn't have time to dry it. I have excessively curly hair, and left unattended, it tends to resemble an overused mop. I had only just pulled on a pair of jeans and a T-shirt—the first things that came to hand—when the doorbell rang.

Detective Louise Estrada stood there, accompanied by one of the fingerprint people from yesterday. I swallowed my disappointment, not entirely sure if it was disappointment or something more like relief, that it wasn't Ryan on my doorstep. Estrada's eyes were concealed behind large round sunglasses, making it difficult to know what she was thinking.

She didn't bother giving me a good-morning. "We're here to take your fingerprints. That didn't get done yesterday. Can you please put the dog outside or lock it up while we're here?"

I peeked outside. The police van and a marked cruiser were parked in front of my house. Once again, the neighbors were either at their windows or on their front porches, pretending not to be watching. Mrs. Macintosh—three doors to the west—takes her two miniature Dobermans for a fifteen-minute walk every day (regardless of the weather) at six AM and six PM. It was now quarter to seven, and she was dragging the confused dogs out of the house. Mr. Gibbons—on the opposite side of the street, two doors to the east—was getting a very early start on trimming his front hedge, which was already so immaculately trimmed he might have used a plumb line.

Violet was eager to greet our visitors, but I picked her up, took her into the office, and shut her in. Estrada didn't remove her sunglasses the entire time she was in my house. Perhaps she feared I could read her mind.

"We'll have to take your prints for elimination," she said.

"That shouldn't be necessary," I replied. "They're on file."

Her eyebrows rose above her glasses. "Is that so?"

"Not because I've ever been accused of a crime, but I have offered to assist the police on other occasions." I refrained from adding that my well-intended offers of assistance had been strongly rebuffed.

"Humor me," she said, and I did so.

I knew the routine, but I allowed the fingerprint tech to explain it all to me. I rolled my inked thumb on the provided paper. "My uncle Arthur lives here also. He's out of town right now, and I can't say when he'll be back."

"Are his prints on file too?"

"I don't know."

"What's his name?"

"Arthur Clive Doyle."

"Have you thought of anything you should have told us last night?" Estrada asked.

"No. I told you the whole story."

"Sure you don't want to change a few details here and there?"

I wiped my fingers on a tissue. "Nothing to change, Detective."

"We'll be in touch," Estrada said.

I didn't bother to ask her what the police had discovered (if anything) since last night. She kept her face impassive, and her words were polite enough, although short, but her entire body bristled with hostility toward me.

I had no idea what I'd done to make her dislike me so.

Once they'd left—watched by an enormous crowd, only some of whom pretended to be going about their business—I galloped down the hall, freed Violet, and got ready for work. I should have stayed home and cleaned up the mess, both from the previous night's break-in and then the police activity, but I'd get around to that later. I decided to dispense with a second shower and a hair wash, but I changed out of the jeans and T-shirt into a pretty summer dress of white cotton sprinkled with large pink flowers, secured with a thin black belt, and slipped my feet into black ballet flats. When I'd opened the door to my visitors, the big yellow ball of the sun had been rising over the ocean into a cloudless sky and the fresh salty air had blown in on a light, warm breeze.

Violet stays at home every day when I go to work. Every day, judging by the look on her face, you'd think it was the first time she'd been abandoned. Shortly after Moriarty set up residence in the shop, I thought it would be nice if the dog came with me sometimes. She could spend the day in the office, and I could take her for short walks when I wasn't busy. We'd come through the front door of the Emporium, the dog trotting happily at my side, and Moriarty had flown across the room in full attack mode, teeth and claws bared, hair rising. Suffice it to say that after I'd swept up shattered china, righted the bookshelves, and calmed the trauma- tized dog as best I was able, I'd decided not to try that again.

On days when I didn't have breakfast at home, my first stop of the working day was Mrs. Hudson's Tea Room for tea and a blueberry scone dribbled with white icing. If my mother could see what they called a scone in America, she'd have a heart attack, but I have to admit I greatly prefer the ones Jayne makes to the dry rocks with raisins my mother baked every Monday of my childhood. For afternoon tea, Jayne changes the recipe and bakes what she calls a tea bis- cuit (which seems like a scone to me) but the menu still says scones because, she tells me, that's what people expect to have with their tea. Why Americans have to confuse everything by using the same name for two different things is beyond me.

This morning, all the tables were occupied; Jocelyn was bustling about with laden trays, and Fiona was busy behind the takeout counter.

"Busy morning?" I asked Fiona when it was my turn to be served.

"Is it ever. You got the last of the scones. You and Jayne were seen last night at the site of a murder. And left in the presence of the police. People are talking."

I spun around. Everyone behind me suffered whiplash as they turned their heads and pretended not to have been trying to listen in on our conversation.

"Is Jayne in the kitchen?" I asked Fiona.

"Yes."

"Glad to hear she made it home alive," I said.

I took my breakfast through to the Emporium. At the sound of the key in the lock and the door opening, Moriarty strolled down, as he always did, from the upper floor. He arched his back and hissed at me in his usual greeting.

"Good morning to you, too," I said.

I keep his litter box in the staff washroom and his dishes in the office. I filled the bowls and emptied the box. He never thanks me, and I'd soon learned that I might lose a fingertip if I tried patting him while I poured kibble and refreshed the water.

I went onto the office computer and checked the local news. The killing at the West London Hotel was the feature story, as could be expected, but it provided few details. According to Irene Talbot, staff reporter, the deceased was named as Mary Ellen Longton of Boston. West London Police Detective Ryan Ashburton was asking anyone who'd been at the hotel yesterday evening to . . . blah blah blah.

I'd given the card of the rare book dealer I'd met on Monday to Ryan, but not before jotting down Grant Thompson's number for myself. I gave him a call.

"I appreciate the recommendation, Gemma," he said once we'd exchanged greetings and I'd told him why I was calling. "Not that I'm likely to get any business out of the local police, but word spreads and that's important for a newcomer. Maybe I'll even get a mention in the paper."

"Did you examine the magazine?"

"Far too briefly, and in the presence of a room full of cops. I didn't open it past the cover page. I want to do that in a controlled environment and when I have time to do it properly. But based on far too quick of an examination, I'd say it might well be genuine."

"Worth a lot then?"

"If it's complete, it's probably priceless. Meaning worth whatever anyone is willing to pay."

"Do you collect yourself?"

He laughed. "I specialize in Victorian and Edwardian detective novels and the golden age of English crime writing. I have a few first editions, and I buy and sell others, but mostly I act as a middleman for people who do collect at that level."

"Did the police say what they plan to do now?"

"Not to me, but surely they'll be trying to find the owner. They're working on the assumption that the dead woman stole it."

"Perhaps," I said.

"What does that mean?"

"Just that unexpected people can legitimately come into possession of unusual things."

"Do you think you might have a claim to it?" he asked.

"Me? Hardly. I found it. It wasn't given to me, by the legal owner or otherwise."

"Finders keepers?"

"Losers weepers. But not in this case. Thanks, Grant. You'll let me know if you hear more?"

"That I will," he said.

I opened the store and a few customers drifted in. I half-expected Ryan to call me, but my phone remained stubbornly silent.

Shortly after eleven, a man walked through the door. I'd never seen him before, and he didn't look as though he were on vacation. He was dressed in a perfectly fitted, dark-gray business suit—Armani maybe?—and silk tie with gray-and-pink stripes. He was in his late sixties, lightly tanned and expensively groomed, with recently manicured hands and iron-gray hair cut short. He took a quick look around my shop, not able to stop his lip from turning up in disapproval. He saw me watching from behind the counter, forced a stiff smile onto his face, and crossed the room with quick, confident steps.

"Mr. Kent," I said. "My condolences on the loss of your father."

His smile died, and he studied me through wary, hooded brown eyes. "Do I know you?"

"No," I said. Businessman, wealthy, would have left Boston about two hours ago, waiting until the worst of the rush-hour traffic was over, timed to arrive shortly after the shop opened, before we'd get busy. He could, of course, have been an employee or even a lawyer for the Kent family, but I didn't think so, not with that degree of arrogance on his face. That, plus the same square jaw and too-close-together eyes I'd seen last night in a twenty-year-old photo of the Kent patriarch.

"But you know me? Or did you know my father?"

"Your family has been in the news."

"Unfortunately, yes. I'm on my way to the police station. They called me last night to say that some . . . items stolen from my family had been located. I was driving by and saw your store. The Sherlock Holmes Bookshop and Emporium. Very unusual. It looks as though you specialize in Holmes and Conan Doyle collectables."

"We're primarily a bookstore, but we also stock all the paraphernalia that goes with it." I didn't bother to point out that the most direct route from Boston to the police station does not go down busy Baker Street.

"Are you the owner?"

I extended my right hand. "Gemma Doyle."

"Doyle?"

"No relation."

"Colin Kent."

We shook hands. His, I thought, was clammy.

"Do you buy, Ms. Doyle, as well as sell?"

"I have to get my stock somewhere. The contemporary books are all new, not used, but we have some second editions of the original Holmes books, and I occasionally come across a first edition. I have collectable magazines . . ." Did I imagine the look of interest that crossed his face? Perhaps not, but Moriarty chose that unfortunate moment to jump onto the counter, and Colin's attention was distracted.

"What a beautiful cat." He stretched out a hand, and Moriarty allowed himself to be petted.

"My late father was a Holmes collector," Colin said. "Over his lifetime he accumulated a substantial amount of stuff. He bought, but never sold. Not only books but memorabilia as well. We haven't gotten around to having the collection fully appraised yet. Would you be interested in having a look when we're ready to bring interested parties in, Ms. Doyle?"

"I might be." I didn't go on buying trips. Uncle Arthur handled that sort of thing for me, and not often. Sellers usually managed to find their own way to our doors. "As well as books, my customers like plates and teacups with pictures of Holmes and Watson, that sort of thing." Jayne had mentioned that she'd like to have a full line of Sherlock tea sets. I doubted that Kurt Frederick Kent Jr. was the sort to accumulate teacups, although you never know what will strike a rabid collector's fancy. Colin Kent was a businessman, and I decided to play my cards (not that I had any) very close to my chest. Let him think I was playing hard to get. "Did your father have things like that?"

"Uh . . . I'm not sure. He had eclectic tastes."

Meaning the son had no interest in his father's collection when Kurt was alive, and his interest now was in what he thought he could sell it for. I couldn't condemn the man for that. It was common enough. Collecting is a highly individualistic hobby, as any perusal of garage and estate sales would show.

"But those aren't valuable," I said. "Teacups I mean. I'd love to get my hands on copies of the original *Strand* magazines . . ."

His eyebrows twitched.

"Or even a *Beeton's Annual*. Condition is always important, of course."

"Once the inventory is complete, I'll be in touch if I find something of interest."

"I'd appreciate that. Do you know if he had any first-edition books?"

"I believe I've seen some old books on the shelves. It's not something I'm knowledgeable about. It seems fascinating, but I never could find the time."

"You'll want a rare book dealer to have a look at them. Because Holmes was so popular in Doyle's own time and the popularity never waned, most of the books aren't rare and thus not particularly valuable. But there are exceptions."

"Thanks. I appreciate your time. I'll be in touch. Can you tell me the best way to get to the police station?"

I gave the directions, and he left. *Interesting that his first priority was checking out my shop rather than talking to the police.* I popped my head into the tea room and called to Fiona. "I'm closing for half an hour." I locked the connecting door, dashed upstairs for my bag, and then headed out. Fortunately, the police station isn't far from Baker Street. Colin Kent didn't look to me like much of a walker. By the time he went for his car, drove through the busy streets, and found a place to park at the town offices, I could be there too.

I set off at a trot. It was a lovely day, warm and sunny with a sea breeze that ensured it didn't get too hot. It was early in the season, but summer had arrived prematurely in Massachusetts this year, and the tourists were taking advantage of it. They were out in force, smiling and shopping. I didn't like leaving my place closed during the day, but Ruby wasn't scheduled to come into work until noon, and I decided proving I didn't commit a murder was more important than the possible sale of a $7.99 paperback or a $15.00 jigsaw puzzle.

I hadn't been inside the police station since Ryan left town, but nothing had changed. Unlike the rest of West

London, the town's police didn't cater to tourists in search of the authentic coastal New England experience.

"Is Detective Ashburton in?" I asked the officer at the dispatch desk.

"Who's calling?"

"Gemma Doyle. It's about the incident at the West London Hotel last night." I attempted to look helpful.

The officer reached for the phone, and at that moment Colin Kent came in. He started when he saw me. "Didn't I just leave you?"

"I remembered an important matter."

"You're not following me, are you?"

"Why on earth would I do that?" I said innocently. "Your visit simply reminded me of a question I have for the police."

He didn't look as though he entirely believed me but said no more.

"Can I help you?" the officer asked him.

"I'm here to speak to Detective Ryan Ashburton. He's expecting me. Name of Kent."

"I'm here." Ryan came through the inner doors. He shook hands with Colin and eyed me suspiciously. "What brings you here, Gemma?"

"Mr. Kent and I were talking about his father's estate, and that reminded me of last night."

"Do you have additional information for me?"

"Not information as such, but questions have arisen in my mind." I turned to Colin. "Were full records of your father's collection kept while he was alive? Would you, or people representing you, notice if anything has gone missing since his death?" I had no interest in the state of the late Mr. Kent's collection, but I wanted to start making myself part of the conversation. When Ryan took Colin through those locked doors into his office, I intended to go with them.

"Not really," he said. "My father was very ill in his later years, and his grip on reality was, sadly, slipping. Which is why that awful woman, Mary Ellen Longton, was able to—"

"We'll get to that," Ryan said. "If you have some fresh information for me, Gemma, take a seat. Otherwise, I'll come by later. We still have things to discuss."

"I uncovered some interesting information on the Internet last night," I said.

"So did I," he replied. "We'll compare notes later."

Detective Estrada had come out of the inner sanctum while we talked. She stood beside the dispatch desk, her arms crossed over her chest, watching us.

Ryan held the door open. "Come on through, Mr. Kent." I stepped forward.

"Gemma," Ryan said, "I need to talk to Mr. Kent in private. I haven't forgotten you." He shut the door in my face.

Estrada threw me a look that would frighten small children. It certainly frightened me.

*   *   *

Jayne pounced the moment I was back in the shop.

"What's happening? Are you okay?" She wiped her hands on her floury apron.

"Why wouldn't I be?"

"I got a call from Robbie. He said you were down at the police station and you'd been arrested."

"I was not arrested, and why does Robbie know my whereabouts anyway?"

"Someone called to tell him you were seen going into the police station."

"If everyone who walked into the police station on a sunny summer's day was under arrest, the streets would soon be empty, Jayne."

"I know that. But you closed the shop in the middle of the morning. You never do that."

"Kurt Kent's son—"

"I hope his name's Clark."

"It is not. It's Colin. He popped in this morning on his way to a meeting with Ryan. I was hoping to be party to their conversation, but no such luck."

"Why would he come here?"

"I . . ."

The chimes over the door sounded and a tall, thin, frumpy woman walked in. I suppressed a groan.

"What on earth is going on here, Gemma?" She wagged a long bony finger at me. "My brother's sister-in-law works at the West London Hotel, and he called me this morning, to say the both of you had been arrested for murder! Of course, I told him I didn't believe a word of it. But, well, when I looked across the street a few minutes ago and saw that the store was closed, naturally I felt it was my duty to investigate. Nothing worse for business than a closed and boarded-up shop front on the street."

"As you can see, Maureen," I said. "We're standing here in front of you. Unjailed."

She tried not to look too disappointed. "The busy season has arrived early. Gossip is not good for business either."

Business at the tea room had only this morning proved just how good for business gossip could be. I simply smiled at her and said nothing.

"Speaking of business," Jayne said. "Time to get back at it."

"I've a line on some Sherlock loo paper," I said to Jayne. "All in good taste, of course."

Maureen looked around the tea room. "*Nothing* you two sell is in good taste." With what she no doubt thought a witty parting shot, she left the building.

Jayne and I grinned at each other. "What would a day be without a rain shower?" Jayne said.

"She's more like a thunderstorm." Maureen owned Beach Fine Arts, located across from us at 221 Baker Street. (Yes, Great Uncle Arthur had tried to buy that building first, but it hadn't been for sale.) It was a souvenir shop that, despite its name, sold nothing at all fine. Just the usual tourist kitsch along with some of Maureen's own paintings. Her art, I suspected, came from paint-by-numbers boxes.

Maureen thought the Emporium tasteless and tacky and was always trying to get it shut down on the grounds that it lowered the status of the street. The good people of the business owners' association pointed out that I paid my taxes and ran a profitable business, but Maureen had decided that getting rid of me and the Sherlock Holmes Bookshop and Emporium was her goal in life. The occasional visitor would get confused and wander into number 221 in search of "Sherlock

Holmes's store." When that happened, I could hear Maureen's screech if I happened to be standing near the front window.

She didn't mind Mrs. Hudson's Tea Room though. Shoppers needed somewhere to go for refreshments, and the tea room kept them from leaving the shopping district in search of lunch.

"Let's hope that's the only thunderstorm today," I said.

"You're not seriously going to stock toilet paper are you?"

"No. Just trying to get a rise out of Maureen."

"It worked."

"That's not exactly challenging."

The chimes tinkled again and three women, beach-hatted, sun-tanned, laughing, and laden with shopping bags, came in.

"We need to talk things over," I said to Jayne. "Now is obviously not the time, and we have too much to discuss in the afternoon business meeting. Let's meet for a drink at the Blue Water Café after the store closes."

"Okay." She returned to the tea room and her cucumber sandwiches and scones.

Chapter 7

Ryan Ashburton came to the Emporium shortly after one. Ruby had arrived, and the shop was busy. Next door, the lunch crowd spilled out the doors of the tea room.

Ryan stood in the doorway, just looking around, while I hid behind a life-sized cutout of Martin Freeman as Dr. John Watson. A customer tried to get past him, and he quickly stepped aside with a muttered "sorry."

"If you need any help, be sure and let me know," Ruby said.

"I'm looking for Gemma."

"She's around somewhere. Gemma! Someone to see you!"

I stepped out from behind Martin. "Ryan, what brings you here?"

"Do you have someplace private we can talk?"

"Follow me." I led the way upstairs to the office. A wide-eyed Ruby watched us go. Moriarty followed.

My office is more of an overflow storage room, coat closet, and place where paper goes to die. I swept a pile of *Strand* magazines (current issue) off the visitor's chair for Ryan, and I took the seat behind the desk. Moriarty leapt onto a carton of books waiting to be unpacked, the better to follow the conversation. Uncle Arthur bought the building for the address and for its Cape Cod charm. If I'm ever looking to move, I will not get premises in which we have to be constantly carrying boxes of books up a narrow set of stairs and back down again.

"No doubt," I began, "by now, you've determined that the deceased woman found at the West London Hotel is Mary Ellen Longton, previously the private nurse to reclusive millionaire Kurt Kent Jr. Mr. Kent mentioned Mrs. Longton in his will, and his family is contesting the will on the grounds that he wasn't mentally competent at the time. A sad but not uncommon tale. Mr. Kent was a Sherlock collector and, as much as I hate to make assumptions, we can assume the magazine in question is part of this disputed estate. We can also assume that Mary Ellen hid it in my shop fearing someone was after her, intending to either steal it or repossess it pending the result of the legal action regarding the will. Her fears were obviously well grounded, and whomever she was hiding from found her and killed her. That person then went to my house and began searching for the magazine. The search was interrupted either when we arrived or when a confederate told them we were on the way."

Ryan stared at me. "We can assume all that, can we?"

"You look surprised. Don't tell me you didn't also uncover that information?"

"About Mr. Kent, and the will, and the nurse, yes. It's public knowledge, and it was confirmed by Colin Kent. I'm not entirely convinced, however, that Mary Ellen Longton hid this magazine in your shop."

"But I told you that's what happened."

"Detective Estrada wants to arrest you," he said.

I smothered a cry of indignation. "She's mistaken."

"Don't you want to know why?"

"Why? I know why. Because she's a small-minded small-town cop with lots of ambition and little imagination, that's why."

"Don't make an enemy of her, Gemma."

"Enemy! I'm not in the business of making enemies of anyone. I've told you what happened. What we now have to determine is—"

"*We* have to do nothing. This is a police investigation. It has nothing to do with you."

"Of course it's to do with me. I found the body. I was given possession of a half-a-million-dollar magazine, although I wasn't supposed to know that. My house was broken into and searched. I hate to think what might have happened if Uncle Arthur had been home and surprised the intruder."

"I'm ordering you to stay out of it."

"You're ordering me? That's preposterous. I'll do what I have to do to clear my good name."

"Gemma, Louise finds the story of you happening to find the magazine hidden in the shop and then tracing the woman to the hotel difficult to swallow, and I have to say I see her point."

I was gobsmacked. He held up his hand. "You're smart and you're exceptionally observant. Not everyone understands that, Gemma."

"So that's what this is about, is it!" I leapt to my feet. "One more time, we'll list all my faults. Of which, apparently, being smart is top of the list. If I am so smart, Mr. Big-Shot

Detective, then you tell me why, if I had stolen the magazine and killed the woman, I'd make a public display of trying to find her at the hotel, and then *call the police*!"

Moriarty hissed at Ryan. For once, even the cat agreed with me.

"You're too smart for your own good sometimes." Ryan got to his feet. We glared at each other over the top of my cluttered desk, watched by the keen-eyed Moriarty. "Maybe this one time, you've tried a double play, a triple cross, and tripped yourself up."

"That's absurd!" My fury mounted.

"You're too clever by half, Gemma," he yelled, "and that's always been your problem. It was a mistake coming here. I should have let Estrada interview you."

The office door flew open. "What on earth is going on?" Jayne said. "It sounds as though someone's being murdered in here. I can hear you all the way through to the tea room, and every one of our customers has stopped what they're doing to listen in."

"A minor disagreement." I dropped back into my chair.

"I'm interviewing a reluctant witness," Ryan said.

"Reluctant! I'm anything but reluctant!"

"Stop it." Jayne looked back and forth between us. "I suggest a cooling-off period. Gemma, the shop is full, and your attention is needed. Detective Ashburton, I doubt you want the entire town of West London knowing police business."

"I need to talk to you, Ms. Wilson," he said. I couldn't help but notice how attractive Ryan was when he was flustered. I gave myself a mental slap. That was over and done with, and good thing too. He would always be, first of all, a cop.

"The lunch rush is slowing down, so I can spare the time now," Jayne said. "Why don't you come to the tea room, Detective? We can talk in my kitchen. I'll even provide coffee and a sandwich."

Ryan didn't look back, but Jayne threw me a questioning look over her shoulder. Moriarty smirked and settled down to wash his whiskers.

I remembered to breathe deeply. I let a few minutes pass, and then I lifted my head, pointed my chin, and sailed down the stairs. Seeing that Ryan had left without dragging me in handcuffs, kicking and screaming, to an impromptu hanging, the customers had returned to minding their own business.

Maureen swooped down on the store. I sometimes wondered if she had my place bugged so she'd be able to respond instantly to the slightest impropriety. "Really, Gemma. Did you have to make such a scene? It doesn't reflect well on the other business owners on this street."

"Is that the police I see going into your place, Maureen?" She had her back to the window, and I was facing out into the street.

She whirled around. "What? Heavens yes, I think it is."

"You'd better get back and see what they want. I hope they don't damage any of your fine art in their search of the premises."

She ran.

Okay, so I lied. But I didn't feel like defending myself to her. Or to anyone.

I turned around. Ruby ducked her head, trying to pretend she hadn't been watching me, but she wasn't fast enough.

As I helped customers and rang up purchases, I kept replaying the conversation with Ryan over and over in my head. He hadn't come right out and said he believed I'd stolen the magazine and killed the woman. He only suggested that others, Detective Louise Estrada in particular, might think so.

Fortunately, Jayne had been with me the entire time yesterday evening, from discovering the magazine to finding the dead body to coming home and realizing that my house had been searched. Jayne had the most innocent, wide-open face of anyone I'd ever met. She'd tell the police what transpired yesterday, and that would put all their suspicions to rest.

*   *   *

"I knew I'd find you two here," Irene Talbot slid into a seat opposite us in Mrs. Hudson's Tea Room. It was quarter to four, and Jayne and I had just sat at the table in the window alcove for our regular afternoon meeting. Irene plucked a smoked salmon pinwheel sandwich off my plate. "Any coffee left?"

I was about to say "no," but Jayne got to her feet. "I'll see what I can find." On her way into the back, she flipped the sign on the door to "Closed" and locked the door.

The sandwich disappeared and a strawberry tart followed it. "Help yourself," I said.

"Thanks," Irene said. "Don't mind if I do. It's been a heck of a busy day, I can tell you. Not often we get a murder in our sleepy little town, never mind one that goes unsolved for a whole twenty-four hours. Usually they either find the killer still at the scene in a state of shock or down at Pete's bar telling everyone she deserved it." She pulled a pen and a notebook out of her giant handbag.

Now that Irene was here, I might as well make the best of it. "What have you learned?"

She set about telling me everything I already knew. Jayne put a coffee mug on the table and began to sit down. "Any more of those sandwiches left?" Irene asked. "They're great."

Jayne headed back to the kitchen, and Irene sipped her coffee. She sighed in appreciation. "Best coffee in town."

"Drop the act," I said. "You don't have to play friendly, well-meaning journalist with me. You've told me nothing that's not common knowledge." Mary Ellen's identity and the details of her dispute with the Kent family had been the lead story on the local radio news late this morning. I hadn't had the radio on, but I had been provided with all the details by Jocelyn, Andy Whitehall, several of my neighbors, Uncle Arthur's euchre partner (also grandmother to Officer Johnson), and the woman who worked at the accessory store next to Beach Fine Arts. There had been no mention of my name in the press, but Jayne had been described as "the owner of the popular West London café Mrs. Hudson's, who discovered the deceased and called the police."

"I don't want to see my name in your paper, Irene," I said. "I am not an interested party, I just happened to be on the scene with Jayne."

"Nonsense," she said. "You're very interested. You told me yesterday you found something of the deceased woman's and were trying to return it. Do you want to tell me what that was?"

"No comment."

"I'll find out anyway, you know. I have my sources."

Jayne put a fresh plate on the table. "Strawberry tarts are finished, but I have some brownies left."

"Thanks. What about you, Jayne? You were there yesterday. Is there anything you think the people of West London need to know?"

"No."

"Have you given a statement to the police?"

"I was interviewed by Detective Ashburton last night and again earlier this afternoon," Jayne said. "Everyone who was at the hotel yesterday was probably interviewed."

"Were you interviewed, Gemma?" Irene asked.

I began to say "no." Jayne interrupted me.

"Was she ever! I'm surprised you didn't hear her and Detective Ashburton yelling at each other all the way over at the *Star* offices."

"Is that so?" Irene forced her face into a surprised look. Not many people can act, which is why there's a profession for those who can. Easy to tell this tidbit of information wasn't anything new to her.

I sipped my tea. We smiled at each other.

I was saved from more smiling by a loud rap on the door. A man stood there, holding his hands to the glass, peering in. He saw me, waved, and knocked again. I'd never seen him before.

"Can't he read?" Jayne said.

"Let him in," Irene said. "He's with me."

"We're closed," I pointed out. Jocelyn was stacking chairs upside down on the tables prior to sweeping the floor, and Fiona was clearing what few leftovers there were out of the display cabinet.

"You'll want to hear what he has to say," Irene said.

I gave Jayne a nod, and she opened the door. The man who entered was short and slightly built. His gait tilted heavily to the right, the result of a bad knee. He wore faded jeans, bagging from wear at the knees and in the seat; a Boston Red Sox T-shirt; and heavy work boots. He peered at us through small black eyes from under a Red Sox ball cap. He gave me a nod and a weak smile. He was missing a tooth on the upper right side. A workingman—construction, most likely—unable to get work because of the injury to his knee and considerably down on his luck. The acrid scent of cigarette smoke, fresh as well as stale, permeated his clothes and emitted from his every pore. His stubby fingers were stained a deep yellow.

"Have a seat, Mr. Longton," I said. "Or is that just your mother's name?"

He threw Irene a look. "You told her."

"No," she said, "I didn't."

"Jayne," I said. "Would you mind asking Fiona to bring another coffee and maybe one or two of those brownies?"

One hardly had to be Sherlock Holmes to recognize this man as Mary Ellen Longton's son. Anyone could have figured it out. Anyone who bothered to observe and correlate the known facts. I've found that almost no one does. If I'd passed Mr. Longton in the street, I wouldn't have given him a second glance. But as Irene had invited him to join us after telling me she wanted to talk about Mary Ellen's death and the police investigation, combined with his small stature, the same furtive mannerisms as the late woman, and some similar facial characteristics, it was obvious they were closely related. He was in his midforties; therefore, he was most likely to be her son rather than a brother or grandson.

Jayne sat down in the chair next to me, and Mr. Longton slid into the bench seat beside Irene. Ever so slightly, Irene inched away from him.

Outside, people and cars passed by. The parking enforcement officer was writing up a ticket for an SUV parked in a loading zone.

Fiona brought another mug of coffee and a plate containing a selection of pastries.

Mr. Longton muttered his thanks. Fiona made no move to leave us, and Jocelyn's sweeping was bringing her ever closer.

"Gemma Doyle, Jayne Wilson, this is Roy Longton," Irene said. "Roy came to me because he has some questions about his mother's death."

"That's natural enough," I said. "But I don't see what any of this has to do with us. Let the police handle it. I have some experience with the WLPD, and Detective Ashburton is more than competent."

"You found her body." He spoke properly for the first time. His voice was surprisingly high-pitched, squeaky almost. He gripped his mug. The tiny nicks and scars on his thumbs and the badly healed gash on the right palm confirmed that he'd been a construction worker.

"We found her by accident," Jayne said.

"She was in your store, next door there"—he pointed with his chin—"a couple of hours before she died. What did you talk about?"

"We talked about nothing. We didn't meet," I said. "The shop was crowded when your mother came in and she left soon after."

"Why'd you go to the hotel then?"

I glanced at Irene. "I'm assuming you know. So why are you asking us that?"

"She left something with you," Roy said.

"I don't have anything of hers."

"She worked for that miserable old man. She was good to him. She treated him right. His family was happy enough to leave him alone to rot in that big house until he died. My mother was the one who looked after him. She deserved to get something for all that."

"I assume she was paid," I said.

"Sure. Paid peanuts. Why shouldn't he leave her a little gift? Something to remember him by."

"Sounds fair to me," Fiona said. Jocelyn nodded.

I ignored them and spoke to Irene. "I fail to see what this has to do with me."

"You're the Sherlock expert," Irene said.

"I'm nothing of the sort."

"He, the old man, left my mother something from his collection. I'm thinking you can help me get it back."

"What Mr. Clark left to your mother, if he left anything, is with the police." I deliberately used the wrong name. Jayne gave me a surprised look, but Roy Longton didn't appear to even notice. Not that close to his mother then, at least not in her final months.

Irene flipped through her notebook. "I thought the man's name was Kent. Not Clark. I have to admit, I thought of Superman too."

"My mistake," I said.

"They're rich," Roy said. "They've got everything. They can afford fancy lawyers. My mom, she didn't have much. But she had her honesty. She was a good woman. The old man owed her, and when he died, his family threatened to sue her. She was on the run. What else could she do? She couldn't afford a decent lawyer. Now they're going to come after me."

"So unfair," Fiona said to Jocelyn.

"That's why Roy contacted me." Irene took the last brownie. "The power of the press is the only weapon the underprivileged have against the rich and powerful."

"You and your mother must have been very close," I said.

"Yeah, we were. Yeah." His eyes slid to Jayne sitting beside me.

"Did Mr. Kent leave anything to you?" I asked.

"Why would he do that?" Roy said. "He didn't know me."

"Just wondering." I pushed my chair back and stood up. "I'm going out after work, so now I need to go home and let the dog out. Nice meeting you, Roy. Don't forget our meeting tonight, Jayne."

*   *   *

Violet greeted me effusively, and I did the same for her. I took her leash down from the hook by the back door, and we headed out for walk. Since a dog came into my life, I've found there's nothing like time spent walking her to engage in some serious thinking. Something about meandering along at the pace of a happy dog, with no particular place to go, clears the mind wonderfully. Although right now, I'd rather my mind wasn't cleared.

It bothered me deeply that Ryan thought I might have had something to do with the death of Mary Ellen Longton. After all we'd once meant to each other, he couldn't possibly think I'd kill a woman for a magazine? I didn't know Louise Estrada. I didn't know anything about her world view or her thought process. Maybe she was influencing Ryan without him even being aware of it. She was an attractive woman. He was an attractive man. Though surely, if they were more than colleagues, I'd have noticed the signs.

Then again, maybe I didn't want to see any signs.

A squirrel ran down a tree trunk and darted across the grass. Violet made to follow, and the abrupt jerk of her leash pulled me out of my thoughts.

I took her home, filled the food and water bowls, and went back to the Emporium.

*   *   *

Jayne was perched on a tall, colorful stool when I arrived at the Blue Water Café. Andy stood behind the bar, his elbows resting on the shiny mahogany, a huge adoring smile on his face, and the light of love glowing in his eyes. Brian, the bartender, slid a martini glass containing a lurid pink-and-yellow concoction topped with a bright-red cherry toward Jayne, and she thanked him with a brilliant smile. I thought Andy was going to faint.

I'd come directly from the shop, but Jayne had been home first. She'd changed into a red skirt that flowed in waves above her knees, a crisp white shirt with a deeply curved neckline, and strappy sandals with three-inch heels. When she crossed her bare legs, Andy wasn't the only man who gulped and took a second look.

I lumbered across the deck in shoes suitable for spending a day on one's feet and joined them. "Hey, Gemma," Andy said. "What can we get you?"

Jayne took a delicate sip of her drink. She rolled her eyes in pleasure. "This is so good."

"Sauvignon Blanc for me, please," I said.

"Andy heard something about what happened last night," Jayne said. "I was about to fill him in."

"To tell him that we were simply innocent passersby caught up in an unknown person's tragedy, you mean?"

"We were?"

"Yes, Jayne. We were."

"Keep your secrets then," Andy said. "I'll get it out of you in due course."

"Thanks." I accepted a glass of wine from Brian.

"Better get back at it," Andy said. "We're full again tonight."

He walked away, returning to the mysterious depths of his kitchen. I swung my stool around to check out the view. The restaurant overlooked the small harbor, and the outdoor seating area was perched on stilts above the water. The harbor faced east, toward the stormy waters of the Atlantic, but this stretch of the coast was protected by a sandbar lying a few hundred feet offshore. Big charter fishing crafts and small private sailboats were returning to port, moving slowly through the calm waters of the inner harbor. A seaplane flew low overhead, and far above it, the passage of a commercial jet drew a line of white vapor across the blue sky. Seals played under the pier or followed in the wake of the fishing boats, and sea gulls swooped though the evening sky on the lookout for dinner. The beam from the West London lighthouse flashed above it all.

"Cheers," I said, and Jayne and I clinked glasses. Our seats were against the railing on one side, and on the other side, two elderly couples had gathered stools into a circle. They were not on their first drinks of the day, and their laughter filled the deck.

"So," I said, keeping my voice low, "What did Ryan have to say?"

"I want the scoop first."

"What scoop?"

"What's the story with you and him?"

"I told you, there is no story. We dated once, for a short while, and it didn't work out." I took a slug of my wine.

"Seems to me there's still a lot of feeling between the two of you, judging by the way you were yelling at each other earlier."

"He was almost accusing me of murder, Jayne. I'm allowed to yell."

"I'll grant you that. But what about the way you blush when he talks to you and you can't look him in the eye?"

"I do not blush," I said around another mouthful of wine.

"You're not the only one who can be observant, Gemma. Hope you're not driving tonight, not the way that drink's going down."

I put the glass on the bar. "It's been a difficult twenty-four hours. If you must know, the end of our relationship was . . . difficult might be the word. He got a job in Boston and moved away. Now he's back. That's all."

"It's obviously not all. He still likes you, Gemma. He likes you a lot. His face is as readable as yours."

"Be that as it may, it wouldn't work. We met when a series of nighttime arsons struck some of the stores along Baker Street. The police investigated, of course. I soon pointed out to them, in the person of newly promoted Detective Ashburton, that it was obvious that the owner of the jewelry store at 195 Baker Street—"

"There's no jewelry store at 195 Baker."

"Exactly. He, the store owner, set up the other crimes as a smoke screen for his ultimate intention, which was to burn his own business to the ground and thus claim the insurance money, not only for the store but for the contents as well, which themselves were fake, as he'd sold the genuine jewelry to his mob debt collector. Ryan and his senior detective, a fat, balding fellow by the name of Rick Mertz—who has, fortunately for the good people of West London, gone on to a comfortable, if totally undeserved, retirement—at first suspected me of being the arsonist." And that's why my fingerprints are on record with the West London police.

"Because you knew the details."

"Because I took the time to observe what was going on. Fortunately, the guilty party wasn't particularly clever—desperate men rarely are—and I was able to convince Ryan, if not his superiors, where and when to catch him in the act, and the case was brought to a successful conclusion."

"That doesn't explain why you broke up with him."

"I attempted to help on some of his other cases. He didn't want my help. His stubborn male pride got in the way. I might have said that publicly. That was a mistake."

"No kidding," Jayne said.

"Everything okay here, ladies?" Brian asked.

"I'll have another," Jayne said. "Can I also see the bar snacks menu, please?"

"Gemma?" he asked.

"What?" I blinked.

"Do you want another glass of wine?"

"No thanks." He handed Jayne the small menu, and she flipped it open. I leaned back in my chair and closed my eyes with a sigh. My relationship with Ryan had not ended because I tried to help the police with their cases. Yes, that had always been a sticking point between us, but the climax had been far more personal than that.

I'd made the unpardonable error of saying "yes" before giving him the chance to pop the question.

We'd gone to one of West London's finest restaurants, on Ryan's suggestion. It was a gorgeous early summer evening, much like this one, and I knew something special was in the air.

When the main course was over and the plates taken away, he'd cleared his throat, looked around the restaurant, caught the waiter's eye, blushed to the roots of his hair, patted his jacket pocket and said, "Gemma."

And I, *far too clever for my own good*, had enthusiastically replied. "Yes!"

"Yes what? I haven't asked you anything."

"Yes, I'll marry you."

The color drained from his handsome face. "How did you know?" He looked, frankly, horrified, but I blundered on, not noticing.

"You're wearing your best suit and a brand new tie, if I'm not mistaken. You've gone to the trouble of shaving after work, which you don't normally do. You've even polished your shoes. You have a touch of sweat on your brow, but this room isn't hot. Somewhat the contrary, I think. They've turned the air conditioning on too early. The bulge in your jacket pocket is the size and shape of a ring box. You gave the waiter an unobtrusive nod that had him grinning like a fool, and if I'm not mistaken, he's bringing the champagne now. Veuve Clicquot, excellent choice."

"Gemma," Ryan said. "I . . . I . . . can't."

"Can't what?" I asked in all innocence.

He stopped patting his jacket pocket and looked straight at me. "I can't do it. I'm sorry. I love you like crazy, but everything I think, you know it before I do. There will never be any surprises. No secrets."

"Isn't that a good thing? No secrets between us?"

"There's such a thing as good secrets, Gemma. Birthday presents. Surprise parties. Marriage proposals."

"I'm sorry," I said. "I can try not to notice . . ."

"No, I'm sorry. This was such a mistake. I guess I hoped that for once, you'd just enjoy the evening. Yes, you can try. But then you wouldn't be you, Gemma, and how miserable would that make you? You'd blame me."

"I wouldn't . . ."

"You would. Whether you wanted to or not." He stood up. "I've been offered a job in Boston. I was about to turn it down, but I've changed my mind. I'm sorry, Gemma. It's not going to work. I'll take care of the check on my way out."

He left me sitting there, surround by the hum of conversation, the clinking of silver, and the dying light of the candle on our table.

The waiter gaped at me, towel draped over his arm. "Don't bother opening that bottle," I said.

I'd managed to get out of the restaurant and halfway home before I started to cry.

But Jayne didn't need to know all the details.

"So that's the story," I said. "A promising romance that came to naught. Happens to us all. What did he have to say to you over coffee and sandwiches?"

"He didn't tell me anything. He asked questions about last night. I told him what happened, and that's all."

"Ryan knows me, as you pointed out. He believes me. But I'm worried about that Detective Estrada. She's got a shifty look about her. If she discovers Ryan and I once dated, and it's hardly a secret around town, she might try to get him taken off the case."

"So? We didn't do anything."

"Miscarriages of justice have been known to happen, Jayne. And I don't intend to be the victim of one. Now let's examine the events surrounding the situation."

"Want anything?" the bartender asked. "Andy says it's on him."

"How nice of him," Jayne said. "I'll have an order of bruschetta. Gemma?"

"What?"

"Do you want something to eat?"

"No thanks. I'll have some of yours."

"In that case bruschetta and the calamari, please." She handed him the menu with a smile.

"That Mary Ellen Longton is—or I should say, was—involved in a legal quarrel with the estate of her previous employer is not in dispute. That the previous employer was a Sherlockian tells us why she was able to take possession of the magazine. Either he left it to her in his will, and she took off with it before the presumptive heirs knew what was happening, or she stole it the moment he kicked the bucket."

"'Kicked the bucket'?"

"Isn't that a phrase you Americans use?"

"I'm surprised to hear you using it."

"I'm trying to fit in."

"Her son says the magazine was left to her in the will."

"No, her son says she was left *something* in the will. He obviously doesn't know what that is. And I would advise you to take everything he has to say with a grain of salt. He has an agenda of his own. It might be worth dropping a word into Ryan's ear to check Roy Longton's alibi for last night."

"You don't think her own son would have killed her?"

"Right now, Jayne, I have not the slightest idea of who would. All I know is who didn't. You and me. Someone followed Mary Ellen Longton to West London with the intention of retrieving the magazine. They may or may not have intended to kill her, but that's irrelevant."

"Not to her." Our food arrived and Jayne selected a slice of bruschetta. It was too early in the season for the tomatoes to be fresh and local, but they did look delicious, so I helped myself also. The herb toppings, I knew, were fresh and local, having been grown by Andy in the small greenhouse on his property.

"First, let's examine events around the time that may be relevant. Donald Morris told me he's searching for a copy of the *Strand* that has been rumored to have come onto the market. I wondered at the time why he was interested, as the *Strand* isn't at all uncommon unless it has some distinguishing feature such as a signature or notation by Conan Doyle. In that case, it would be possible, almost likely even, that such an item would be in the possession of a wealthy, long-time collector. Question: Is Donald genuinely looking for this rumored *Strand*, or was that a ruse to get me to reveal that I am in the possession of the much more valuable *Beeton's*?"

"You didn't have the magazine when Donald first mentioned it to you."

"Excellent point. Still, we have to ask to what lengths Donald would go to obtain the magazine."

"You can't be thinking Donald Morris killed Mary Ellen?"

"He's a fanatical collector, Jayne. And a collector without much in the way of funds. Donald is on our list."

"We have a list?"

"We will shortly." I wiped my fingers on my napkin and selected another piece of bruschetta. "Next, Grant Thompson. Rare book collector and dealer."

"Oh, yes. The handsome one."

"Is he? I hadn't noticed. He came into the shop the day before The Small Woman. Coincidence? Unlikely. Was he hunting her? My shop would be an obvious place for her to go if she wanted to sell the magazine but hadn't done enough research to know that I'm just a small-town, main-street retailer. I didn't think to ask Ryan if Grant showed any prior familiarity with the *Beeton's* when he examined it at the police station." I popped the last piece of bruschetta in my mouth, dug in my pocket, and pulled out my phone. "I'll do so now."

Jayne's left hand was holding a piece of calamari. She put her right hand on my arm. "That might not be such a good idea. You said he told you not to get involved."

"But this might be important information."

"Who's next on this list?"

I put the phone away and selected a piece of calamari. "Kurt Kent's son Colin. Ryan called him last night to tell him what had happened, and he came to West London first thing this morning."

"Nothing unusual about that."

"No, but what did attract my attention was that he stopped at the Emporium before going to the police station. I can't help wondering why he did that."

"You would think the police would be his first priority," Jayne said.

"Yes, you would. If not Colin himself, what about the other heirs? We have to ask the same questions about the jewelry I found in Mary Ellen's hotel room as we do about the magazine. Had Mary Ellen stolen it, or was it bequeathed to her and she decided to head out of town lickety-split before the will could be contested?"

The loud group next to us was told their table was ready, and they moved away. Two young women hopped onto the vacated stools. I eyed them, wondering if we'd have to save this conversation for another time. They immediately took out their phones, and their fingers began to fly.

I lowered my voice anyway, just to be sure, and leaned toward Jayne. "And then there's the bridge bus tour group."

"What about them?"

"They were in the shop the same time as Mary Ellen Longton." I mentally pulled up a view of the Emporium as it had been yesterday afternoon. The Small Woman came in. She spoke to no one, at least as far as I could tell, and I soon lost track of her. The women of the bus tour were shopping, chatting, laughing. No one appeared to be acting suspiciously, whatever that might mean. Then again, we were very busy. I might have missed something. I hated the thought. "I wonder if any of them noticed anything. It might be worth asking. I don't suppose they told you where they were going next on their tour?"

"Nope. You want that last piece of calamari?"

I waved my hand.

"What about Ruby?" Jayne asked.

"Ruby? My new assistant? What about her?"

"She saw the magazine, Gemma. She might not have realized the value of it, but your reaction told her something was up."

"True," I said. "But I don't see it. Even if she did decide she wanted the magazine, she, along with only you and me, knew The Small Woman didn't have it any longer. Plus, she'd left the shop when I discovered the postcard from the West London Hotel, so how would she know where to go? I suppose she might have decided to steal the magazine from me, but I find it impossible to believe that the murder of Mary Ellen Longton and the ransacking of my house are not directly related."

"Remember," Jayne said, "that 'once you have eliminated the impossible, whatever remains, no matter how improbable, must be the truth.'"

"Spare me," I said.

127

Irene Talbot came onto the deck. She was with a group of men and women I didn't recognize, but I took to be out-of-town reporters. Freelancers, probably, snooping around for something—anything—of interest. The death of Mary Ellen Longton hadn't gotten any press outside of Cape Cod, no doubt because it wasn't particularly newsworthy. Give it time though. A rich man, a wealthy family, a greedy (according to some) private nurse, a disputed inheritance ending in murder. The stuff sensational cases are made of. Irene spoke to her companions, gestured for them to follow the hostess to their table, and approached us.

"Hi, Jayne. Gemma. Lovely night, isn't it? My mom says it's going to be another record-breaking summer in terms of the numbers of tourists."

"Good for business then," Jayne said. "If not for getting a last-minute table at a restaurant."

"Want to tell me what this afternoon was about?" I asked. "Bringing Roy Longton to Mrs. Hudson's to meet us?"

"Can't you figure that out for yourself? Maybe if he twitched his right eyebrow or something."

I was suddenly angry. "Don't treat me like a fool, Irene. You didn't tell him to drop by for tea and tarts because you thought I needed a new friend."

She lifted her hands. "Okay, don't bite my head off." She glanced around the room, checking no one was listening. "This is all on the down low, you understand. Even my," she gestured to the other reporters, "buddies over there don't know yet. Someone I know, who just happens to work for the WLPD says that a magazine was left in the Emporium, and that's why you went to the hotel in pursuit of Mary Ellen Longton."

"Hardly in pursuit."

"Don't shoot me, I'm only the messenger. I said, 'Who cares about some magazine?' but my friend went on to tell me that a rare book dealer showed up at the police station this morning to examine it. He told them it was worth thousands." She studied my face. "You don't look surprised."

"If I wanted you to think this was news to me, Irene, I would look surprised."

"She can do surprised," Jayne said. "Flabbergasted, even."

"Considering that your contact told you this magazine is currently in the protection of the police," I said. "I still don't understand why you brought Roy Longton to meet me."

Jayne sipped at her drink, her eyes watching me over the rim of the glass.

"Mary Ellen gave the magazine to you, Gemma," Irene said. "Before she died. That might give you a claim to being the rightful owner."

Jayne spat pink liquor all over herself and Irene. The intrepid reporter yelped and leapt out of range, swatting away beads of liquid forming on the front of her shirt. A young, handsome male waiter appeared instantly, clutching a handful of cocktail napkins. He basically shoved Irene aside and helpfully dabbed at Jayne's blouse.

"Is everything all right?" Brian, the bartender, asked. "You okay, Jayne?"

"She'll live," I plucked the napkins out of the waiter's hand. "Thank you for your help. I can manage here." I handed the napkins to Irene and spoke to Brian. "Another glass of wine for me, please." The table of reporters was watching us. Seeing as to how nothing further seemed to be happening, they returned their attention to their beer bottles.

I accepted the fresh glass and took a sip.

Irene continued to dab. "This is an expensive shirt, I'll have you know."

"Sorry," Jayne said.

"Let's get one thing straight," I said. "Mary Ellen did not give me anything. She hid her property and scampered, no doubt intending to come back for it at a better time."

"Why would she do that?" Irene asked.

"If I knew that," I snapped, "I'd know who killed her and why. Good heavens, Irene. Are you telling me you told that man, her son, that I own the magazine?"

"I merely pointed out that if you can prove she gave it to you, willingly and without being coerced, then yes you'd have a claim."

"Cool," Jayne said. Brian brought her a fresh drink to replace the one that was now soaking into Irene's nice shirt.

"I want no part of this," I said.

"You could stake your claim. Tell the court she intended it to go to a good home, and who better to take care of it than a noted Sherlock Holmes aficionado?"

"Who better?" Jayne agreed.

"Which I am not," I growled.

"You could give it to Arthur," Jayne said. "He'd love to have it. Or you could use it to attract customers to the shop."

I almost yelled at her, but I noticed the twinkle in her eyes in time.

"This conversation is over," I said. "I don't have any claim to the magazine, and it's a moot point because I don't happen to have it. The police do. The Kent and Longton families can fight it out in court."

"Which is the problem," Irene said. "Roy's Mary Ellen's only child, and his parents are long divorced. It's perfectly obvious he can't fight the Kent family legally. All they have to do is delay, and any money he has for legal fees will run out, probably in the middle of the first billable hour."

"I hate to point this out to you, Irene," Jayne said. "But Gemma isn't rolling in the big bucks either."

"Not that Gemma has any claim to stake," I replied.

"I thought Roy should meet all the players, that's all," Irene said.

"I am not a player. And don't tell me you bought his grieving son act, never mind all that about what a loving, kind woman she was to the dying old man abandoned by his heartless family."

"Whether I believe it or not is irrelevant. It makes good copy."

"This is a pointless conversation," Jayne said. "As of right now, no one has the magazine."

"Nor the jewels," I said.

I knew that had been a mistake the minute the words were out of my mouth. If Irene had been a wolf, she would have thrown her head back and howled to the moon. Instead she said calmly, "Jewels?"

"Looks like your buddy Mr. Longton's holding something back from you." I took a sip of wine. Then I took another sip to give myself time to calm down. I gazed out to the harbor.

Shadows were lengthening and the incoming boats were deep-purple smudges against the dark water.

"Do tell, Jayne," Irene said.

Jayne clamped her lips shut and shook her head. I returned to the conversation. "Are the police saying anything about suspects? This all might have nothing to do with anything we've been talking about, you know. A random killing, maybe. Mistaken identity even."

"I got the feeling," Irene said, "that Detective Ashburton's convinced it's because of that inheritance."

I changed the subject abruptly. "Do you know why Ryan Ashburton's back in West London?"

She leaned in between Jayne and me. Instinctively, we slid closer. "That detective they brought in from Chicago when Rick Mertz retired didn't work out too well." She made gestures as though she were drinking. I'd not had much contact with the new detective, but when I had, the careful placement of his steps, the ever-so-slight slur to his words, and the scent of breath mints that trailed behind him like sharks following a fishing trawler were surefire clues that the guy had a serious drinking habit. "When he was . . . not exactly fired, but sent off to plague another police department, they lured Ryan back as head detective. He'd done well in Boston and was ready for the promotion. You know his dad's not been well since last summer, when he had that bad fall off the ladder when painting the house?" I nodded. "Ryan wanted to be closer to his folks. Plus, I heard he missed the Cape." She gave me an exaggerated wink. "He might have missed other things in West London too. You know anything about that, Gemma?"

"No," I said.

"Not everyone was happy to see Ryan Ashburton back in town," Irene said.

"Meaning?" I asked.

"Louise Estrada, so my department sources say, wanted the job. She wasn't happy when they brought in an outsider and promoted him over her."

"Ryan is hardly an outsider," I said.

"He left West London for the bright lights of the big city. To her, that makes him an outsider."

Meaning, I thought but didn't say, *she thinks she has something to prove.*

"Was she qualified?" Jayne asked.

"I can't really say. She's always seemed competent enough to me, but who knows what goes on behind the scenes." Irene turned around to check out her friends. They waved to her, drinks in hand. "I gotta go. There's a beer there with my name on it. You will let me know if you hear anything, won't you, Gemma?"

"I will," I said. "If you stop spreading rumors about me."

She gave me a wink and walked away.

"That was interesting," Jayne said. "You don't really think . . ."

"No, I do not. Even if I did have some extremely nebulous claim to the *Beeton's*, I wouldn't want to go up against the Kent family in court either. Let's just drop it."

Andy came up between us and laid a hand lightly on our shoulders. "Did you enjoy your appetizers?" he asked Jayne.

"They were absolutely delicious. So nice of you. Thank you."

"It's always my pleasure, Jayne." He looked deeply into her sea-blue eyes. "Can I get you another drink?"

"Better not," I said. "She's had two already."

"Gemma! You're not my mother, and I'm not driving."

"No, but I need you sharp and alert."

"Well, that's not going to happen. I'm meeting Robbie soon."
Andy's face fell.

"There he is now." Jayne waved frantically. The object of
her affections slouched across the crowded deck.

"I'll get back to the kitchen then," Andy said. "Going to
be a busy night."

"Never give up." I gave him what I hoped was an encouraging smile.

"Hey, babe." Robbie kissed Jayne loudly on the lips while
Andy slunk away. "Yo, Gemma."

Andy was a lovely man. He was attractive, gainfully
employed, a marvelous chef, and a successful businessman.
Robbie was a slovenly layabout who could barely summon up
two brain cells to rub together and dabbled in what he called
art but no one else did. Andy clearly adored Jayne. I watched
Robbie leer down the front of her shirt, and I knew what Robbie saw in her.

What Jayne saw in him was the mystery.

I hopped off my stool. "I'm off home. See you tomorrow,
Jayne."

"Bye, Gemma. Try not to worry. Everything will turn out
okay." She leapt to her feet and gave me an impromptu hug. I
hugged her back. When we separated, I feared Robbie would
try to grab me as well, but he was too busy snatching my
vacated stool out from under a woman in her seventies who
was preparing to lower herself onto it.

I went home, but I did not try not to worry. I was already worried. If there's one thing I am not, it's the type to sit around and worry unproductively.

Not only was the idea that I might have some claim to ownership of the magazine ridiculous, it was dangerous. Not least because it would give Estrada a reason to believe I had motive to kill Mary Ellen Longton. Might she try to argue that, when I realized Mary Ellen had left the magazine behind, I turned around and killed her so I could keep it? She might try to claim that I promised to split the proceeds with Jayne and thus convinced her to lie for me, negating my alibi.

Rather than take Violet for a walk, I let her into the enclosed yard to do her business while I made myself tea in a mug I'd salvaged from the Emporium when it suffered a small chip. It proclaimed "I am SHERlocked." Once Violet was back inside, I carried my tea into the den and took my iPad out of the secretary. The entire room was covered in a fine coating of fingerprint power, as were the living room, mudroom, and kitchen. I still hadn't tidied up after our mysterious visitor had tossed my house. I'd better get that done before Uncle Arthur came home. He'd immediately know something was wrong: even I'm not that untidy.

I opened the iPad and immediately forgot about housework.

I'd started to draw up a mental list of suspects: Donald Morris; Grant Thompson; Roy Longton; Colin Kent; other heirs of the late Kurt Kent Jr. I knew what Donald, Grant, Roy, and Colin all looked like, but not the other potentially interested parties.

I started with what was once called the society pages and is now the gossip blogs. The Kent family was wealthy, although not extravagantly so, and the patriarch's reclusiveness provided some fodder to the gossip mill. His eldest granddaughter, who went by the improbable name of Sapphire, chewed up a great deal of available media space. Twice married, twice divorced, childless, age thirty-nine, she'd been photographed many times getting out of limousines at the hottest night clubs (and showing a heck of a lot of leg and bony cleavage while going about it) or strolling on a Caribbean beach in a bikini made of dental floss while pretending not to notice the cameras following her. I studied her face carefully, but other than the same hooded eyes as Colin, her father, nothing looked familiar. I found pictures of Colin and his brother George arriving in court to contest their father's will. Colin I'd met, and although the family resemblance between him and his brother was strong, I was positive I'd never seen George before. The brothers were accompanied by their lawyer and by George's son Alexander, both of whom I also did not recognize. It would seem as though in the Kent family, business was left up to the men. Kurt had a daughter, I'd read, and it took a substantial amount of searching to locate a picture of her. She kept a low profile and was never mentioned in the gossip blogs, but it's almost impossible to keep yourself completely off the Internet, and eventually I found her. Her name was Judy, and although she was married, with one daughter called Rebecca Charmaine, she appeared to have kept the Kent name, as that was the one by which she was always referred. Judy seemed to be somewhat of an equestrian and had won a ribbon in dressage at a show in Upstate New York last January. To my considerable disappointment, I didn't recognize her either. I was about to close the computer and give up for the night, when something in a photo of Judy caught my attention, and I expanded the image on the screen.

And there she was. I let out a long breath, as I took a moment to wonder how detectives ever accomplished anything in the days before the Internet. In one of the pictures of Judy and her horse accepting their award, another woman was standing beside Judy. Her name was Elaine Kent, and she was, the article said, Judy's sister-in-law.

Armed with a name, I quickly found further details about her. Elaine Kent was married to Colin and was the mother of Sapphire. She was Kurt Kent Jr.'s daughter-in-law.

She'd been in the Sherlock Holmes Bookshop and Emporium on Monday, as part of the bridge group bus tour.

Chapter 8

I called up memories of the tour group. The women had all been of an age—midsixties to early seventies—and a type—moderately affluent. Their hair varied from dyed-blonde-covering-gray to gray. They were all white, all of middle height, and their weight ranged between slim and softly plump. Their clothes and jewelry were indicative of practical but well-heeled women on vacation. I flashed through mental images of them in the Emporium and searched through the crowd for Elaine Kent. She hadn't stood out from the rest, hadn't been paying any particular attention to any one thing, and hadn't been sneaking about. At least not when I was watching, which was, admittedly, not all the time. I remembered seeing her flicking through a copy of *How to Think like Sherlock* by Daniel Smith. She bought the book. I'd been behind the cash register, accepted payment, put the book in a store bag, wished her a good day, and went on to serve the next person. I hadn't seen her again.

Her payment. She'd paid by credit card. The record of her transaction would be on the store computer. I considered retuning to the Emporium tonight to check the receipts, and thus confirm my suspicions, but decided it could wait. I was positive Elaine Kent had been in my shop at the same time as Mary Ellen Longton.

And that could be no coincidence.

I considered what to do next. I pulled out my phone and studied it. I hadn't called Ryan Ashburton in a long time, but I still had his number. I played with the buttons. I'd been told, more than once, that the police didn't need or want my help.

So be it.

I needed to find out if Elaine was still on the tour and talk to her if she was. But I hadn't arranged the visit, Jayne had. The women had been wearing "Hello, my name is . . ." stickers on their chests, but they didn't have the name of the tour company on it. Their young guide had been dressed in generic navy-blue Bermuda shorts, a blue-and-white-striped shirt, and a plain blue ball cap. I hadn't seen any identifying company name or logo on her. She'd carried a clipboard, but it had been a plain brown one, and I hadn't been close enough, or interested enough, to read the papers on it. I called Jayne. It went immediately to voice mail. Drat! She must still be with Robbie. I left a message. "Jayne, it's Gemma. Ring me as soon as you get this."

*   *   *

Mrs. Hudson's Tea Room opens at seven in the tourist season for the benefit of those heading out on a fishing trip or wanting to get an early start to their holiday. Jayne makes most of her baked goods herself, so that means she's up bright and early.

So bright and early, the sun hadn't yet made an appearance when my phone rang.

"What's so urgent?" Jayne said.

I blinked sleep out of my eyes. "Huh?"

"I've only just turned on my phone. You called me last night. You said it's urgent, so I knew you wouldn't mind me calling you this early."

"Right." I lay back against the pillows. The room was pitch-dark, lit only by the glow of the phone and the numbers of the bedside clock. "The tour company that brought the bridge players to the tea room, what was its name?"

"You called me last night, while I was enjoying a lovely evening with Robbie I might add, to ask that?"

"Do you remember?"

"Yes, I remember. New England Holiday Tours."

"What's their number?"

"I don't have it at home, Gemma. I can call you when I get to work."

"No need. I'll look them up. Do they operate out of Boston?"

"I think so."

I hung up. The time was 4:24. Too early to call the offices of New England Holiday Tours. Outside, a car drove slowly down Blue Water Place, throwing its lights across my bedroom walls. Someone else heading to work extremely early or sneaking home after a late night. Now that I was awake, I might as well get up.

From her bed on the floor, Violet opened one eye. Clearly she was not impressed with the time. Nevertheless, she stretched and yawned and followed me down the hall.

While Violet checked to see if any squirrels had invaded our property in the night and the kettle boiled for my tea, I looked up the bus company. I found nothing out of the ordinary on first glance. A long-standing tour company that ferried visitors around Boston and to Cape Cod in spring and summer and took them on foliage-viewing expeditions in the autumn. I didn't see mention of bridge groups, but as well as their packaged tours, they offered "private, customized small-group trips to suit your individual needs."

I filled in the time until the company's office would open by delving into the world of Sherlock Holmes collecting. Despite the fact that I own a shop called the Sherlock Holmes Bookshop and Emporium, it's not something I know a great deal about. Uncle Arthur knows more about the high-priced world of first editions and rare magazines than I do.

I hadn't spoken to Uncle Arthur since Tuesday when he called to tell me he was leaving town. I didn't want to contact him now. I wouldn't be able to tell him why I was interested without him worming the full story of Mary Ellen Longton and *Beeton's Christmas Annual* out of me. And then he'd turn the Triumph around on a dime and come home. As long as a murderer was running free, I'd just as soon Uncle Arthur stayed away. He might see mention of a killing in West London in the papers, depending on how far he'd gotten in the past two days, but my name hadn't appeared in the stories. Arthur was an intelligent man, interested in almost everything he came across, particularly people. But he'd declared long ago that this "Interweb-thing" held no appeal for him. He carried a flip-phone only because I put my foot down and insisted that when he was away I needed to be able to contact him in case of an emergency.

The Sherlock discussion boards were aglow with the news that Kurt Kent Jr. had died and speculation that his vast collection would soon be up for auction. The excitement dimmed when it was revealed that the will was in dispute and nothing would happen until the situation was resolved. Some members posted that they'd attempted to speak to one or another of Kent's children and had been rudely rebuffed.

No surprise there. *Sorry your dad's dead, can I get my hands on his stuff?*

I clicked backward through time, looking for any mention of Kurt Kent prior to his death. I found a great deal. The Kent collection hadn't been seen by anyone outside the immediate family and household staff for almost twenty years. Every time a piece of valuable Sherlockania came up for auction and the winning bidder had been anonymous, it was speculated that Kent had bought it. Some collectors were not happy. It was an outrage, they said, that one wealthy man should be able to keep artifacts such as these from the enjoyment of others.

Was it possible an enraged Sherlockian had killed Mary Ellen in an attempt to get the magazine?

I let out an exasperated breath. *More suspects.*

But surely if a mad collector had come to West London in pursuit of Mary Ellen and her magazine, they would pop into the Emporium? I couldn't see anyone who was that much of a fanatic leaving town without paying the shop a visit.

Unless, of course, they were a regular visitor and knew I didn't stock the sort of items that would drive a collector into a murderous frenzy.

By eight o'clock, Violet had fallen asleep in front of the cold fireplace, and I'd consumed gallons of tea and more than a respectable amount of toast and marmalade. I placed a call.

"Good morning. New England Holiday Tours, bringing you the best of beautiful, historic New England. This is Janice. May I help you with your vacation plans today?"

"Uh. Not exactly. I'm calling from Mrs. Hudson's Tea Room in West London. One of your tour groups visited us on Monday. One of the ladies left something behind. I'd like to talk to the tour guide, if I may."

"Let me check." I heard computer keys clicking.

"Yes, West London. We had a private tour make a stop in your lovely town."

"A bridge group."

"That's correct."

"Can I have the number of the tour leader?" I knew she wouldn't give it to me. Always worth a try, though.

"Why don't I get in touch with her and have her contact you?"

"I'm not at work this morning, but she can ring me at home." I rattled off my number. "Thanks."

They were efficient at New England Holiday Tours, I'll give them that. I was rinsing out the teapot when my phone rang, and a woman's voice asked, "Is this Jayne?"

"No, it's Gemma Doyle, her business partner. You brought a group of bridge players into the tea room and then the Sherlock Holmes Bookshop on Monday."

"So I did. I'm Alicia. The office said there was a problem."

"Sorry, Alicia, there's no problem. I needed to talk to you. I'm trying to contact one of the ladies on your tour. Elaine Kent?"

"No one by that name's with me. Sorry. Maybe you're thinking of another group?"

"Is the tour still together?"

"Yes, we're in Truro tonight and tomorrow, and then returning to Boston."

"Are all the original members still with you?"

"We lost one. As you can imagine, for a bridge group, that's not good. The numbers have to be divisible by four. I've tried to take her place, but I don't really know how to play."

"Lost one?"

"Mrs. Kirk. Ellen Kirk had a death in her family. Very sudden, she said. It was the morning after our visit to West London. She was very upset, but frankly, I wasn't entirely surprised she left us. She didn't seem to be enjoying the tour much, and she wasn't making friends. She wasn't even a good bridge player, and I overheard some of the women complaining about not wanting to partner with her."

"How did she seem when you left my bookshop?"

"Seem? Normal enough. I guess. Oh, now I remember. She was very late getting to the bus. I always tell the women, we leave on time whether they're on board or not, but I don't really mean it. This time I was about to tell the driver to go when Mrs. Kirk came running up. She was . . . 'flustered' is probably the best word. She plunked herself down in her seat without so much as an apology. She went straight to her room when we got to the hotel and didn't even come down for dinner."

I had little doubt this was the woman I was after. When people employed a pseudonym, they often used the same initials, thinking it would be easier to remember. Still, I needed confirmation. "Can I send you a picture of the woman I'm interested in? You can tell me if it's this Mrs. Kirk."

"I guess that would be all right. You haven't told me why you want to talk to her."

"Haven't I? I'll send the picture now. Just a text back to me saying yes or no will suffice. Thanks for your help."

"Okay. Oh, one thing . . ."

"Yes."

"You don't play bridge, do you? The ladies are very unhappy, and I'm getting desperate."

"Sorry. No."

I pulled up Elaine Kent's picture on the iPad, cropped it to take out her sister-in-law and the horse as well as all the wording, and texted it to Alicia.

She replied in less than a minute: *Can't say for sure. But might be.*

Chapter 9

"Might be" wasn't a yes. But it was close enough for me to investigate further. If Elaine Kent had been on the bridge tour, and if she'd left suddenly, she had almost certainly done so because of the death of Mary Ellen Longton. Meaning either Mrs. Kent had been responsible or she knew who was. It was also very likely she'd gone straight home.

In my perusals of the business and family affairs of the Kents, I'd discovered that Colin Kent, the eldest son and CEO of Kent Enterprises since his father's illness, lived in "the historic, stately Boston mansion" purchased by Kurt Kent Sr. in 1957.

The Internet is a marvelous thing, and a few minutes of searching gave me the address of said *stately historic mansion*. In her day, Mr. Kent Sr.'s wife, Juliette, entertained extensively to raise money for various charities, and she was particularly fond of throwing champagne and afternoon tea garden parties at the mansion.

There hadn't been a party at the house since Mrs. Kent's death, but a historian had kindly put her memories of attending such a garden party up on the Internet for me to find, including the address of the house. I put the computer away, satisfied with my morning's work. Moments later, my phone rang. I felt a small fission of pleasure at seeing the name Grant Thompson on the display screen.

"Good morning, Gemma. I hope I haven't woken you."

"Not at all. I've been up for hours."

"I thought you might be an early riser." A soft chuckle came down the line. "I've been wondering if there's any news about the *Beeton's Annual*. I called the police station, but the detectives won't talk to me. I'm eager to do a proper examination of it."

"Sorry. Nothing," I said. "They don't talk to me either."

"I hate the thought of that precious magazine, that fragile one-hundred-and-thirty-year-old paper, tossed into the back of some police locker."

I shuddered in sympathy. "Without climate control."

"Handled by people not wearing white gloves."

"The police station building is old. It's close to the sea, meaning damp."

"They might even have rats."

We both groaned.

"Unfortunately, the police don't seem to have set the protection of the magazine as their first priority," Grant said. "The disbelief on their faces when I told them its possible value was obvious."

"I don't think Detective Estrada entirely trusts me either. But I do have an idea. I'm glad you reminded me. My uncle Arthur plays tennis with the chief of police's father. I'll ask him to place a call. We can try to get at the police that way."

If I could get hold of Arthur. He had a tendency to forget to charge his cell phone. That he never forgot to do anything else made me think he forgot on purpose.

"Small towns," Grant said with another of his warm chuckles. "Gotta love 'em."

"And I do," I said.

"Are you free for lunch today, Gemma? We can talk about the Sherlock papers and . . . other things."

"Sorry," I said, pleased at being asked. "I'm going to Boston later."

"Will you be back in time for dinner?"

"I should be," I said, *very* pleased at being asked.

"Let's do that then. You're the local, name the place."

"My favorite is the Blue Water Café down by the harbor. It gets busy, so you should make a reservation."

"Is eight o'clock too late?"

"The store closes at nine on Thursday, but my assistant's working today, and she can close up." I thought quickly. I could leave the store in Ruby's hands before eight, rush home and change, and be at the café by half eight. "Eight thirty?"

"Perfect. See you then, Gemma." His voice lingered over my name. I hung up with a smile and got ready for work.

I didn't have to be a detective—reluctant one though I might be—to remember that Thursday is sticky bun day at the tea room. Jayne could charge people for walking past on the sidewalk, so intense is the scent of warm pastry, hot cinnamon and sugar, and melting butter drifting out the doors. I greeted several Thursday-morning regulars waiting patiently in line as I headed for the kitchen. I found Jayne and Jocelyn rolling dough, their cheeks and the tips of their noses dotted with white powder.

"Did you have an explosion in the flour bin?" I asked.

"Something like that," Jocelyn muttered. The bell on the industrial oven sounded, and she slipped on heat-proof gloves before opening the door.

"This must be what heaven smells like," I said. Jocelyn took the gorgeous, glistening, scented spiral rolls out of the oven and laid them in the cooling racks. I breathed deeply.

"What's up?" Jayne asked. "We're busy."

"I'm going to Boston. Do you want to come?"

"You mean today?"

"I mean now."

"Why would I want to go to Boston, and, perhaps more to the point, why do you?"

I glanced at Jocelyn, who'd turned away from us to get a bag of sugar off the shelf, and touched my lips.

Jayne rolled her eyes. "Give us a minute, will you please, Jocelyn? Those croissants are ready to go out front."

"Sure." She lifted the tray and left.

I quickly told my friend what I'd learned last night and this morning. "I need to talk to Mrs. Kent."

"And accuse her of murder? That's unlikely to end well, Gemma."

"The least I can do is confirm that this woman is the one who was in the Emporium, and thus in West London, on the day her late father-in-law's private nurse was murdered. All I have is a poor photo taken off the Internet, a maybe from the tour group leader, and my suspicions. Not enough to take to the police. I want to go to the Kent home and see the woman for myself. Only then will I be sure."

"I'm in the middle of the day's baking."

"I can wait a couple of hours. Ruby comes in at noon today. She can look after the shop in my absence."

"If I say no?"

"Then you'll miss a nice outing to Boston and the chance to see a *stately historic mansion,* once famous for its garden parties."

"Meaning you'll go without me."

"Is that in doubt?"

"No. Okay, give me two hours. Jocelyn should be able to manage by herself after then."

*   *   *

If I didn't have to earn a living, I'd keep the bookstore as my own private library. I wouldn't let anyone else come in. I could regularly order the newest books and reread old favorites. The shelves would be neatly organized, and I'd never have to search for anything misplaced by a careless employee or absent-minded customer. If I got rid of the life-sized cutouts, the puzzles, the coffee mugs, and all the other assorted junk (sorry, merchandise), then I could expand the bookshelves. I might even be able to purchase a few first editions. For my own reading pleasure, of course.

But as I am not independently wealthy and I do have to stock what customers want to buy, I enjoy being alone in the Emporium before opening. It's quiet and peaceful, and everything is in its proper place. Just me and the books. And Moriarty, glaring at me over the arm of the chair in the reading nook.

I unpacked a box of new books, pleased to see that the reprint of *The Moonstone* by Wilkes Collins I'd ordered some time ago had finally arrived. As I organized the gaslight shelves to make room for the new arrival, I breathed in the scent of paper and ink and the bindings of a good book. The door to the tea room was closed, but a trace of cinnamon drifted in to mix with the new book smell.

Heaven on earth. I chose a copy of *The Moonstone* for myself, took it upstairs to the office, and put it in my tote bag to take home.

A new line of coffee mugs from the contemporary BBC TV show, featuring quotes from the programs and pictures of the main characters, was proving very popular with my customers. So popular were they that this morning, they were out of order on the shelf. That would never do. I spent a few minutes organizing them into a straight line with their handles all facing in the correct direction, and I'd stepped back to admire my handiwork when the phone beneath the sales counter rang. I hurried to answer it. "Sherlock Holmes Bookshop and Emporium."

"Gemma Doyle?"

"This is she."

Moriarty jumped onto the counter.

"My name is Edward Manning, from Manning's Rare and Antiquarian Books in New York City." The voice was deep and rumbling. An older man, his vocal cords seasoned by decades of cigars and whisky.

"Yes?"

"You've come into possession of a rare copy of a magazine. I'd like to make an appointment to view the magazine with the intention of making you an offer, depending on the condition. You're in Cape Cod, I understand. I can be there tomorrow. Say ten AM?"

"Huh? I mean, you're mistaken, Mr. Manning. I don't own such a thing."

"My sources tell me you're about to inherit it."

"Your sources?" For a brief moment I wondered if Great Uncle Arthur had a possession he'd not told me about. For an even briefer moment, I wondered if something had happened to Great Uncle Arthur and this was how I was being informed. Then I remembered what Irene had told me last night. "Your sources are mistaken. I'm not in line to inherit anything."

"Perhaps you don't understand the value, Ms. Doyle. I looked up details on your . . . store . . . and see that you are strictly retail." Judging by the tone in his voice at the last word, he might have suggested that I dealt in trafficked human body parts. "Which is why I'm prepared to do you a favor and give you a fair and just estimate and offer."

"Good-bye." I hung up. *Oh dear.* Word was spreading. Not only was it spreading, but it was wrong. Mr. Manning hadn't named the magazine. I wondered if he even knew. What had Irene told me? Someone in the police station had tipped her off about the *Beeton's.* I could imagine the scene. Grant had said the room was full of cops when he did his initial estimation. It was unlikely, although not impossible, that a sworn officer was Irene's informant. It was more likely a case of two cops going for coffee after Grant left—one saying to the other, "Imagine a magazine worth thousands of bucks!"—and having been overheard by an eager clerk or a passing citizen.

However it had happened, this situation did me no good. Now I had more than Louise Estrada's suspicions to worry about. Someone had killed Mary Ellen Longton, very possibly in pursuit of the magazine. If that someone thought I was next in line to take possession of it . . .

All the more reason to go to Boston. I would talk to Elaine Kent and tell her I had no legal rights to her father-in-law's property, and I didn't want it in any event.

Moriarty's narrowed amber eyes watched me think. "You want me to keep it, don't you?" I said to him. "Aside from the fact that I don't have it, and thus can't *keep* anything."

He did not reply.

*   *   *

Ruby arrived for work precisely on time. That was not a common occurrence. She looked somewhat the worse for wear, which was a common occurrence.

"Are you all right?" I asked.

"Yes," she snapped.

"Just asking."

She sighed. "Sorry Gemma. I didn't sleep well last night, and I think I might be coming down with a cold." Her face was pale and her eyes rimmed red, but her breathing was fine and she wasn't sniffling. I suspected her condition had more to do with the sleepless night, probably caused by the consumption of excessive quantities of alcohol, than any potential illness. She gave Moriarty a scratch behind the ears, and he rewarded her by rubbing against her arm.

"Don't be sneezing on our customers," I said. "Jayne and I will be out for the rest of the afternoon. If you have to go home, call Lorraine and see she if she's free." Lorraine Dobbs was a friend of Jayne's mother. She'd once owned her own clothing shop but had retired a couple of years ago. She worked in the tea room on busy weekends and in the Emporium if I was in a pinch.

I began to leave when I had a thought. "Ruby, you were here when I found the magazine hidden in the bookshelves on Tuesday. I'm sure you realize the woman who left it here is the one who was murdered that night."

She nodded. "Everyone in town's talking about it."

"Is your father likely to be interested in something like that?"

"Gosh, no. Why would he?"

"You told me he's a Sherlock fanatic."

"Oh, right." She shrugged. "He reads the books, but he doesn't have any interest in collecting stuff."

"What did you do on Tuesday, after you left here?"

"I didn't go around to a hotel to kill a woman, if that's what you're asking."

"I'm only trying to place everyone."

"If you must place me, and I don't see that it's any of your business, I went home, and then met up in Hyannis for a drink with a friend. I stayed at his place until the next morning. That really is none of your business." She glared at me. "Okay?"

"Okay," I said. "If you need me, I have my phone with me."

I headed home to get my car. A strong wind was blowing off the ocean, and as I hurried along the boardwalk, I felt the touch of warm salty air on my face and ruffling my hair. I remembered my conversation with Grant this morning and tried calling Uncle Arthur. It went immediately to voice mail.

"Hi, it's me, Gemma. Something interesting has happened here. A book collector came into the shop and told me about an original and rare Holmes magazine that's turned up in West London. Imagine that. Anyway, the magazine is at the police station as there's some dispute, so I understand, about provenance." I tried to keep my voice light, uninvolved, just being nice and doing a small favor for a new friend. Whether I could fool Uncle Arthur or not was another matter. He knew me so well. I didn't want him turning around and coming home. He was a strong man, mentally and physically, but he was approaching ninety and no match for a determined killer. Those tennis games he told me he played with the police chief's father every Sunday? I long ago began to suspect the two old men had abandoned the courts in favor of McGillivray's Irish Pub, where rather than exchanging volleys, they exchanged stories of chasing down pirates in the Gulf and chasing up mob-connected hit men in Boston. "He—my collector friend, I mean—is concerned that the police don't know how to take proper care of the magazine. I thought maybe you could have a word with Jack and ask him to have a word with the chief. Thanks. Hope you're having fun." I hung up. Just as well he didn't pick up; he'd ask questions I didn't want to answer.

I had to go into the house to get my car keys, which means I had to deal with the crushing weight of guilt when Violet realized I wasn't taking her with me. She loves nothing more than a ride in the car, but there's no room in the Miata for her if I have a passenger. "Sorry," I mumbled, grabbing the keys and fleeing the house.

A few minutes later, I parked the car in the loading bay behind the tea room and went in to get Jayne.

She was, as I should have guessed, not ready.

"Sorry, Gemma. Last-minute rush on the cinnamon buns, so I decided to make another batch, and then I realized that the egg delivery hadn't come yet, so Jocelyn had to make a dash to the supermarket."

"You can call me The Mad Dasher," Jocelyn said with a grin.

"I asked Fiona to wrap up a couple of yesterday's muffins and pastries for us to eat on the way," Jayne said.

You would think, seeing as to how Jayne worked in a bakery and thought about food all the time even when she wasn't working, that she'd be enormous. I eyed her tiny, petite frame and decided that life was not fair. "Let's go."

"Give me a couple of minutes," she said. "I have to get these tarts decorated." She pointed to a tray of glistening fruit pastries, piping hot from the oven. A bowl of perfect, tiny bright-red raspberries sat on the counter beside them.

"I can drop a raspberry on top of a tart, Jayne," Jocelyn said. "But . . ."

I took my friend's arm. "No 'buts.' I'm leaving. Now. If you want to come, that means you are too."

She untied her apron and tossed it onto a chair. Jocelyn handed her our survival pack, and we went out the back way to the car. It was another gorgeous day, not a cloud in the sky, so I put the top down and we headed to Boston.

"The Blue Water Café seems to be doing well," I said, apropos of nothing, once we'd left West London itself and were heading north on Route 136 toward Highway 6, which would take us west and off the Cape. It was midday on a Thursday in June, but traffic was already building, as city dwellers headed toward the hotels and summer homes and beaches for what was predicted to be a fabulous weekend. I had to shout to be heard.

"It's a great place, good location," Jayne replied.

I gave her a sideways glance. "Andy is a great cook."

"Yup."

"I've always wanted a man who could cook. Haven't found one yet."

"Um-hum."

"Even the best cook can't run a successful restaurant if they can't manage a business. He's good at that too, don't you think?"

"Um-hum."

"Jayne, you know that Andy . . ."

"Duck!" Jayne shouted.

We were coming into a bend; fortunately for the other cars on the road, I did not duck.

I did, however, see what had alarmed Jayne. We were outside of West London now, but a WLPD car was heading our way.

I kept both hands firmly on the wheel and my face pointing straight ahead. My eyes, however, slid to one side. Two people were in the car and their heads turned as I sped past.

"It's them," Jayne said. "Maybe they didn't notice us."

"In this car? Oh, dear, they're turning around." I watched my rearview mirror. Yep, the cruiser had made a turn onto the verge of the road and was now speeding up. I pretended not to notice and kept driving, sticking precisely to the speed limit. It was hard, however, to keep not noticing when lights and sirens came on. For the briefest of moments, I reminded myself that the Miata could easily leave their clunky old Ford Vic in the dust. But as I had no desire to reenact the climactic scene of *Thelma and Louise*, I slowed, flicked on my turn indicator, and pulled over. The patrol car came to a halt behind me. Both doors opened and Louise Estrada and Ryan Ashburton got out. They were dressed in plain clothes, but Estrada pushed her jacket slightly aside so I could see the gun at her hip. As if I was going to take off in a blaze of dust, exhaust fumes, and glory.

"Good morning, Ryan," I said when he appeared at my side. "Lovely day for a drive." Estrada stood by the passenger door, feet apart, hands on hips, sunglasses shielding her eyes, scowl firmly in place.

Ryan pushed his own sunglasses onto the top of his head. "Where are you going, Gemma?"

"Why do you ask?"

"Because you're involved in a murder inquiry, and you were ordered not to leave West London."

"I was?"

"Yes, you were."

"Sorry." I wasn't pretending to be innocent. I'd totally forgotten that minor detail.

"We're not exactly fleeing," Jayne said. "You can search the car if you want. We don't have suitcases, never mind our passports and two one-way airline tickets to Brazil."

Ryan ignored her. "Gemma?"

"I can't go for a drive with my best friend on a pleasant day? If you stop everyone on this road, you're going to be very busy."

"Look—" Estrada snapped. Ryan held up one hand, and she bit off the rest of her sentence.

"It's midday in the middle of the week," he said, "and you're both responsible businesswomen. Something took you away from the store."

"I notice," I said, "you're returning to West London. I might ask the same of you."

"Gemma! You don't ask the questions here. I do."

"The estate of the late Mr. Kurt Kent is said to have a substantial collection of Sherlock Holmes–related items. I spent some time this morning on the Internet reading discussion boards. People are showing a lot of interest in his collection. I want to try to get some things for the store."

His blue eyes were usually the color of the ocean on a sunny day. Right now a hurricane was moving in. His jaw clenched. He didn't believe a word I was saying, but he wasn't ready to accuse me of anything nefarious yet. Not in the presence of Estrada at any rate.

"You were told to stay in West London," she said. "We can bring you in for disobeying an order, you know."

"When do you plan to be back?" Ryan asked.

"Before the shop closes today. As you said, I am a responsible businesswoman." I indicated Jayne. "We both are."

Jayne nodded. "Highly responsible."

"Be sure you are," Ryan said.

"I—" Estrada began to protest, but Ryan silenced her with a look. "You're wasting your time," Estrada said, determined

to get in the last word. "You know what those rich old families are like. That estate's locked up tight in a legal dispute,
and it'll be some time before it's all unraveled. Tough enough
when the nurse was the heir, but now that she's dead, her relatives are coming out of the woodwork."

"Did she have much of an estate of her own?" I tried to
sound as though I had a casual interest. Just curious.

"She didn't have a spare penny, or so it seems, except for
what she got from old man Kent. Her son's claiming that what
was left to her in the old man's will should now go to him."

I glanced at Ryan. He was standing by the car, watching me, letting Estrada talk. Neither of them seemed to have
heard the rumor that I was interested in making a claim. Give
them time.

"You mean the magazine?" I asked.

"He also left her some of his late wife's jewelry," Estrada
said. "As you can imagine, that didn't go down well with the
sons and the daughter."

"Expensive jewelry?" Jayne asked.

She whistled. "Oh, yeah. Stones as big as a rock."

"I can understand the family being upset about losing
their mother's jewels," I said. "They probably don't care too
much what happens to the magazine, though."

Estrada snorted. "Nothing's too small to get the lawyers
fighting over it."

"Speaking of the magazine, what's happening to it?"

"The son's demanding we hand it over, but as it's evidence
in a murder investigation, that's not likely to happen for a
good long time. Same with the family jewels."

"Has anyone had another look at it? Other than the initial examination by Grant Thompson?"

"Not yet," Estrada said.

"If it is an original, it's very delicate. Paper is highly fragile. It doesn't keep well unless it's properly cared for. Any amount of rough handling or improper storage could reduce the value considerably."

"Don't you worry your pretty little English head," Estrada said with a barely controlled sneer. "It's safe and sound. We won't touch it with our dirty fingers."

Ryan took a step backward. "We'll let you be on your way, Gemma. Be in West London by dark tonight. Don't get your hopes up about being able to buy the magazine or anything else from that estate any time soon."

I put the car into gear and we sped away (keeping strictly to the speed limit, of course). In my mirror, I watched Ryan and Estrada return to their car.

"Wow," Jayne said. "She sure doesn't like you, does she, Gemma?"

"No, she doesn't. And that worries me."

"Although she can be the chatty one when she wants to be."

"Ryan didn't stop her, which I find interesting. I wonder if he realized she was telling me they'd found jewelry among Mary Ellen's things—information that hasn't been publicly released. Fortunately, I don't have to pretend that I don't know about it anymore."

I had revealed nothing and learned a lot. The police had been to Boston to talk to the Kent family lawyers about the will. The only reason they would do that would be if they believed Mary Ellen was killed because of the items she'd inherited from her late employer. Meaning, it had not been a random killing. Not that I thought it had been, but it was nice to have my suspicions confirmed. The main issue, however, might not be the magazine, but the jewelry.

Elaine Kent wasn't Kurt's daughter, but she was his daughter-in-law. She might well have expected to inherit some of the nicer pieces of jewelry upon his death. Had she been promised something particular? Say, a nice brooch of big diamonds with an enormous sapphire in the center?

What was the name of the party-girl granddaughter? *Sapphire.*

Easy to assume the girl, or her mother, would inherit the stone after which she was named.

Ryan had done me a favor, letting Estrada tell me what they knew and not pressing me as to where Jayne and I were going. Time to return the favor. When I got home, I'd fill Ryan in on what I'd learned about Elaine Kent and her visit to the Sherlock Holmes Bookshop and Emporium.

*   *   *

The Kents' *stately historic mansion* was situated on a street of similar stately historic mansions. Very few of the homes were visible from the road, hidden as they were by huge old trees, thick shrubbery, tall fences and locked gates, or expansive, carefully maintained lawns and long curling driveways.

The hair on the back of my neck prickled as a hundred security cameras followed us down the winding streets.

"That's the one," I said to Jayne as I slowed and made the turn.

The property was surrounded by a high, thick hedge inside of which I could see a wire fence. The gate at the entrance was firmly shut. A small guardhouse squatted inside the gate, and after a moment a man came out of it. He was young, tall, and well built and wore the uniform of a private security firm.

"No admittance," he said. His eyes ran appreciatively over both Jayne and the Miata.

I gave him a smile. "Good afternoon. Is this the Kent residence?"

"Yeah."

"I am here to see Mrs. Elaine Kent." I pronounced each word carefully, emphasizing my English accent. Some Americans, I have found, react better to that. As though I have returned to the colonies in order to claim my rightful place as Lady of the Manor. My mother's family is minor (extremely minor) aristocracy (penniless aristocracy), but I can do Maggie Smith as the Dowager Countess of Grantham when needed.

"She ain't home."

"That is unfortunate. I've come some distance to speak with her. When do you expect her to return?"

He shrugged his massive shoulders. They were, I thought, disproportionate to his small bullet-shaped head with its big floppy ears.

"Is she not home or just not receiving guests?" Jayne said.

"I don't know. I've a standing order of no visitors, that's all." The hem of his trousers was scuffed, his trainers dirty, and he sported a highly unattractive goatee. His uniform could do with a good wash.

"Have you been on duty long today?" I asked.

"Came on at noon."

It was two thirty now.

"So you're not entirely sure who's at home?" Jayne said.

"Look, lady, all I know is *no visitors*."

I opened my door, and he just about jumped out of his skin. I made no move to get out of the car and slammed the door shut with considerate force. A crow squawked at us from the canopy overhead. Otherwise, all was quiet. "Sorry," I said, "my shirt was caught in the door."

I rummaged in my bag for a business card. I held it out to him. He eyed me but made no move to take it.

"Would you give this to Mrs. Kent, please? She can ring me at that number. I have business that should interest her."

"I'm no messenger boy."

"Next time you're talking to her then," Jayne said.

"I've never talked to her. I've never talked to any of them. They drive in. They drive out. I open the gate, and then I shut it behind them."

I shoved my unwanted card into my pocket. "Very interesting. Good day, sir." I backed onto the street.

"Waste of time," Jayne said.

"Nothing is ever a waste of time." Fortunately, the Kent property occupied the corner of the street. I simply drove around the corner and stopped the car.

"What are we doing?" Jayne asked.

"Looking for ingress," I replied.

"What? We're not going to sneak in!"

"It would appear that we have to."

"Come on, the place is a fortress. I bet they have cameras everywhere, even if we get over that fence. And I'm not climbing fences."

"They might well have cameras, but no one's watching them." I edged the car forward and scanned the shrubbery. "Excellent."

"What's excellent?"

"Gap in the fence up ahead. The hedge is covering it, but not very well."

"We can't simply park here. We'd be noticed in a neighborhood like this one. Someone would be calling the cops in minutes."

"You're probably right. I saw a suitable place to leave the car not far away."

A few streets over, the properties were much less ostentatious and the lots so small, comparatively speaking, the houses could be seen from the road. One of those houses appeared to be hosting a child's birthday party this afternoon.

A cluster of brightly colored balloons danced in the air above the mailbox to which they were tied, and SUVs and luxury cars crowded the driveway. I could leave the Miata on the street, and it would look as though it belonged to late-arriving partygoers.

"What makes you think no one's watching the cameras at the house?" Jayne asked.

"That security guard has remarkably little interest in his job, but no one seems inclined to remove him from it. I took a quick glance inside the guard house and saw a bank of display screens, all of which were blank. He was watching his phone when we drove up and, with considerable reluctance, came out to see what we wanted. He's not exactly bright and alert. The condition of the fence also indicates that security here is but a pretext."

"What's wrong with the fence?"

"Jayne, you need to pay more attention to your surroundings. I immediately noticed several gaps, as well as places where the wire is rusting, thus easy to penetrate. And the hedge is badly overgrown, giving cover to anyone trying to break in."

"Didn't you notice the 'Beware of Dog' sign on the gate?"

"Of course I did. At the same time as I noticed that not only does the guard not have a dog with him, but nothing barked when I opened the car door and slammed it shut as loudly as I could."

I parked the car in front of the party house, and we trotted down the calm, leafy streets back to the Kent property. When we reached the spot I'd identified, I bent over and took off one of my shoes.

"What are you doing?" Jayne said.

"Ensuring no one's coming. Be quiet." I shook an imaginary stone out of my shoe and listened. Birds chirped in the trees, but otherwise all was quiet. This wasn't a neighborhood where residents walked anywhere. It was the middle of the afternoon and getting hot. Staff who walked from the bus stop would have arrived at work long ago, and joggers and runners would have been out before the heat settled in. I put my shoe back on and slipped into the shrubbery. Jayne followed.

I pushed branches and the rusted fence aside, and we scrambled through to emerge on the lawn at the east side of the house.

"The things I do for you," Jayne said as she picked leaves and twigs out of her hair.

We were exposed standing out in the open, so I loped quickly across the grass to another, smaller hedge closer to the house. This one was also badly overgrown, and I slipped inside. I gestured for Jayne to do the same. She grumbled as a broken limb scraped against her cheek and I told her to shush. From between branches, I peeked out and studied the property.

The lawn on which Boston's elite had once gathered to sip champagne and Darjeeling and nibble on crustless sandwiches while exchanging the latest gossip and business news, and incidentally drop a few pennies for charity, was choked with crabgrass and dandelions. The hedges were a tangled mess, and the decorative bushes unpruned. Last year's leaf fall cluttered the no-longer-neat perennial beds where daisies, bellflowers, hosta, and ornamental grasses struggled in vain against the weedy onslaught.

"What now?" Jayne asked.

"You have blood on your cheek," I said.

She squawked and wiped furiously at it.

"We ring the doorbell, of course," I said. "Like any proper visitor."

We kept to the hedge until it reached a wall of the house. It was a marvelous old building: golden, weatherworn stone; tall beveled windows; several brick chimneys. I glanced in the windows as we passed but could see little, as the light of the sun reflected back at me. The driveway made an expansive circle at the front of the house before ending at a four-door garage. All the doors were closed, and no cars were parked outside. The drive itself was large enough to accommodate rows of horse-drawn carriages carrying hoop-skirted ladies and mustachioed gentlemen to balls and concerts. The garage doors desperately needed a coat of paint, and the surface of the driveway was chipped and pitted and potholed. Giant stone urns marched in straight lines up the steps and guarded the front door. Once, they would have overflowed with colorful flowers and topiary, but now they contained nothing but dry dirt and a few struggling weeds.

I climbed the steps. Jayne scurried behind me. I rang the bell, and in response, chimes echoed throughout the house. No other sounds followed.

"Not at home," Jayne said. "Let's go."

"I would have expected a maid," I replied. "Colin lives here, I know, and thus I assume his wife does also, but I don't know about their daughter or any of his siblings. I was planning to ask, but that so-called security guard doesn't seem to know or care what goes on here. Let's have a peek around."

"Gemma, we're trespassing."

"So we are." I jumped off the front steps and went to a window. I put my face up against the glass and cupped my hands around my face. A hallway, dark and foreboding. "Interesting that this place has been allowed to fall into rack and ruin."

"You said the old man had been ill for a long time. I guess he lost interest in the garden."

"There's a lack of interest, and then there's serious neglect. I wonder if the inside of the house is as bad as the outside."

Jayne might have muttered something like "I don't want to find out."

We crept around the house. Spacious lawns, an acre at least, stretched down a slight incline to end at a patch of heavy woods. A large fountain dominated the center of the lawn. A tall, graceful woman clad in classic flowing stone robes poured water out of a Greek vase into a pool at her bare feet. The woman had no nose and numerous cracks ran through her stone garments. No water spilled from her jar, and dead brown leaves floated in the mucky rainwater in which she stood.

"Sad," Jayne said.

A wide staircase led from the back lawns to a veranda running the entire width of the house. I imagined partygoers sipping champagne and chatting while light spilled through the French doors and a round, white moon hung over beautiful gardens and water tinkled in the fountain. Occasionally a couple would slip away from the party to talk softly and exchange stolen kisses in the deep shadows beneath the ancient trees.

Wasn't my imagination getting away from me.

The veranda appeared to still be in use. Terracotta pots containing multicolored coleus and yellow and white begonias, lush with blooms, lined the stone walls. A thoroughly modern glass-and-aluminum patio table was set up by the doors, six chairs arranged around it. The furled sun umbrella and matching chair cushions were bright with color. Three ceramic pots of yellow begonias sat in the center of the table. I put my finger into the dirt and it came out slightly moist. As there had been no rain in this part of Massachusetts for several days, the plants had been watered by hand.

"Now we really are trespassing, Gemma," Jayne said.

"Anyone home?" I yelled, rapping on the French doors. "It's Jayne and Gemma from West London. We tried the bell, but no one answered. Hello?" Nothing moved, inside the house or out. I began to turn away, thinking we could do nothing more here but creep out again, when a shimmer of light coming from the far side of the house caught my eye. Water. A swimming pool perhaps. I crossed the veranda and turned another corner. It was a pool, and it was full. The water was slightly cloudy and a few leaves floated in it, but it wasn't totally neglected. Lounge chairs were laid out, and a book and a white mug rested on a small round glass table. The chair beside the table had its back to me, but I could see the bottom of someone's feet and bare legs. Judging by the hairless calves and brightly painted red toenails, it was a woman.

"Sorry to bother you," I said in a good loud voice. "But we did knock. Perhaps you didn't hear." I marched across the patio to the chair. "I'm Gemma Doyle and . . ."

The woman lying there was in her midsixties, five foot five, plump but not fat. Her ash-blonde hair was expensively cut and colored. She wore what at first appeared to be a white sundress with a pattern of red flowers.

Only when I got closer did I realize the red flowers were splashes of blood. A knife pierced the woman's chest, and she was very dead.

Chapter 10

It took all of my considerable powers of persuasion to convince Jayne to return to the Miata and get the heck out of town.

"Don't touch anything," I yelled, as she ran toward the woman and stretched out her hand as though to remove the knife.

"We have to help her."

"We're too late." Drops of blood had fallen down the woman's chest and splashed onto the patio stones, where they'd dried in the sun. There wasn't a lot of blood on her clothes, and what little there was had also dried. I knelt beside her and, taking great care as to where I put my hands, leaned over her and lightly touched the side of her neck with the back of my hand. Cold and still. The blade had pierced her heart, and she'd died instantly.

I studied her face. Her eyes were open in shock, but I knew without a shadow of a doubt she'd been in the Emporium on Tuesday, purchasing a copy of *How to Think like Sherlock* and pretending to be part of a bridge group holiday.

I got to my feet. I held my hand over the coffee mug on the small side table but felt no warmth. The cup was about half full, and cream had formed into a skin on the top.

"Let's go." I grabbed Jayne's arm, and she turned a pale, shocked face toward me. I gave her a tug, and she stumbled after me. We ran across the veranda, skirting the table and chairs, past the empty windows, around the unseeing stone woman and her empty vase, across the remains of a once-lush lawn, through the tatters of the fence and then the hedge. We stepped out onto the street, and I kept us to a brisk, but not too fast, pace. Unfortunately, it was not the middle of winter, and we weren't wrapped in heavy coats, scarves, and hats. I could only hope security cameras were focused on the entrance to properties, not the middle of the street.

The children's party was still in full swing, and the Miata was just one high-end car among others. We hopped in, and I drove sedately away.

Jayne fumbled in her bag for her phone.

"Put that away," I said.

"We have to call the police."

"We will. In due course. We couldn't help her, Jayne. It was too late for that, probably by several hours." The mug on the table had contained coffee gone stone cold. Coffee, more likely to be a breakfast drink than something consumed midafternoon around the pool.

"Did you recognize her?"

"It was Elaine Kent."

"The woman who'd been part of the bridge tour?"

"The same."

"The guard'll tell the police we were there."

"He will also tell them we drove away when refused admittance. One hopes he was enough on the ball to have marked down the time of our visit. Good thing we were earlier stopped on the highway in Cape Cod, heading toward Boston, by none other than the investigating detectives."

"If we have alibis, then why are we running away?"

"We're not running away. We're engaging in a strategic retreat. I do not want to have to explain my reasoning to the Boston Police—that gets so tedious—and then wait for them to contact the WLPD, who will probably want Ryan, at best, and Estrada, at worst, to come down and confirm I am a person of interest in a West London homicide."

"I don't think I touched anything, other than pushing a few bushes out of the way, but you rang the bell and knocked on the veranda door."

"I used my knuckles. No fingerprints. I held my hand above the coffee cup to check the warmth of the contents. I didn't touch it."

"Gemma, dare I ask why you go around consciously not leaving fingerprints?"

"As I said, I find it extremely tedious to be the subject of police interest. With few exceptions, their pedestrian minds have trouble following my line of reasoning."

"My pedestrian mind has trouble following you sometimes."

I turned my head and gave her a smile. "But you do anyway."

Her smile in return was strained. "Because you're my friend. Do you have any idea who might have killed Mrs. Kent?"

"No. I simply don't have enough information about her personal or family relationships. It might have nothing to do with the inheritance or with Mary Ellen, but I find that so impossible to believe that I'll assume, until proven otherwise, that the two killings are directly related. I find it extremely interesting that no one answered the door."

"Because the woman of the house was dead, Gemma."

"No maid. Middle of the day, middle of the week? In conjunction with the sloppy security and the state of the gardens, I suspect the family has fallen on hard times."

"Hard times?"

"As in short of funds. The patriarch is recently deceased, his will is in the courts, but I'd expect his children would still have some money. Colin should be getting a handsome salary as CEO of the companies. The state of the garden indicates the place hasn't had money spent on it for a good long time. If the old man was confined to the house, he'd naturally lose interest in the grounds, but letting it fall into such a state indicates far more than simply lack of interest. It's not as if he was likely to have hefted a rake or pruning scissors and done the gardening himself even when he was hale and hearty. The value of the house and property is being undermined by the lack of maintenance. The gardeners and full time maids were let go when Kent couldn't afford to keep them on, same for the security. The guard's uniform said he was with Boston Home Protection Services. I'm going to look them up, and when I do, I suspect I'll find the sort of outfit people only hire when they can't get anything better."

"Gemma, need I remind you that this is better left to the police?"

"I don't trust Estrada. I fear she's the sort of single-minded detective that, once she's fixed on a suspect, won't consider other options. However, Ryan needs to know that I can identify

Elaine Kent as having been in West London on Monday. When we get home, I'll give him a call."

"Are you going to tell him what we found here?"

"I'll say we were refused admittance and drove away. That is the absolute truth."

"But not the whole truth."

"I'll decide at the time what to reveal. If I have to." I took a quick glance at Jayne. She was staring out the window, watching the scenery whip past. A lock of hair had freed itself from her ponytail and blew around her face. She lifted a hand and tucked it behind her ear, whereupon it promptly worked itself lose. Trapped in her hair, a dead leaf fluttered behind her head like a flag, and a streak of blood had dried on her cheek where she'd been scratched by the bushes.

I checked my own hair and found twigs and leaves. I pulled them loose and threw them to the wind. "If the police talk to you, don't even try to lie. Lay the whole story out and tell them I forced you to leave the scene."

"You forced me?" That strained smile again.

"Convinced you, then." Jayne had the most open, honest face I'd ever seen. If she tried to lie to Estrada, she'd be clapped in irons before she knew what was happening.

Leave the lying to me. Every time.

"Use the GPS," I said to her. "Find the location of the nearest high school."

"We're going to school?"

"On further reflection, I've decided that we can't simply drive away. Someone needs to call nine-one-one, but I don't want it to be from our phones." Mrs. Kent had a family. Her husband would be home from work soon, perhaps her daughter. She might have young nieces and nephews, or children of friends, stopping by later for a visit. I couldn't leave her body to be found by kids or someone who loved her. Even worse would be if no one cared that she hadn't been seen for a while, and she wasn't found for some time. It was spring, but the forecast for the next few days was for temperatures in the high seventies.

"Found one," Jayne said. She gave me directions.

I turned into a pleasant middle-class neighborhood. The houses had been built in the '50s or '60s, big lots with small houses for large families. Most of the properties were well maintained—grass cut, flowers planted, picket fences painted. Mailboxes formed a straight line at the end of driveways and a few flags fluttered from white porches.

I drove past the high school, again keeping strictly to the speed limit. It was three thirty, and classes were getting out. Groups of teenagers clustered at the school gates or walked singly or in pairs down the sidewalk. Some of them were smoking, and almost all were on their mobile phones.

Excellent.

I turned the corner and parked the Miata in the shade of a huge old oak tree. I put the top up. A convertible is a very noticeable car. "Stay here," I said to Jayne.

"Gemma, what are you doing?"

"I'll explain later." I dug in my wallet and counted out a grand total of five dollars in one dollar bills. "Do you have any money?"

"I might. Are you buying us snacks for the drive home? I'm not hungry, Gemma, but I could use a bottle of water."

"Fifty bucks should do it."

"Fifty dollars for water?"

I held out my hand, shaking it impatiently. She gave me two twenties and a ten.

"I'll be right back. Please don't use your phone while I'm away."

"Why not?"

"Better not to have any record of it being in Boston at this time." I stuffed the money in my pocket. "Just a precaution. In the meantime, you might want to tidy up a bit. You look like you've been dragged through a hedge backward. Which, come to think of it, you have." To the sound of Jayne's screech when she pulled down the visor mirror and saw her reflection, I popped the trunk of the car. I found a Boston Red Sox ball cap and a long blue scarf, and slammed the trunk shut. I pulled the hat low over my face and wrapped the scarf around my neck. Not much of a disguise, but all I could do at a moment's notice. I trotted down the street, turned the corner, and walked toward the school. A light wind lifted the edges of the scarf and it trailed behind me. I didn't have to wait long before two boys came my way. They were fourteen or fifteen, sauntering along with not a care in the world. They carried bulging backpacks and wore their trousers slung low but not obscenely so.

"Hi," I said, Boston accent firmly in place. "Sorry to bother you, but I need to use your phone. Do you mind?"

They eyed me. The taller one had the barest touch of whiskers on his upper lip. The shorter one sneered openly at me. "As if."

"Is it an emergency?" the taller and better-mannered one asked.

"No," I pulled my lip up to one side, in quick rapid movements. As expected the boys stared, while trying not to, at it. "I need to make an important call, and my phone's dead. I promise you it won't be long distance, and I won't take more than a minute. Less, even." I pulled a bill out of my pocket. I tried to look harmless and helpless. More lip twitches. "Twenty dollars?" If questioned by the police, the nervous tic would replace every other characteristic in their minds.

"I guess that'll be okay," the taller one said.

"Forty," the short one said.

I sighed heavily and handed over forty dollars. The tall one pulled his phone out of his pocket and entered his password. I took it from him and walked a few feet away. I turned my back to them and held my head down. The taller boy stayed where he was, but the smaller one walked around me. He didn't trust me not to run with the phone. He was a smart, although rude, kid.

I faced directly into a bush and dialed 9-1-1.

"Police, fire, or ambulance?"

"Police." I kept the Boston accent but lowered my voice, hoping to sound like a teenage boy. "There's a woman dead at 864 Elm Trail. I . . . I'm sorry, but I climbed the fence, just for fun, like, and there she was. Dead, I'm sure of it. She'd been knifed." My voice trembled with emotion. "She's by the pool. I'm sorry."

"What is your name, sir?"

"I . . . I don't want to say. Sorry."

"Please stay on the line, sir."

"Sorry." I hung up. I tried to be surreptitious about wiping the entirety of the phone down with the edges of my scarf, but the short one gave me a very strange look.

"Thanks." Still holding it by the scarf, I handed the phone back. Then I walked away in the direction I'd been going. I let them watch me for a few moments, and when I reached the next corner, I turned around. The boys had continued on down the street. No doubt I was already forgotten as they argued over how to use their ill-gotten gains.

I walked as quickly as I dared, well aware that a running woman would attract a lot of attention, back to the Miata.

I jumped into the car. "We're outta here." I took off the scarf and hat.

"You going to tell me what you were doing just now?"

"I called nine-one-one and told them what we found at the Kent home. I couldn't leave her for her family to find."

"I'm glad you did. But where did you go? Did you see a pay phone?"

"In a manner of speaking."

"Won't they be able to trace the call?" Jayne said. "And fingerprint the phone. Or did you use your tongue to press the keys?"

"Most amusing. Tracing the call will take them time." I didn't know if the police would even bother to do more than send a patrol car around to the house. The guard would tell them no one had gone in. Would they then consider it a prank call and drive away? It was up to them. I'd done what I could. "By then we'll be back in West London. Now, let's go home. I've had enough of Boston for one day."

Chapter 11

As we approached the outskirts of West London, Jayne said, "Am I allowed to use my phone now?"

"Go ahead."

She called Fiona to check in, and on being told they'd managed just fine without her, she asked me to take her home. Right now, she said, she wanted to be alone. "I'm supposed to be meeting Robbie later, but I'm going to cancel. I don't want to have to put up a cheerful front."

"Brilliant idea," I said. "In that case, a quiet dinner alone at the Blue Water Café would be just the ticket." And if Andy happened to see her there, sad and lonely, and stop by to offer her a kind word, all the better.

"No," she said. "I'm going to stay in and watch trashy TV. They don't need me at work, and I'm not in the mood for going out."

She had an apartment in a well-maintained, modern townhouse complex not far from the harbor. I dropped her off. Despite the two-hour drive back from Boston, her face was still pale and her hand had shaken when she called Fiona.

I felt a sudden twinge of guilt. Poor guileless Jayne. I couldn't put her in the position of attempting to lie to the police and, when she eventually slipped up and confessed all, possibly be charged with obstruction. "If the police question you about today, don't even try to lie to them," I reminded her. "Answer all their questions as truthfully as you can. And remember what I said: It's all my fault."

She gave me a weak smile. "Take care of yourself, Gemma." She got out of the car. I watched until she was inside with the door shut behind her.

I drove straight to the Emporium. My phone rang as I was about to get out of the car. Irene. I didn't particularly want to talk to her, but she might have some information I needed to know.

"Gemma, did you hear what happened?"

"As I don't know what you're talking about, Irene, I can't say if I know or not."

"Ryan Ashburton's been taken off the Longton murder, and Louise Estrada is now in charge."

Not good. Not for me, anyway. "Do you know why?"

"I can't reveal my sources, of course, but I hear she found out that you and Ryan used to be an item, and she went to the chief to say that as you are—her words, Gemma, not mine—the prime suspect in this case, Ryan can't be involved."

Prime suspect. Definitely not good. The afternoon sun was beating down on the car. I'd put the roof up and turned the engine off, but a chill ran down my arms and I shivered. "Did Ryan put up an argument?"

"He said you and he are not together anymore and pointed out that the permanent population of West London is small.

If he was disqualified from every investigation involving someone he knows, he might as well go back to Boston."

"That makes sense. But the chief didn't buy it?"

"He bought it just fine and said Ryan would remain the lead detective. Unfortunately, immediately after they all left his office, Louise looking like she was about to explode, or so my contact says, the chief got a call from his dad."

"Oops."

"Yup. The chief's dad was calling at the request of his good buddy Arthur Doyle to advise the WLPD that they should immediately hand the Sherlock Holmes magazine over to a book expert for proper care and storage. Because the police facilities in West London are not adequate for the job."

That wasn't what I'd asked of Uncle Arthur. All I wanted was a quiet word in the chief's ear that the magazine needed to be handled carefully.

"Louise said that made it obvious you intended to take ownership of the magazine, on the grounds that Mary Ellen Longton had given it to you, which suggests that you killed to get it . . ."

I sputtered.

"Ryan said that was ridiculous. Anyone who loves old books would be concerned for its care. Louise yelled at him that he was blind to your guilt, he yelled back, and the chief got mad at the both of them and said Ryan was off the case. He went back into his office and slammed the door. You know our chief. All he wants is peace and quiet until he can collect his pension."

"Then he should have taken a job working for the public library."

"Don't bite my head off, Gemma. I'm only the messenger."

"I appreciate it, Irene. I really do. Talk to you later."

Inside the Emporium, Ruby was behind the counter, ringing up a copy of *Jewel of the Thames* by Angela Misri for a regular customer.

"Birthday gift for your granddaughter?" I asked.

"Hard to believe she's going to be twelve. Seems like only yesterday her dad was twelve."

A couple of people browsed, and an elderly lady was ensconced in the reading nook, flicking through a graphic novel version of *The Hound of the Baskervilles*, while Moriarty snoozed on her lap. No one appeared to need immediate assistance. "Why don't you gift wrap that, Ruby," I said. "On the house."

The customer beamed at me. "That's nice of you, Gemma. Thanks."

"All part of the service. I'll be in my office, if you need me." I climbed the stairs and dropped into the chair behind my desk. I kicked off my shoes, closed my eyes, and sighed. Then I made a long-overdue phone call. Ryan might be off the case, but he still needed to know what I knew. It would be up to him to decide what he wanted to do with the information.

"Any luck in Boston?" he asked.

"Waste of time, like you said. We arrived at the Kent home, but the security guard told us he had orders to admit no one. I couldn't even drive in to turn the car around. How's your investigation going?"

"Gemma, did you call to ask me that? You know I'm not going to answer."

"Just fishing," I said, because I knew he'd expect me to do that. "I have some information for you."

"Do you want to meet?"

I pride myself on being a good liar when necessary. But not when Ryan Ashburton's lovely blue eyes are gazing deeply into mine. "Far too busy. Ruby's been swamped while I was away."

"If you say so," he said.

"Kurt Kent's daughter-in-law Elaine might have been in West London on Tuesday as part of an organized bus tour that came into the shop and the tea room in the afternoon. That's why I went to Boston earlier. I wanted to confirm my suspicions before taking them to you. I wasn't able to talk to the woman." That was true enough. "I thought I should let you know."

"What makes you think it might have been her?"

"I was searching for information on the Kent family—out of interest, since I have become, unwillingly, involved in their domestic drama—when I saw a picture of her in an old newspaper article. I'm pretty sure it's the same woman, but I wanted to double check."

"Interesting," he said. "What's the name of this tour group?"

I told him. "The woman's traveling under the name of Ellen Kirk, but she left the tour abruptly. A death in the family, or so she said."

"How do you know all that?"

"I phoned the tour company."

"Gemma, don't get involved . . ."

"In your investigation. Yes, yes. I'm trying to save you time, Ryan."

He cleared his throat. That meant he was about to give me bad news. I'd not told him I knew the news already. "I'll pass what you've told me onto Louise. She's in charge of the case now."

"Why not you?"

"She found out that you and I . . . were once friends. That creates, she says, a conflict of interest, as you are a person of interest in this case."

"She's new in town," I said. "Things are different here than in New York City."

"How do you . . . ? Never mind."

"Everyone in West London—full-time residents, anyway— is friends with everyone else. And if not friends, then enemies."

"I know that. I pointed it out, and the chief agreed with me. But then . . . well something else happened to strengthen Louise's hand, and the chief caved."

"Is she a good detective, Ryan?"

"Yes." The assurance in his voice made me feel slightly better. "I still have work to do. A burger shack near the Sound beach had a break in last night. Bringing the miscreants to justice is now my top priority." He tried not to sound bitter.

"I didn't kill anyone, Ryan," I said.

"I know that, Gemma. You take care, and please, please try to stay out of trouble. We—I mean, Louise does have some other leads in this."

"Among them, I hope, Mary Ellen Longton's son, Roy."

He groaned. "I will not ask how you know about him."

"Ryan, don't try to make me sound like some sort of evil genius with a finger in every pot. Irene told me about him. He came to her because he wants press support for what he sees as a forthcoming battle with the Kent family over his mother's inheritance. Which he now considers to be rightfully his."

"Okay, I'll buy that. He's in town and he's another one making a lot of noise about us handing the . . . items found . . . over to him."

"Another one? As well as Colin Kent you mean? Anyone else?"

"Other than Colin and you, Gemma, no."

"I don't want any part of this. I keep telling people that and no one believes me. Don't tell me you think I'm dumb enough to suppose I have a claim to the magazine just because it was hidden in my shop."

"I have never believed you to be dumb, Gemma."

I sucked in a breath. I didn't like the tone in his voice one little bit. I'd been disappointed when he'd been taken off the case, thinking Estrada had it in for me. Maybe all Estrada was doing was picking up on signals from Ryan.

Now I was being paranoid.

Just because you're paranoid, doesn't mean they're not out to get you.

I shook the thought away. He'd loved me once; I knew that. Our relationship didn't work out, but that didn't kill the feelings we still had for each other. Did he still have feelings for me?

"Well, I don't want it, and I certainly don't want the hassles that go with it. So there. Is it possible Roy killed his mother? Matricide is an extremely rare crime, but it does happen."

"I suppose I can tell you that he doesn't, so far, have a good alibi for the time. And that's all I'm going to say on the matter."

"Thanks."

"I interviewed Jayne yesterday about the events of Tuesday."

"Yes."

"You might be able to wiggle your way out of any uncomfortable situation, but Jayne Wilson can't. She says she was with you at the estimated time of Mary Ellen Longton's death, and I have to tell you, Gemma, I believe her."

I felt the weight of the world fall off my chest. "I knew you would."

"I doubted you, and I let . . . maybe some of my personal feelings get in the way. I'm sorry about that."

"Thanks," I said. "Your confidence means a lot to me."

"Perhaps we could . . . uh . . . get together for a drink some time," he said. "When this is over."

"I'd like that." I hung up the phone, full of thought.

I had not killed either Mary Ellen Longton or Elaine Kent.

Estrada was a good detective.

Put those two facts together, and I should have been relieved, able to go about my business confident of not being arrested.

But I wasn't.

All I wanted to do was sit and think, but I did have a business to run. I went downstairs.

The store was empty of customers. Ruby was at the sales counter, standing over Moriarty, who lay on his back with his eyes closed, his feet in the air, and his belly exposed. She was rubbing at his soft fur and cooing gently. "Who's a nice boy? Who's a beautiful cat?"

"I'm back," I said.

Ruby squeaked, and Moriarty rolled over. He hissed at me before jumping down.

"You scared me there," she said.

"Sorry to interrupt your private moment," I said with a laugh. "Everything okay here?"

"Moderately busy, but the phone hasn't stopped ringing all day."

"Why?"

"All calls for you. No one would tell me what they wanted. A few said they'd call back. Some left numbers." She pulled a stack of pink phone memo slips out of the drawer.

"That's odd. I'll check them in the office, but I'll come out if you need me."

"Sure."

I climbed the stairs once more, flipping through the messages. I didn't recognize any of the numbers. Most were from Boston, two from New York City, one from somewhere in California. Very strange. I chose one at random and called. An answering machine picked up.

"You have reached the desk of James Finegram Editions, specializing in books of distinction. Please leave a message . . ."

I slammed the phone down. Book collectors. These were all book collectors and dealers. The only possible reason they'd have for calling me is that word must be spreading that I might be in line to inherit the *Beeton's,* and they're hoping I'm going to sell it.

I felt Detective Estrada pounding another nail into my coffin.

I opened my office computer and called up the store's e-mail account. The screen filled with new messages. I deleted all the emails from names I didn't recognize. Such was my haste in hitting the delete button that I almost got rid of an urgent letter from one of my suppliers.

He told me that release of the hottest new Sherlock Holmes pastiche novel had been delayed when, at the last minute ("last minute" meaning "on the eve of printing tens of thousands of copies"), it had been found to contain an enormous error. At the climax, Sherlock reveals that the killer is none other than John Watson! That would have been a shocker indeed, but apparently (drat, now I knew the ending) the guilty person was the good doctor's long-lost identical twin brother, James Watson, and no one—not the author, editor, copy editor, proofreader, or advance-copy reviewers—had noticed the misplaced first name.

I groaned. If word got out of what the typo was (thus prematurely revealing the killer), orders of the book would sink to unseen depths. I'd done up posters and put them in the window, announcing the pending arrival of the book, and cut back on other orders to give the new novel plenty of shelf space. Now I'd have to order more stock of other titles to fill the gaping hole in the shelves.

I wanted to check online and see what was happening with Elaine Kent. But first, I'd decided I better get some work done.

Ruby's head popped into the office. "Gemma, I'm still not feeling well. I think I'm coming down with something, so I made a doctor's appointment for tomorrow at noon. I need the time off."

"That should be okay. I'll be here."

I reflected that Sherlock Holmes hadn't had a business to run while he was hot on the trail of a criminal. I emailed my supplier back, asking him to keep me posted on the new book, and ordered more copies of books I had in stock already.

By the time I finished that, I had an e-mail from the publicist for the author of the unfortunate pastiche novel asking if the author could come to the Emporium for a book signing. That my earlier invitation to such an event had been rudely rebuffed, on the grounds that my premises weren't large enough to accommodate the expected crowds, made me think they were desperate to save the book.

I generously replied that we were *extremely* busy over the summer months, but I could probably squeeze him in.

Only once I'd sent that off and deleted another unread message from a rare book dealer was I able to lean back in my chair and think.

Had my trip to Boston caused the death of Elaine Kent? I am not so full of myself that I think every event in life circles around me, but I had been looking into ("interfering with," as Ryan calls it) the affairs of the Kent family. I hadn't announced my suspicions to the world, but I hadn't kept them entirely to myself either. I'd told Alicia at the bus tour company who I was looking for. I'd told Jayne. We'd been in the back of the bakery at the time. Jocelyn had gone out front with the tray of fresh croissants, but she could easily have stood at the door listening. So could Fiona. So could any of the customers, come to think of it. The swinging doors that open into the kitchen are located beside the display of loose teas and assorted tea-making paraphernalia we offer for sale. Then again, according to my calculations, by the time Jayne and I were making plans to go to Boston, Elaine Kent was already dead.

I'd talked to Alicia shortly after eight. She'd said she was in Truro, which is more than a two-hour drive from Boston. Easy enough to check if she was telling the truth, as she was in charge of twenty-three bridge players eager to get a start on their day. She could, of course, have called someone in Boston immediately after speaking to me and sent them around to do the deed. I could see no motive, but then again, I knew absolutely nothing about Alicia.

I glanced at the clock on the shelf above my desk. It had been a gift from Uncle Arthur when I took over the business. It was of modern manufacture and kept perfect time but had been handcrafted to look like a timepiece Captain Jack Aubrey might have in his quarters on HMS *Surprise*.

Seven o'clock. Where, I thought, had the time gone? All I'd had to eat today was toast and marmalade in the morning and a leftover blueberry muffin on the way to Boston. Jayne and I had not had our 3:40 business meeting in the tea room. Perhaps I could sneak in time for a quick dinner.

Dinner! I mentally slapped myself upside the head.

I was supposed to be having dinner tonight with Grant Thompson. How could I possibly have forgotten?

Perhaps, I thought with a sigh, I'd deliberately not wanted to remember that he and I had talked early this morning. And that I'd told him I was going to Boston.

He'd called me from his cell phone. I assumed he'd been in West London, as he suggested we meet for lunch. But that was at eight o'clock. Easy enough to get back to the Cape by noon if he'd been in Boston.

I cursed the lost days of landlines and set area codes and prefixes. Without police resources—and I could image Detective Estrada's reaction if I asked her to run a check for me "as a favor"—I had no way of knowing where Grant had been calling from.

Boston?

He was interested in the *Beeton's*. Any rare book dealer would be, particularly one who specialized in Victorian and Edwardian detective fiction. How far did that interest go? Had he gone to Boston to see what else the Kent estate might have for sale?

What of it? It would be natural enough for him to want to find out that information.

According to what I'd read on the Sherlockian discussion boards, there was a great deal of interest in the Kent estate. I knew little of Massachusetts laws of inheritance, but surely if the will was in dispute, nothing could be sold until the estate was settled. Certainly not the magazine and the jewelry that were at the heart of the fight.

No outsider had seen the Kent collection for many years. I thought about the house and the gardens, crumbling slowly into ruin. It was possible the old man had put every last penny of his family's money into his hobby. Or maybe he refused to sell his beloved items to raise desperately needed funds. It had happened before. To the family's horror.

Was that why Elaine Kent had been in West London? Was she following Mary Ellen, trying to locate the disputed magazine and jewels? If they were all the items the family still owned of any substantial value, then they'd be even more desperate to get them back.

When the will was settled and the magazine put up for sale (if it was, and judging by the state of the Kent property it would be) it would likely go to auction. It might bring in an enormous sum. Seven years ago, no one had been willing to pay four hundred thousand pounds for a similar magazine, but conditions may have changed in the interim. The price might go even higher, particularly if something of interest had been written in it—a note by Sir Arthur Conan Doyle, perhaps, or maybe even a handwritten correction. Only today I'd heard about a book on the verge of being released that contained a plot-changing typo. Could it be possible that Conan Doyle himself had made a change in the margins of the *Beeton's* and *A Study in Scarlet*, as we know and love it today, wasn't as the author had intended? My heart pounded. I forced myself to calm down. That was nothing but speculation.

Still, speculation is what fortunes are made—and lost—on.

Grant had seen the magazine. Yes, he said he'd not opened the cover. Was that true? Had the police momentarily turned their backs, and had Grant taken advantage of the opportunity?

I swung back to my computer. I pulled up several of the unread emails from the deleted folder and skimmed them quickly. Not one of them said the name of the magazine I supposedly owned. They all alluded to "an item" of interest that I might be wanting to sell, and one of the men from New York told me he collected copies of *The Strand* magazine.

They didn't know it was *Beeton's Christmas Annual* of 1887. Irene's police department source (and thus probably the source of all the rumors) hadn't named it, and he hadn't known its value. Thousands he'd said, thinking that was a lot of money. And it was. But not compared to the upper limit that the *Beeton's* could potentially fetch.

Only Grant Thompson knew exactly what was in police possession.

Had he decided to make a deal, right now, with the Kents for the magazine? Offer them a reduced sum, but cash in hand, rather than waiting, maybe years, for it to possibly go to auction. Upon hearing that I was going to Boston later, had Grant Thompson assumed I wanted to be the first to make a deal and decided to beat me to it?

Had he gone to the Kent estate and . . . ?

I was getting way ahead of myself. I had no reason to suspect Grant of anything of the sort.

Except that I had told him I was going to Boston today. I knew nothing about him other than what he'd told me and the few things I'd observed. I'd only met the man once and talked to him on the phone a couple of times.

Once again I swung around to the computer and did a Google search. I found a web page for his rare book business. It looked legitimate, including testimonials from satisfied clients.

Now that I was on Google, I searched the online Boston news. Yup, there it was. Top of the page. At approximately three thirty this afternoon, police had been called to the home of the late reclusive multimillionaire Kurt Kent Jr., where they found a female, recently deceased. Police were not revealing the cause of death, but the intense official activity around the mansion indicated they were treating it as a possible homicide.

I read on. Acting on an anonymous tip, police had arrived at the Kent home where they found Mrs. Elaine Kent, wife of the CEO of Kent Enterprises, dead next to the pool. The woman's daughter, Sapphire Kent, arrived home after a brief vacation in New York City to find police stopping anyone from entering the property. She became hysterical and had been whisked quickly away from the gathering press and into the house.

I let out a long breath: I'd done the right thing. If I hadn't called the cops, Sapphire would have been the one to find her mother lying dead at the side of the pool. A photo of Sapphire, once again flashing a lot of skin as she got out of a limo, graced the article. The killing was getting a lot of media attention already, no doubt due to the wealth and reputation of the Kents, the ongoing battle over the will, and Sapphire herself. The less respectable papers would want a shot of her weeping inconsolably. Preferably with several shirt buttons undone.

I then looked up Boston Home Protection Services, the name on the security guard's uniform. They had a web presence, but it was sloppily done, and the most recent update had been almost a year ago. A couple of testimonials from grateful clients, which may or may not have been paid for, and a few pictures of highly attractive and professionally groomed men and women, almost certainly models, shining flashlights into dark corners. Otherwise, the web page gave me little other than a phone number and address and a statement that if I called today, they would provide me with a "free estimate to best determine your security needs."

Boston Home Protection Services was either a fly-by-night operation or a front for organized crime or the intelligence services. I decided on the former.

I next headed for the muckraking websites. To my infinite relief, I read that, unofficially, the police were giving the time of Elaine Kent's death as early morning. The security guard we'd encountered said no one had called at the home, except for a "pretty little blonde in a fancy red sports car" who he'd turned away. The "pretty little blonde" had not argued with him.

Hey, I thought. *I was there too!* What was I? The Invisible Woman?

Once I got over being offended, I was quite pleased. The blonde was probably, he added, calling on Sapphire. Not a very good witness, if it came to that. I'd specifically told him I was there to see Mrs. Kent. If the guard was telling the Boston cops that one blonde woman had stopped by wanting Sapphire, they'd be highly unlikely to come in search of me. When we'd been stopped on the highway, I'd told Ryan and Estrada we were going to the Kents', and later I'd told Ryan we'd been turned away.

Maybe the Boston police wouldn't connect the killing to the recent goings on in West London, and Estrada wouldn't hear about it.

A girl can hope, can't she?

I considered erasing all traces of my search for information on the Kent murder from my computer, in case the police came looking, but I decided to leave it. Natural enough for me to be interested in the family. When the first hit brought up the death of Elaine Kent, I searched for more. Wouldn't anyone?

I didn't want to have to evade, if Estrada did ask, any knowledge of Mrs. Kent's death. Which would be a moot point anyway if the police traced the 9-1-1 call to me. Even now, they'd probably be swooping down on two unwitting teenage boys. I hoped the boys would get a kick out of being the object of a homicide investigation. I'd done all I could to disguise myself in the boys' presence, and I'd wiped my fingerprints off the phone. But it was still possible they'd trace it to me. I'd parked the Miata out of sight of the boys, but all that was needed was for someone to take a picture of it, license plate and all, or a security camera to catch it, and the police would have me. That didn't bother me terribly much. It was no secret we'd been to the Kent house, and the most I could be charged with was trespassing and leaving the scene. I had an alibi for the time of the murder. I'd been seen around West London, in the tea room and the Emporium.

A burst of noise from the shop pulled my head out of deep, perilous thoughts. Time to remember I had a business to run.

A group of women were gathered around the table containing Sherlock knickknacks, laughing uproariously. "I know exactly who to give this to for Christmas," one of them said. She picked up a three-inch-tall china statue of the Great Detective, hatted and clamping on his pipe. "Eddie's mom."

"Is she a Holmes fan?" I asked.

"She absolutely hates the whole thing. She wants to be a writer, you see, but for some reason, she can't convince a publisher of her genius. Therefore anyone who's had any success is just a hack. My mother-in-law hates popular culture, almost as much as I hate her. The perfect gift. She'll have to put it out when I'm around. Wouldn't be proper not to. I'll also take Doctor Watson and any other characters you have."

"Excellent," I said. Now there's a house I don't want to be invited to for Christmas dinner. I went up to the storage room and found a box containing the full set. As well as Holmes and Watson, it came with a stout woman representing Mrs. Hudson, a scowling Detective Lestrade, a snarling dog, presumably the Hound of the Baskervilles, and assorted other characters, both male and female. I never cease to be amazed at what some people will buy.

Ruby rang up the set while I packed it all into an Emporium bag.

A family group came into the shop, and the children immediately headed for the kids' book section. They'd raised their children to be booklovers. I heartily approved.

"Unlike Mary's mother-in-law, my husband adores Holmes," one of the women said. "I can't wait to tell him about this store." She placed a deerstalker hat on the counter along with a jigsaw puzzle. "You and he would get along so well."

"We would?" I said.

"He can talk about Sherlock Holmes for hours. He tries to talk to me, and I try to act as though I'm interested. I like the books just fine, although they're a bit old-fashioned for my taste, but really, how much detail do I need in my life? You must just love Holmes to want to work here."

"He's far too stodgy for me," one of her friends said, putting *Treachery at Lancaster Gate* by Anne Perry on the sales counter. "You can't trust a man who doesn't like women."

"He liked that opera singer well enough. The one who outwitted him. What was her name?"

"Irene Adler," I said.

"I meant women as a group. Now that"—the friend pointed at the cover of *Lancaster Gate*—"is more like it."

"I loved what the new show did with Irene Adler," another woman said, handing me a Benedict Cumberbatch wall calendar. "Showing up naked. Martin Freeman was so uncomfortable. It was hilarious."

Others of their group bought books, and they all left, still laughing.

I ran my eyes around the shop. "Looks like you've had a good day."

"Pretty busy all around," Ruby said. "It's amazing what junk some people will buy."

The parents were browsing while their children flicked through the books. "Hey," I said. "Watch what you're saying there." I might *think* the same, but I would never say it out loud.

"Sorry," she muttered. "I get sick of all this stuff sometimes."

"Then you might want to consider handing me your resignation." I wasn't joking. I couldn't care less what Ruby thought of Sherlock Holmes and all the assorted offshoots (I sometimes find it all a mite excessive myself) but I didn't need an attitude like that being expressed in front of my customers.

"Sorry. You're an intelligent woman. What appeals to you about this"—she waved her hand toward the Sherlock dish towels—"stuff?"

The family placed their selections on the counter, saving me from having to answer.

Hadn't Ruby told me at her interview that she'd gotten her love of Sherlock from her father? She might as well ask her dad that question.

Quite a lot appealed to me about Sherlock Holmes. Not the least his intellect and the way people didn't always understand him. I loved the Arthur Conan Doyle books; I liked some of the TV or movie adaptions, particularly Jeremy Brett as Holmes and the BBC's *Sherlock* with Benedict Cumberbatch, and I enjoyed the Mary Russell books. I didn't pore over every bit of minutiae or debate with fellow Sherlockians about whether Sherlock was a woman in disguise or why Watson's leg injury, suffered during the Second Afghan War, mysteriously moved between his leg and his shoulder. I didn't fill my house with trinkets; I didn't collect Holmes memorabilia at all. But I didn't look down on anyone who did. No doubt Ruby's dad was the same.

"We're looking for a nice place for dinner," the woman asked as her husband passed Ruby his credit card. "Can you make any recommendations?"

"If you go early, the kids will enjoy watching boats returning to the harbor from the deck of the Blue Water Café," I said. "If you and your husband are dining alone later, it's a very romantic setting. Good food any time of the day."

She touched her husband's arm, and they gazed adoringly at each other.

Late dinner it would be.

They left, passing Donald Morris on their way out.

Donald headed directly for the magazine display. He picked up the most recent copy of *Strand* and flicked idly through it. If Donald hadn't already read the current issue, and memorized most of the lines, I'd eat the last remaining deerstalker hat. (Note to self: Order more hats.)

"Looking for anything in particular, Donald?" I asked.

"No. Nothing," he squeaked. Today's T-shirt said, "You Know My Methods."

I took a step closer, lowered my voice. "Are you still interested in a particular magazine?"

Beneath his coke-bottle lenses, his eyes widened. "I might be, Gemma, my dear. What have you heard?"

"That a certain estate might be desperate to sell off its collection."

"That's what I've heard too," he whispered. "The community is on high alert, Gemma. A few pieces have been said to be making their way onto the market under the table."

"Avoiding pesky legal complications."

"Exactly! Such a bother. Kurt Kent's collection is one of the most comprehensive in private hands in the world today. His heirs appear to have little interest in keeping it." He tapped the side of his nose. "They've been making a few discreet, very discreet, inquiries."

The best way to extract information is always to simply pretend you know all about it. People love to share their knowledge, the more secret the better, and they'll grab any excuse to do so.

I winked at him. "Inquiries, yes."

"You've heard of something, Gemma!" he shouted and then, realizing what he'd done, made an apologetic face and lowered his voice again. "What are they offering you? You can tell me. The price is sure to be well under what it would get on the open market. I've been told that before Mr. Kent died, some of his less scrupulous relatives snatched parts of the collection fearing, as happened, it would get tied up in court and they might end up with nothing. A bird in the hand and all that, right, Gemma?"

"Right." A copy of *The Strand* from August 1891, which contained "The Red-Headed League," was on display. Not a rare issue, and not in good condition, I was selling it for fifteen dollars. I ran my fingers lightly over the plastic wrapping. Donald gasped. "You don't mean . . ."

"Shush," I said.

"Of course." He glanced furtively around the shop. No customers were in at the moment. Ruby watched us from behind the counter.

"Have you met recently with some of your fellow collectors?" I asked.

"We've talked by e-mail. No one's revealing too much. Naturally."

"Naturally." I could imagine them hunched over their collections, rubbing their hands together and scheming how to get the better of their colleagues. For objects that no one had seen but everyone thought everyone else had.

"I've also heard that you're the rightful heir of a magazine of some significance," Donald said. I was about to repute it, when he sniffed. "Don't get your hopes up on that, my dear."

"I have no hopes at all. But why are you so sure?"

"I didn't spend twenty years as a family law attorney to think the nurse has any case at all. And her heirs have even less."

"Of which I am not one. I didn't know you'd been a lawyer."

"Hated every minute of it," he said. "When my father died he left me an ample enough—albeit small—inheritance that if I lived simply, I could quit my practice, move to Cape Cod, and devote myself to Sherlock Holmes, Doctor John Watson, and Sir Arthur Conan Doyle, as had long been my dream."

"If you're talking to any of your fellow enthusiasts, be sure and mention that I have no legal claim to anything of Mr. Kent's, will you?"

He nodded.

"When the items in the collection do become available, I suppose Boston will be the place to be," I said.

"So that's where he is."

I was baffled at that one and had to drop my pretext of knowing all. "Where who is?"

"Why, Arthur, of course."

"Why would Uncle Arthur be in Boston?"

He gave me a sly glance. "You sent him on a buying trip, of course. You can't fool me, Gemma."

Now it was my turn to tap the side of my nose.

"Too bad I didn't know he was there," Donald said. "We could have met for dinner last night."

Chapter 12

"You will keep me informed, won't you, Gemma, dear?" Donald Morris asked.

"You can count on it," I lied.

"I like to think that our long years of friendship and mutual love of Sir Arthur and his greatest creation mean we can dispense with formalities such as haggling over value."

"Consider it dispensed."

He waved to Ruby and almost skipped out of the shop.

Hadn't that been a highly productive conversation? I'd wanted to learn something about what was happening with the artifacts of the Kent estate. Instead I'd learned something even more interesting: Donald Morris had been in Boston last night.

Anything of substantial value owned by the Kent family would be far beyond Donald's means, but most collections include minor objects as well as the valuable ones. Had he gone to the Kent home hoping to buy some of the lesser items that weren't currently under legal lock and key? Anyone who'd been to that house would come to the same conclusions as I had. The family needed money. Badly.

Had Donald, realizing that, attempted to haggle to cut a deal for something more valuable? Had Elaine laughed at him, and so he killed her?

With a pang of disappointment, I had to admit I couldn't see it. Inoffensive, mild-mannered Donald Morris killing someone? They say anyone's capable of murder if provoked enough, but what distinguishes one person from another is how they react to what they've done. If Donald had killed her, I'd have found him weeping over the corpse and telling me he didn't mean it. No doubt he would have had a Holmes quote at the ready. I'm not well enough versed in the canon to know if there's an appropriate one, but I was sure he'd be able to come up with something.

"He's an odd one, that guy," Ruby said. "All these Holmes fanatics are weirdos."

"Not all. Many people enjoy the intricacies of the stories and the historical setting. It's their hobby, like model trains. People such as my uncle Arthur." I gave her a warning look. *Don't you dare criticize Uncle Arthur.*

She got the hint and flushed.

"Some of the modern novels or short stories that take their inspiration from the Holmes canon are brilliant," I said. "It takes a lot of imagination to take something old and make it new again."

"You're right. I read a couple of those short stories the other night, and they were clever. I was just wondering what Donald wanted."

"What he always wants," I said. "Something he can afford that's escaped everyone else's notice."

At that moment, a police car pulled up out front and parked (illegally, I might add) in a loading zone. Louise Estrada got out of the passenger side, a uniformed officer joined her, and they headed for the Emporium. I considered making a break out the back door into the alley, but Ruby was muttering under her breath, so I knew she'd seen them even though she pretended not to. If I asked her to lie for me and tell them I was long gone, she'd point dramatically in the direction in which I'd fled and say, "She went thataway."

I greeted the new arrivals with a smile, while Ruby scurried into a corner and began rearranging the games and puzzles. "Good afternoon, Detective," I said. "Looking for gifts today or something for yourselves? A little token for your grandmother maybe, Officer Johnson?"

"Let's cut the friendly chit-chat, okay," Estrada said. "I want to know what you and Jayne Wilson got up to in Boston this morning. Does murder follow you everywhere, Ms. Doyle?"

Ruby's eyebrows hit the ceiling.

"Perhaps we can talk in my office," I said.

"In your office or down at the station," Estrada said. "It's all the same to me. For now, anyway."

The three of us climbed the stairs. I took the chair behind my desk, and Officer Johnson leaned up against the closed door, feet apart and arms crossed over her chest, while Estrada sat in the single visitor's chair. Her black eyes were like chips of coal in her olive face. I almost expected to see a spark of red flash in their depths. The sleeves of her blouse were elbow length, and when she shifted her shoulders, they slid up to reveal paler skin. So the color on her face and hands was from being outside dressed in work clothes. That might account for the almost invisible trace of paler skin on the third finger of her left hand. Either she worked all the time or she didn't know how to relax and have fun when she wasn't working and her husband had left her because of it. Or perhaps she left him because he didn't understand her ambition and her schedule. I didn't think I was in the position to ask. Her clothes showed no traces of recent contact with a baby or toddler—no sticky patches on the shoulders or handprints on the hips of her trousers. Then again that might not mean she was childless; older children were less likely to leave physical traces of their passing. That she was from New York City, I had no doubt at all; even to an Englishwoman, the accent was unmistakable. She smoothed some of the rougher edges most of the time, but slipped up once in a while, and she occasionally put the emphasis on the wrong part of a syllable. She'd been brought up in a rough neighborhood and had worked hard to make something of herself.

An admirable trait. I would have taken the time to admire her, if she wasn't looking as though she was eager to arrest me the moment I slipped up. "Let's skip the beating about the bush," she said, although I hadn't said a word, much less beat about any bush. She pointed a finger at me. Unlike the rest of her, which put me in mind of a dark, sleek racehorse, always ready to bolt out of the starting gate, her fingers were short and plump. Her nails were chewed to the quick, and a fresh but healing tear on her left pinkie finger marked where she'd tugged at a hangnail only hours ago. "You went to Boston this morning. You were seen on the way. The security guard at the Kent home identified a car very similar to yours as arriving at 2:34 seeking admittance. Two women were in it. He described them as being much like you and Ms. Wilson. I have a photograph of you on file, and I'll be dropping in on Ms. Wilson to ask her for one when I leave here. Any reason he won't pick the two of you out of a photo line-up?"

So he had remembered me after all. More to the point, he remembered my car. I'd have to consider getting something a bit less noticeable. "Not at all." I related the story of our arrival at the gates and being refused admittance.

"What did you do then?" Estrada asked.

I could quite comfortably lie my way out of it. But Jayne couldn't, and that would look even worse than giving them the truth when asked. It didn't appear that anyone had yet traced the anonymous 9-1-1 call to me, but I couldn't count on that never happening.

All my subterfuge hadn't bought me any time at all. *Too clever by half.*

I told Estrada everything.

"You didn't think to call the police?"

"We were, of course, very upset. Not thinking clearly. I feared the killer might still be around, lurking unobserved in the bushes. All I wanted to do was get as far away from there as possible." If Estrada or the uniformed officer had been men, I might have allowed myself a little shudder. Maybe beseeched them with my eyes to offer me protection.

Instead I kept my face impassive. "End of story. We came home."

"Did you go into the house itself?"

"No. I knocked on the door, but no one answered. I was curious to see what an elegant old Boston mansion is like, so we poked around the yard a bit. And then we found Mrs. Kent."

"They have lots of fancy houses in England," Officer Johnson said. "Or so I've heard."

"We don't all live in Downton Abbey," I replied. Although my mother is a distant relation of the Carnarvon family—whose home, Highclere Castle, served as the stand-in for the house in the TV show—we've never been extended an invitation to visit.

I doubted Estrada was interested in the story of my mother's relations and what had brought about their fall from grace.

"I could arrest you, you know," Estrada said.

"On what grounds?"

"Trespassing. Obstruction of justice."

I said nothing.

"But I won't," she said. "Not this time. The initial report from forensics at the scene says the woman died sometime between seven and ten o'clock this morning. The staff here tells me Ms. Wilson was working in the bakery all morning, and you came in around ten . . ."

"You've been checking up on me."

"Did you doubt I would?"

"No."

"Perhaps more important, considering employees can be offered incentives not to tell the truth, you were observed leaving West London, almost a hundred miles from the Kent home, at twelve thirty by none other than me. You're in the clear. For now, anyway."

"Nice to hear."

"Don't leave town, Ms. Doyle."

"Why ever would I want to do that?"

"Don't get smart with me, Gemma. After the murder at the hotel, you were ordered to remain in West London. Despite you disobeying that order, Detective Ashburton allowed you to go to Boston. Detective Ashburton is no longer in charge of this case. I am. You'll find that I'm not as lenient as he is. Do you understand me?"

"I do."

"Glad to hear it. An initial estimate of time of death is often wrong. If, on further examination, it's found that Mrs. Kent died later, say around three o'clock, shortly after you were seen trying to gain admittance to the property, I'll want to talk to you again. In less pleasant surroundings."

"You'll find nothing to incriminate me," I said. "Now, have you found out why Elaine Kent was in West London on Tuesday?"

"She was?" Officer Johnson said.

Estrada wasn't surprised. I didn't think she would be. Ryan would have told her what I said. "When I do, Ms. Doyle, you will not be the first person I tell. Understand?"

"Perfectly."

"Stay out of this. The Boston PD is handling the Kent investigation, but I am in charge of the one in West London. And believe me, despite what others might think, you are still very high on my suspect list. In fact, at this time, you're the only one there. Good day, Ms. Doyle."

The police showed themselves out.

Estrada didn't frighten me. Or so I tried to convince myself.

*   *   *

Fortunately, booking a table at the Blue Water Café had not been left up to me, because when I arrived, the place was full. I was precisely on time, as I always am, but Grant was already seated. I like punctuality in a man. He got to his feet when he saw me standing at the entrance to the deck and waved. He had a big smile on his face, and my heart might have skipped a beat. Just one. I felt myself smiling in return as I crossed the deck. I'd gone home and spent an inordinate amount of time deciding what to wear, watched closely by Violet. The nice thing about summer, and particularly dining outdoors in summer, is that anyone can dress supercasually and still look good. But I didn't want to look too casual, as if I didn't care what I wore, or too formal, as if I'd fussed. I'd finally selected a plain white skirt, a loose blue blouse worn over a white camisole with a neckline trimmed with lace, and blue suede flats. I accented the ensemble with silver-and-turquoise jewelry Uncle Arthur had brought me from New Mexico. Uncle Arthur always claimed he couldn't bear to be away from the sound of the sea, so I'd expressed surprise that he'd gone to landlocked New Mexico. He said, "Interesting people in the Four Corners." Which I assumed meant he'd followed a woman. I'd had to look up the Four Corners later.

"Busy spot," Grant said once we were seated. The menus were already at our places, but he hadn't ordered a drink yet. He'd been given one of the best tables, tucked into a corner, with an uninterrupted view across the harbor on one side and out to the expanse of the sandbar and the open ocean beyond on the other. The tide was at its highest point. Boats rose and

211

fell gently at their moorings, and water lapped at the stilts of the pier. The night was soft and warm, and the air was full of the scent of the sea mingled with delicious food. But the wind from the east was rising, bringing with it a whiff of ozone, and I knew a storm was coming.

"Unlike some restaurants that get crowded because they're momentarily fashionable," I said, "the Blue Water Café deserves its reputation."

The waiter appeared at our table. "Whatcha havin', Gemma? Buddy?"

Andy struggled to get good, reliable staff for the busy spring and summer months. If they could match the dishes to the customer, he'd once told me, that was good enough.

I ordered a glass of white wine, and Grant asked for a pint of the Nantucket Grey Lady.

"Did you hear the news?" he asked me once the waiter had left.

"News?" I said innocently.

"Kurt Kent's daughter was murdered."

"Daughter-in-law."

"What?"

"Sorry. Yes, I did hear. It was his son's wife, not his own daughter. Tragic." I glanced out over the water, but I kept his face in sight. It was almost dark now, and black clouds were filling the horizon. Along the boardwalk, the lamps came on all at once, and the lights rimming the restaurant's perimeter cast a soft white glow. A single candle in a hurricane vase sat on our table. Grant's face was mostly in shadow, broken by the occasional flicker of the candle.

"Fabulous evening," he said.

I took a deep breath of the sea air. "Storm coming."

"Do you suppose Mrs. Kent's killing had anything to do with the magazine?" he said. "It seems a heck of a coincidence, so soon after that other woman's death not far from here."

The expression on his face indicated mild curiosity, nothing more. Anyone who knew the circumstances of the death of Mary Ellen Longton and the appearance of *Beeton's Christmas Annual* would be thinking the same.

"I don't see how they can't be related," I said. "How did you hear about it?"

"It was in the news. They're a wealthy family."

I leaned back as the waiter placed a glass in front of me. "You talkin' about that killing? Yeah, man, big news. We had a bunch of reporters in here yesterday. Asked if I knew anything." His long earring bounced as he shook his head, clearly disappointed at not being able to be part of the story. "I told 'em I'm just a summer visitor. They sure can drink." He put Grant's mug of beer on the table and walked away.

We laughed. "Good help is so hard to find these days," I said.

"Cheers." Grant lifted his glass, and I responded in kind.

"I called Detective Ashburton this afternoon," he said, "asking if I could finish my inspection of the magazine. He told me to talk to Detective Estrada if I wanted information, but he could tell me that the magazine is in an evidence locker and there it will remain for the time being. I left a message for Estrada. I'm not holding my breath waiting for a return call. But I heard from Colin Kent."

My ears pricked up. I sipped my wine. "When was that?"

"Midmorning maybe. He wants me to handle the sale of the magazine. The police told him I'd seen it."

Midmorning. Around the time his wife was being murdered. "Bit premature, isn't he? It's in the courts."

"That's what I thought, but he said he'd checked my references and as I was already familiar with the item, it would save him time."

"Did he ask you to buy it?"

"I wouldn't purchase it outright; I don't have that kind of money. I'd act as the intermediary, find him a buyer, negotiate the price. I got the feeling, Gemma, that Mr. Kent wants whatever he can get, and he wants it as fast as he can get it."

Which corresponded with my thinking on the matter.

"I've heard your name as possibly having claim to the magazine if you can prove Mary Ellen intended to give it to you."

"I'd love to have it," I said. "If for no other reason than to give it as a gift to my uncle Arthur, who would truly appreciate it. Except for the not-inconsequential detail that Mary Ellen did not give it, or anything else, to me. She hid it from her pursuers, and I was lucky enough—more like unlucky enough—to come across it. She intended to come back later and get it."

He smiled at me. "I'm glad to hear you say that. You don't want to get mixed up in something like this. In my line of work, I've seen a lot of very nasty inheritance battles. Usually the only people who make any money are the lawyers. The so-called winning side ends up having to sell whatever they'd been fighting so hard for to pay the fees, and the losers are completely out of pocket. An ill-considered will or a thoughtless bequest can destroy a family." He shook his head and looked so mournful that for a moment I wondered if he was speaking from personal, not just professional, experience.

"Considering," he continued, "that it's entirely possible the court case might go against Colin Kent and decide the magazine doesn't belong to him, I don't want any part of this."

"Did you tell him that?"

"I saw no need to lay my cards on the table straight off. Who knows, maybe he'll send some other business my way. I asked if there were other books or items of value in the estate that he might consider putting up for auction soon."

"What did he say to that?" I closed my eyes and imagined an enormous library—wood-paneled, with floor-to-ceiling windows, leather chairs, silver ashtrays and cut-glass wine decanters, dust mites under every table—stuffed to the ancient oak rafters with first editions, magazines, novels, and maybe even some books by Conan Doyle's contemporaries that had been gifted to him, signed and personalized by their authors.

"He said he'd get back to me." Grant opened his menu. "Shall we order? What's good here?"

"Everything," I said. "Or so they tell me. I always have the clam chowder to start, followed by the stuffed sole."

"Always?"

"I know what I like. If I order something different and I don't enjoy it, I'll be crushed by disappointment, my evening ruined."

He grinned at me. I smiled back. The waiter appeared at our tableside, pencil poised. "The specials today are . . ."

While he recited, and Grant asked questions, I thought.

So Colin Kent had been on the phone with Grant Thompson around the time his wife was murdered. That in itself meant nothing, but his apparent eagerness to get rid of the magazine as fast as possible might be significant. The Kents had money, even if their circumstances seemed to be restrained at the moment. By all accounts, Mary Ellen Longton did not, and it didn't seem to me as though her son Roy had any either. Did Colin have reason to believe the decision about the will would come his way? Family connections, business colleagues, old private school chums, the right word whispered in the right ear?

Did Elaine Kent know something that might interfere with the expected court decision? Such as that her husband murdered his father's nurse?

Or had Elaine herself killed Mary Ellen, and someone then decided she had to be gotten rid of before that could be uncovered by the West London police? Alicia, the bus tour leader, told me that after their visit to the bookshop, Elaine had gone to her room immediately upon arriving at the hotel and had not been seen again until the next morning.

And speaking of the West London police, might Colin be thinking not of the court decision but of the magazine itself, currently resting safely in the custody of our town's finest? Did he think he could convince the police to hand the property over to him—some pulling of strings, maybe—whereupon he'd sell it *toute suite*? And then present the court with a *fait accomplie*?

Anything that went for the magazine would apply to the jewelry as well. The jewels Mr. Kent had left to his nurse had been those of his late wife. It would be natural for his heirs to want them for sentimental reasons, but after having a look at the state of the family home, I considered it possible, likely even, that they needed them for the cash. Were they so desperate they'd take pennies on the dollar to get cash in hand as fast as possible?

Which led me to the logical conclusion that if Colin Kent was that desperate, one little murder wouldn't stand in his way. Even two.

"Are you okay?"

I blinked. "What?"

"You're a thousand miles away," Grant said. "I asked if you miss England. I do, sometimes. I was lucky to be able to live in Oxford for a while and study at the world's most famous university. Although the people at Cambridge might dispute that." He smiled. He did have a very charming smile. "I loved the history of the place most of all. Centuries of architecture and learning everywhere I turned. Not to mention the warmth of a good sixteenth-century pub on a frosty winter night or a rainy spring day, the fire blazing, a pint in hand, dogs curled up under the tables. The smell of wet dog, damp wool, and burning wood."

"You paint a wonderful picture. So wonderful it makes me confess that I do miss it sometimes. Not on a beautiful evening like this though." It was fully dark now, and the clouds had moved in to cover the moon and stars. "As long as that rain holds off, anyway."

Grant lifted up his arms to indicate the entirety of our surroundings. "I think I'm going to like living in West London. And this restaurant's going to be one of the highlights." He glanced around him.

Instinctively, I followed his gaze.

Ryan Ashburton and two men I recognized as West London cops, now dressed in ordinary clothes, were making their way across the floor to a table. As he always did, Ryan was studying his surroundings, checking all the faces in all the corners. He saw me and the slightest smile pulled at his mouth. Then he saw who I was with, a handsome man, and where, a table for two tucked into a private corner. The natural smile died to be replaced by a forced one. He gave me a nod so abrupt it was almost curt and hurried after his companions.

"The cops," Grant said. "When I called that guy earlier, he told me he wasn't handling the Longton investigation anymore, and I was to speak to the other detective. I figured something more important had come up to take him off a murder case, but he doesn't look all that busy, does he?"

"Everyone has to eat," I said. "Even the police."

Our appetizers were plunked down in front of us, and we dug in. My clam chowder was full of the taste of New England: thick and rich and absolutely delicious. Grant had the shrimp cocktail.

The storm held off, the meal was marvelous, the wine crisp and fruity, the view stunning, and the company excellent, but all I could think of was Ryan Ashburton's solid back presented toward me.

Chapter 13

My beautifully romantic evening with Grant Thompson did not come to its natural conclusion, which was just as well, as I wasn't entirely sure what my feelings were toward him. He was handsome, charming, funny, and clever—and we could talk about favorite pubs in Oxford or attending plays at the Globe Theater in London. But when I searched deep within myself for a spark, I didn't find anything.

We lingered over our meal and coffee for a long time, until Andy himself arrived to say "hi" and incidentally let it drop that they had people waiting for tables. As I stood up, I stole a glance at Ryan, drinking beer, eating wings and nachos, and laughing with his friends. He did not turn around. On the way out, Grant and I passed a packed foyer and a line stretching to the street.

We went for ice cream—French vanilla for me and chocolate chip cookie dough for him—and licked our cones while strolling along the boardwalk, watching all the other people eating ice-cream cones while strolling along the boardwalk and watching their fellow ice-cream-eating strollers.

He walked me home, and we stood together at the front door. An orange cat slipped out of the shrubbery and disappeared around the house. A flash of lightening lit up the sky to the east and the low roll of thunder answered.

"This house must have some history," Grant said. "Or is it a reproduction?"

"The real thing, built in 1756. You'd be disappointed in the interior though. It's all very modern inside." I hesitated. Was that my opening to invite him in for a "nightcap"?

He noticed my hesitation and lightly brushed my cheek with his lips. He smelled of ice cream and musky aftershave. "Thanks for a lovely evening, Gemma. I hope we can do it again soon."

"That would be nice."

He stepped away, and I unlocked the door to let myself in. Violet ran to greet me, and we stood in the doorway, watching him make his way down the street.

The storm arrived a few minutes later, and I hoped Grant had reached shelter in time. The wind howled around the house, causing every old plank and joint to creak. Branches scratched at the windows, and rain pounded on the roof while lightning flashed and thunder rolled.

I love a storm. As long as I'm safe and warm inside.

It was not a night for a walk, so I shoved a reluctant Violet into the yard.

Before heading off to bed, I checked the news and Twitter, but nothing new was being reported regarding the Kent murder. Sapphire had collapsed and been admitted to a hospital for a "rest."

The storm raged all night, but as I slept, my mind was full of the green fields of England and the dreaming spires of Oxford and Cambridge.

*   *   *

The following morning, I'd barely flipped the sign on the shop door to "Open" when Estrada marched through it. Officer Johnson wasn't with her today, but I had not the slightest doubt about the occupation of the man who was. He was large and beefy, with beady black eyes, and nose and cheeks so lined with red veins, you could draw a road map of New England on them. His broad shoulders and the bulge of solidly muscled biceps barely contained under his summer-weight jacket meant a lot of time spent in the gym. His salt-and-pepper hair was cut almost to the scalp, and I suspected his mouth had long ago forgotten how to turn up into a smile. He might as well have had "cop" tattooed in capital letters on his forehead.

The weather had turned, and despite the forecast, the day was cool, dark, and gloomy. Water dripped from every tree, and puddles filled the streets. The police tracked mud across my clean shop floors.

"This is Detective O'Malley," Estrada said. "He's from the Boston PD and is investigating the Kent killing."

I held out my hand, and it disappeared into his massive paw. When I got it back, I refrained from shaking the pain out.

"Interesting place you have here," he said.

"Sherlock Holmes fan, are you?" I asked.

"No," he replied.

People today move around a lot more than they did in the Great Detective's day, so it isn't as easy to tell where someone comes from by the way they talk. After all, I scarcely sound like I live on Cape Cod. But if O'Malley wasn't from Boston and the offspring of a family that went back generations, I'd challenge him to an arm-wrestling match.

Ruby wasn't in yet, so I had to flip the sign back to "Closed." I'd already opened the door leading to the tea room, and the hiss of the espresso machine, the clatter of dishes, and chatter of people exchanging news over their morning coffee break drifted into the Emporium.

"Private?" grunted O'Malley. A man of few words.

"We can go upstairs to my office," I replied. "Detective Estrada knows where it is."

I slid the tea room door closed. At that moment, Jayne came out of the kitchen with a tray of muffins. She threw me a questioning look. I mouthed "cops" and jerked my head toward my office. I twisted the lock.

Moriarty jumped off a shelf and led the way upstairs, his tail high.

This time Estrada stood so O'Malley could take the visitor's chair. I took that to be an indication of rank. Moriarty leapt lightly onto the Boston cop's massive lap and rolled onto his back, allowing O'Malley to scratch his belly with fingers the size of German sausages. "Don't usually care much for cats," he said. "But this seems like a nice fellow."

Moriarty threw me an upside down smirk. I swear he stuck out his tongue on purpose.

"Detective O'Malley," Estrada said, "is investigating the murder of Elaine Kent."

"Is that so?" I folded my hands neatly in my lap.

"You discovered the body?" he asked me.

"Yes."

"You fled the scene."

"I was . . . confused . . . frightened. We were trespassing you see, and I wanted to get away. I . . . I'm sorry."

"Understandable," he said.

Estrada interrupted. "Don't give us that, Gemma. I doubt you've been confused one moment in your life."

Moriarty rubbed his front paws together.

"There you go, little buddy," O'Malley gently put the cat on the floor. Moriarty took a seat on a high shelf to watch the drama. "Detective Estrada tells me you were also the first on the scene of a homicide here in West London, earlier this week. Coincidence?"

"Not at all. Have you been told about the rare and valuable magazine that was hidden in my shop on Tuesday?" He said nothing, but his face told me he knew all about it. "In attempting to return the magazine to the woman who'd left it behind, I came across Mary Ellen Longton's body. Yesterday, I went to Boston intending to speak to Mrs. Kent about the same magazine."

"Attempting to return the magazine?" Estrada spoke to O'Malley. "I've been wondering about that. Gemma didn't have the magazine with her at Longton's hotel. She had, in fact, locked it into a safe in her house. It occurs to me that her intention in going to the hotel hadn't been to return it, but to convince Mrs. Longton to let her keep it. One way or another."

I sighed.

"Interesting," O'Malley said. "The guard at the Kent home told you Mrs. Kent wasn't having visitors, but you broke in anyway. Why would you do that?"

"Sneaked in is the better word. I climbed through a hole in the fence. I didn't think that so-called guard was at all competent. I suspected he'd had no such orders, but he couldn't be bothered to let me in. That would have been work." I deliberately used the word "I" instead of "we" and said nothing about Jayne.

O'Malley's eyes flicked. Yup, I'd guessed right about the reputation of Boston Home Protection Services.

Although, as I have pointed out on many occasions, I never guess.

"You just happened to stumble across two murder victims in less than a week," Estrada said. "You'll forgive me if I'm less than convinced you're an innocent bystander."

"I'd never as much as set eyes on Mary Ellen Longton before Tuesday." My temper started to rise. I forced myself to calm down. "She came into my shop, which is a public place, and in the time she was here, we exchanged not a single word. Same for Elaine Kent."

"Okay," O'Malley said, and I relaxed slightly. "It wasn't anything personal. I get that. But what about this magazine I've been hearing so much about? Did you kill them for the magazine?" Relaxing was clearly a mistake. He might look like a boxer who'd gone too many rounds in the ring, but I'd underestimate him at my peril. I glanced at Estrada. A trace of a smile touched her lips as she noticed my discomfort. "I've seen some strange things in my day," he went on. "But even for me, a magazine worth more than half a million bucks pretty much takes the cake."

"Estimated worth. And that's only if everything about it is perfect and a buyer can be found." I'd been speaking in my haughtiest English accent, hoping to intimidate O'Malley. I didn't exactly switch outright to American, but I gradually let some of the vowels harden. "If, as you seem to be suggesting, I killed Mrs. Longton for the magazine, I wouldn't have turned around and handed it over to the police as soon as they asked."

"Scared you maybe," he said. "When you'd seen what you'd done."

From his lair on the shelf, Moriarty nodded.

"And then, once you'd had time to regret acting in haste, you paid a call on Mrs. Kent to see what other trinkets she might have. When she ordered you off the property, did you get angry? Lash out? Act impulsively once again?"

I bit back a retort: I never act impulsively.

He glanced around the office. Boxes of books, some spilling onto the floor, invoices, publishers' catalogues. A collection of coffee mugs, a new Christopher Lee bust to replace the one recently sold, which I hadn't had time to put on the shelf. Nothing worth much more than fifty bucks. "Do a lot of trading on the side do you, Gemma?"

I didn't like the way he addressed me by my first name. He was trying to come across as my friend. *You can tell me, it'll be just between us friends.* "None. I own a bookstore and gift shop. Everything I sell sits on the shelf for anyone to buy. I only deal in retail."

"Jayne Wilson," he said.

"Who?"

"You seem very protective of Ms. Wilson," Estrada said. "Is there a reason for that?"

"No."

"Knows things about you, does she?" she said.

"Now you're really fishing. There's nothing to know about me. My life is as you see it. I live on Cape Cod. I own a bookstore. I live a simple, quiet life. I even pay my taxes early."

"That's not what I understand. You've been brought to the attention of the police before. Why did you leave England so abruptly?"

"Abruptly? I didn't leave England abruptly. I left . . . for reasons that are absolutely none of your business, police or not."

"Tell me about you and Ryan Ashburton."

"There's nothing to tell."

She turned to O'Malley. "Ashburton is the senior detective in West London. The chief removed him from the Longton case because he has reason to believe Gemma exerts undue influence on him."

I got to my feet. "If you're going to be throwing around accusations, Detective Estrada, I am terminating this interview pending the arrival of my lawyers." I think lawyers, plural, sounds much more foreboding than the singular. Not that I have any lawyer, singular or plural.

"If that's the way you want to play it," she said.

"Hold on here," O'Malley said. "No one's accusing anyone. I'm just asking a few simple questions. I've no interest in Ms. Doyle's past, nor in when she files her taxes. Sit down, please."

Estrada and I glared at each other for a minute, and then I slowly sat down.

"Now," O'Malley said. "I've been informed that your friend was with you yesterday when you went to Boston, as well as at the West London Hotel on Tuesday. Every question I have about you, I have about her as well."

I wasn't sure if Estrada and O'Malley had decided ahead of time to play good cop/bad cop, but it didn't really matter. Estrada didn't like me, and I had better be very careful where I put my feet. And my tongue.

"Jayne's a baker," I said. "And a good one. My great uncle and I own half of her tea room business and she owns the other half. She has no interest, financial or otherwise, in Sherlock Holmes collectables other than the occasional teapot or tea set for use in the restaurant. Her customers like that sort of whimsy. We're friends. We do things together, like friends do. Do you have any friends, Detective?" I bit my tongue. He was good, I'll give Detective O'Malley that. He got me to say the stupidest things. Next thing you knew, I'd be confessing all, just to make him happy.

He grinned at me. "Yeah, I have friends." He lumbered to his feet. "I'll talk to this baker now, Detective. I know you've been told, Gemma, but let me remind you that you're not to leave West London. I'll be in touch."

They left. I scurried after them, tripping over Moriarty in my haste. "Let me show you the way."

"We can find the bakery on our own," Estrada said. "I'll thank you to get back to your business and not interfere."

They went out the front door and around to the tea room using the sidewalk. I watched under the pretext of opening the adjoining door. Estrada spoke to Fiona, who looked past her at me. I nodded. Estrada half-turned and saw me watching. The look she gave me sent an icy chill down my spine.

Directed by Fiona, Estrada and O'Malley went through the swinging doors to the heart of the bakery.

Everyone in the tea room had stopped whatever they were doing to watch the police. Coffee mugs were lifted halfway to lips, croissants and muffins frozen in the act of chewing, conversations cut off midsentence. A baby, unaccustomed to the sudden silence, began to wail.

Jocelyn, obviously told to make herself scarce, came out of the kitchen at a rapid trot and spoke to Fiona. I crossed the room. "Keep working," I whispered. Then I raised my voice. "Nothing's happening. The police have routine questions about the bus tour here the other day."

The customers turned to each other.

"Routine questions."

"Just checking."

"They talk to absolutely everyone, you know."

"I was here on Tuesday. I must have left moments before the soon-to-be-dead woman came in. I wonder if they'll want to talk to me," an elderly woman said hopefully.

I went back to the Emporium and opened up. I stood in the door to the street for a while, watching the traffic. Cars splashed their way down the streets, and pedestrians were keeping their umbrellas close. The sun was hidden by a bank of black clouds and more rain threatened. I was about to turn and go back into the store when my attention was caught by a man coming out of 221 Baker Street.

Roy Longton.

He glanced across the street, saw me watching, lowered his head into the collar of his jacket, and scurried away. I could reasonably assume Roy had not been in Beach Fine Arts to purchase a memento of his visit. What was he up to?

Maureen came out of her shop and stood in the doorway. She glared at me as cars passed between us.

So that was what Roy'd been up to. Asking questions about me. Searching for a weakness or some way of convincing me to hand over *Beeton's Christmas Annual* (which I did not have and had no expectation of ever having).

I went back into the Emporium, but I kept my eye on what was happening in Mrs. Hudson's. Estrada and O'Malley didn't question Jayne for long, to my infinite relief. As soon as I saw them leave, I abandoned a customer in midsentence and hurried into the tea room. Jayne came out of the kitchen. She gave me a tiny, almost invisible nod meaning, *Everything's okay.* She showed no signs of distress, so I believed her. I pushed her into the kitchen. "What happened? Did they tell you anything we don't know? Do they believe you about what we were doing in Boston?"

"I don't want to talk about it, Gemma. I told them the truth about everything, like you told me to. Even though I've done nothing wrong, it was all highly stressful. Right now, I need to be alone, and I need to bake. We can talk later."

"Sure." I went back to the shop. Personally, I've never seen the attraction of being up to your elbows in flour or having all eight of your fingers and both thumbs covered in sticky pastry. Nothing appeals to me about rolling out pie crusts, slicing apples, and sticking my head into steaming-hot ovens. But Jayne thrives on it.

Although at the moment, I could see the attraction of pounding down mounds of rising bread dough.

*   *   *

I hoped I'd seen the last of Detective Louise Estrada today. But it was not to be.

Her timing was excellent, and she waited until I was about to lock up the Emporium for the day before pouncing. I was alone in the shop. The tea room had closed hours earlier, and Ruby had finished her shift. A light but steady rain had begun to fall around dinnertime, and when the street lamps came on, they did little to break the gloom. Windscreen wipers splashed rainwater in all directions, and tires threw up waves. What few pedestrians were still out hurried for shelter. We hadn't had a customer in the store for almost an hour.

Estrada didn't come alone, and I knew immediately that was not a good thing. A line of cruisers squealed to a halt outside, and men and women spilled out. On the other side of Baker Street, Maureen stopped in the act of locking her door to gape.

Estrada came in first, and the others fanned out behind her, spreading rainwater across the floor. At the moment, a dirty floor was the least of my worries. O'Malley was not with her, so this had nothing to do with the Boston murder.

Moriarty rushed to greet her. He wound his entire body around her legs.

"Good evening," I said pleasantly. "How may I help you, Detective?"

The number of people with her could only mean one thing . . .

"I have a warrant to search the premises, as well as your home." She flashed a piece of paper at me.

"On what grounds?" I knew some of the police officers. They came into the Emporium in search of birthday
or Christmas gifts, treated visiting family to afternoon tea at
Mrs. Hudson's, or lined up every morning for coffee. They
avoided my eyes. The ones I didn't know stared openly at me.
They were, I suspected, state police helping with the forensics.

"We finally got Mary Ellen Longton's phone records,"
Estrada said. "She called your number Monday afternoon."

"Which number? My mobile phone, the shop, my house?"

"Here. This place."

She had the warrant in hand, so there was no point in
arguing with her. But I did anyway. "This is a business. We
have customers. People come in here all day long, people I've
never seen before and will never see again. It's not my job to
keep track of them. You're clutching at straws."

"The dead woman phoned you the day before she died. I
believe that's significant, and the judge agrees with me."

"What time was this call?"

"Twenty to four."

At twenty to four on Monday, as on most business days,
I'd been in Mrs. Hudson's preparing to have tea with Jayne
and discuss our day. Ruby had not been working that day, so
I closed the shop for a while. If someone had phoned while I
was out, the voice mail would have answered and asked them
to leave a message. I thought back to Monday, but didn't
remember anything of significance. As I do every time I've
been out of the shop, as soon as I get back in, I check the
phone to see if I have any messages. On Monday afternoon,
if the little red light had been flashing, I would have seen it.

"How long did this supposed call last?" I asked.

"Less than one minute."

"This is a store. We get people phoning all the time to ask about our hours, to check if we have what they're looking for in stock. A call of less than a minute was likely picked up by the voice mail, which gives our opening hours and address."

"About which, I don't care," Estrada said. "I'm not standing here arguing with you."

The eyes of one of the out-of-town people drifted toward the Holmes bookshelf. Another shifted his feet. A third bent over and made clicking noises with her tongue and wiggled her fingers toward the cat. Moriarty abandoned Estrada, who was paying him no attention at all, and strolled over, tail held high.

I held out my hand. Estrada slapped the warrant into it. I read quickly.

"This gives you permission to check the store computers and any paper relating to the business. Apparently you are allowed to do the same at my home, but again only if I have business-related items there. I will, of course, accompany you to ensure you respect those boundaries."

"Don't try me, Gemma."

"Don't threaten me, Louise."

We glared at each other for a few moments. Estrada broke first. "People, we'll do the office first. Is your computer password protected?"

"It is because I keep confidential staff records on it."

"Open it."

"After you."

Estrada marched up the stairs. Moriarty ran after her. There wasn't room in my office for all the people who'd come with her, so I said, "Feel free to browse. If you want to purchase anything, you can come back tomorrow and pay for it. I'll trust you."

"Gemma!" Estrada yelled.

I lifted Moriarty off the keyboard and unlocked my computer. A man in a cheap, crumpled business suit dropped himself into my chair. He flexed his fingers and went immediately to my e-mail inbox. Meanwhile, a woman in an equally crumpled suit dragged my file folder of paper documents across the table and began flicking through it. Estrada leaned up against a wall and watched.

"You have a whole bunch of people here asking about buying a rare magazine," the forensics officer at the computer said.

"You will note that not only did I not reply to a single one of them, I didn't even open most of those emails. I can't help it if false rumors are floating about."

"She's right about that," he said. "Nothing outgoing."

I keep my business accounts in perfect order, and it didn't take long for both of the searchers to lean back and say "Nothin'"

"Because," I said, "there's 'nothin'' to find. Not if you're searching for any communication between me and Mary Ellen Longton or a member of the Kent family, or any mention of a certain magazine."

"Take the computer down to the station," Estrada snapped.

"You can't do that."

"I wouldn't be surprised if you know all sorts of fancy computer tricks. I want a full search of whatever might be under the surface."

I do know all sorts of fancy computer tricks, as she put it. But my business accounts are nothing but respectable and aboveboard. "You're wasting your time," I said.

"It's my time to waste. We'll take these papers as well."

"If you must. I expect it all returned promptly. I do have a business to run."

"All in good time," she said. I imagined all my records gathering dust in the cellar of the police station. I couldn't run the business for long without them, not if the police kept the computer as well. I back up the important details, and my accountant keeps a full set of my financial papers, but I need my supplier numbers and latest order details.

"Your home next," Estrada said.

"Very well," I said. "I'll meet you there."

"Not so fast. You can come with me."

We drove to my house in silence broken only by the steady *swish swish* of the car's windscreen wipers. The boardwalk was empty, the ice-cream stand closed and shuttered, the deck of the Blue Water Café empty. Boats moored in the harbor rose and fell on choppy waves.

Estrada parked on the street, and the small convoy of cars following us did so also. We'd lost two of the forensic officers, who'd gone back to the station with my computer and box of papers.

I unlocked the door, and we went inside. Violet ran to greet me, and she was absolutely delighted that I'd brought my friends for a visit.

Estrada was not equally delighted. "Lock the dog away, please."

"She won't get in anyone's way." Did the woman have a heart of stone? Violet's big brown eyes were shining, her stubby tail wagging for all it was worth, and her entire body shivered with pleasure.

"Lock the dog away, or I'll have it taken to the pound."

Yup, a heart of stone.

I picked the squirming body up. "According to your warrant, you are to search only business-related items. I have an iPad in the antique secretary in the den, and I have a home office down the hall, where I sometimes do business matters. And that's it."

"How do I know you haven't stashed relevant papers elsewhere, or have another computer?"

"Because I'm telling you I haven't. You are not to go upstairs or into any of the bedrooms. Otherwise, I'll have to contact my lawyers." I didn't wait for her to answer but turned and carried Violet away. I put her in my bedroom, gave her a hearty pat, and promised to return. Judging by the look on her face, she'd been abandoned on an ice flow and shoved out to sea.

When I got back, the police were in the den. The secretary was open, and a man held the iPad. I unlocked it, and he sat in my favorite wingback chair to read it. I considered telling him to move but decided I could only fight one battle at a time.

I showed Estrada to the room I use as a home office, where, as before, I unlocked the computer. I keep no business-related papers in the house.

The computer was carted out and taken away. The man making himself comfortable in my den called, "Detective. I've found something."

Estrada's ears almost physically pricked up. She threw me a self-satisfied smirk and sauntered, oh so casually, into the den.

I didn't hurry. I knew what he'd found.

"The history shows a lot of searching for Mary Ellen Longton and Kurt Kent," the man said.

"And what is the date and time of those searches?" I asked.

"Beginning Tuesday around eight."

"After I found the dead woman in the hotel, and after Detective Estrada brought me home. When you would expect any normal person to show some curiosity." I hoped they wouldn't ask how I knew her name or about her relationship with the Kents before that information was made public. Although by now, enough time had passed that I could claim the hotel receptionist had told me, and if she was pressed, she wouldn't remember if she had or not.

Estrada hadn't asked to see my phone, and my quick read of the warrant showed that it wasn't mentioned. That could only mean that Mary Ellen Longton had not called me on that number. No surprise, as she didn't know me, and I didn't know her. I might have been able to argue that the iPad is not a computer, but a smartphone without phoning ability, but I didn't. I thanked my lucky stars that the warrant didn't extend to the phone. The pictures I'd taken in Mary Ellen's hotel room were still on it. If Estrada came across them, I would have had to do some quick talking. I maintain a healthy suspicion of the Cloud, and even though I don't usually keep anything particularly private on my devices, I don't have my photos set to automatically back up or coordinate between the iPhone and the iPad.

"Go further back," Estrada snapped.

"Nothing. Sorry, Detective."

"We'll take that downtown. She's erased it."

"Enough," I said. "You're searching for something that's not there. And no amount of looking is going to find it. I do not give you permission to take my iPad."

Estrada bristled. The man watched us both.

"Jayne Wilson," Estrada said.

"What about her? You don't have a warrant for her, or you would have told me. I'm guessing you tried, but the judge didn't think you'd find anything incriminating among the bulk orders for flour and almonds and receipts for dollar-fifty cups of coffee."

"Why's she covering for you?"

I laughed. And this time it was a genuine laugh. "Jayne is the most honest person I know. If you did some real police work and asked questions, anyone would tell you. They'd also tell you she can't act her way out of a paper bag. If she had done something underhanded, you'd know all about it."

It was probably not a good idea to make an enemy of Detective Louise Estrada. But she was pushing all my buttons, and all at the same time. There were, as far as I had determined, plenty of *good* candidates for the murder of Mary Ellen Longton. Estrada was wasting police resources because of some fixation on me.

She stared at me though narrowed eyes, almost begging me to do something, anything, that would give her cause to arrest me.

In the bedroom, Violet barked.

Estrada blinked. "Let's go," she snapped. "We're finished here."

I saw them to the door and ran to the bedroom to let the dog out. Only then did my legs give way, and I dropped into a chair. Violet nuzzled her nose into my lap, and I stroked her silky, soft head, finding comfort there.

* * *

I don't know how long I sat alone in the dark, the dog's head on my lap, but when I finally roused myself and stood, my back was stiff. I rubbed at my face, and Violet performed a little dance. Not being one to brood on accusations of murder and a police invasion, her expression said, "Play now?"

"Good idea," I said. "A walk will do us both some good."

She recognized her second-favorite word—"dinner" being the first—and ran for the mudroom. I followed with somewhat less enthusiasm. But once I'd clipped on her leash, grabbed an umbrella, and locked the door behind me, I was feeling a good deal better. Since becoming a pet owner, I've found that there's nothing better than walking a dog to give me time to think and, at the same time, put my troubles in perspective.

Rain was still falling hard, and moisture dripped steadily from the trees, but Violet never seems to mind, no matter how wet it gets. She trotted happily ahead of me with her head down, stubby tail wagging, splashing through puddles, checking under bushes, following a trail only she could see. It was past midnight, and the houses we passed were wrapped in darkness. In our peaceful, respectable neighborhood, no one else was out. Not even a single car drove by. I was mentally analyzing the contents of the home computer the police had taken away—hoping I hadn't forgotten something I didn't want them to see—and Violet was sniffing a pile of artfully arranged rocks in an equally artfully arranged garden when she suddenly lifted her head, pricked up her ears, turned, and gave a single warning bark.

I whirred around. All I could see was falling rain and swaying branches, and all I could hear was rain pounding against my umbrella. The lights were off in the house we were passing, and the street lamp high over my head did little to break the gloom.

I didn't bother to call out, "Is anyone there?" If someone was creeping about in the bushes after midnight on a rainy night, they were unlikely to reply.

I lowered my umbrella and snapped it closed. Cold water immediately found its way down the back of my neck, but I could hear better when I wasn't standing in an echo chamber. Not to mention that a furled umbrella makes a formidable weapon.

Violet woofed once again. I let her have her head, and she ran back the way we'd come, all interest in following the trail of passing squirrels or cats gone. I heard nothing and saw nothing but falling rain and branches swaying in the wind, but then again, I don't have the ears or the nose of a dog. Fortunately, I also don't have the attention span of a dog. Violet soon lost interest in whatever was out there. The long hair running along her spine settled down and she turned her attention to the base of a tree.

I noticed only one thing out of place: the scent of tobacco and unwashed clothes lingered on the damp air.

Chapter 14

I was woken around four am by Violet's barking. I groaned, punched down my pillow, and rolled over.

The barking didn't stop. We get a lot of squirrels in our yard, the occasional mouse, and sometimes even a cat. If Violet's outside, she'll chase them, but otherwise she pays no attention.

I opened my eyes and rolled onto my back. The rain had stopped, and all was quiet, except for water dripping from the trees and the barking, steadily increasing in intensity.

Something had her upset. I threw off the covers and jumped out of bed. I grabbed my phone off the night table and crept down the hallway without turning any lights on. The dog was in the mudroom. Light flooded into the rear of the house; the motion detectors over the garage doors had come on. They are not so sensitive as to be activated by a small animal, but we do get the occasional deer around here, and some of the neighbors don't keep their dogs as close to home as they should. Then again, the backyard is fully fenced so Violet can't wander, and I always shut the gate behind me.

I moved my phone to my left hand, slipped open a drawer as I passed and took out a carving knife. When he's home, Uncle Arthur does most of the cooking. As with everything in his life, he takes good care of his tools. He regularly sharpens his Henckels knives.

"Shush, girl," I said.

Violet stopped barking but kept her entire attention focused on the door. I bent down and laid my hand on the top of her head to tell her to be quiet. Her body shivered. Whatever was out there, it was no squirrel or cat. She whined and scratched at the door. The new locks were in place, along with a fresh pane of shatterproof security glass. I peered outside but could see nothing but the light from the garage.

With all the light from the outside, the intruder—if that's what it was—would not be able to see me.

I listened. A car came down the road and carried on past. Close to the house, a branch moved, louder than would be caused by the wind.

Violet growled, low in her throat. It was a sound I'd never heard from her before. She weighs about thirty pounds and has been trained to be nothing but obedient and friendly. I didn't want her going out there.

I tightened my grip on the knife. The lights behind me were off, so I might be able to step outside without being noticed. Then again, I'd be momentarily blinded by the light from the garage. I had the entire backyard to search with a glance. Whoever was out there would be concentrating all their attention on the mudroom door.

I considered going out the front and creeping around, but I'd neglected to lubricate the gate recently, and it squeaked when opened.

At that moment, it squeaked. Violet woofed once more and then turned and trotted into the kitchen. She found her bowl and took a long drink of water.

A few minutes later, the motion detector light went off.

I exhaled.

They—whoever they might be—were gone.

I pulled out a chair and sat in the dark for a long time, listening and thinking, the phone and the knife on the table in front of me. Seeing that I wasn't going back to bed, Violet curled up on the kitchen floor and fell asleep.

I let about half an hour pass. Not even another car had gone by. I stood up. Violet opened one eye.

"Let's have a peek outside, shall we?" I said. She leapt to her feet.

My pajamas had no pockets, so I had to keep the phone and the knife in my hand. I switched on the kitchen light and then the one over the back door. I stepped outside and breathed. The night air was warm and moist, and a breeze ruffled my hair. I smelled nothing out of the ordinary. No scent of tobacco or of unwashed clothes. Whoever had followed Violet and me earlier, this was not the same person. I waved my hands, and the motion detector light came on.

Violet immediately found something to sniff at. A set of muddy footprints led from the gate, up the flagstone path to the back door. I placed the knife on the ground next to one of the prints for scale and snapped pictures. I kept one ear open and my senses alert, but I had no doubt my intruder had left.

The footprints were big, huge even. A very large man, or a smaller man or woman attempting to make themselves look bigger. They'd carefully kept to the path, leaving the imprint of their soles but no impressions deep enough for me to judge the person's weight.

I examined the back door and went around to the kitchen windows but could see no sign of an attempt to force entry. The prints did not leave the flagstone path.

What, then, had my nocturnal visitor wanted? A simple robbery, maybe—a snatch-and-grab foiled when the dog raised the alarm?

Maybe.

I should call the police. But what would I say? My dog had barked in the nighttime? The footprints might be evidence, but no attempt had been made to break in.

I studied the door itself and the ground around, thinking my nocturnal visitor might have left me a warning. Nothing.

I called Violet, and we went back inside. I left the light on over the back door and put the kettle on. I hunched over a cup of tea for a long time, the knife still on the table in front of me.

I finished the tea, put the knife away, and went back to bed. My intruder would not be back. Not tonight anyway.

I wouldn't completely discount that it might be a random burglar, scared off by Violet, but it was more likely to be a warning. A warning by someone who knew me and knew there was no need to leave a note nailed to my door. Someone who knew I'd read the pattern in the footsteps and the behavior of the dog. It had rained heavily today, and the streets were wet, but the shoes in which this person had walked seemed excessively muddy. Those tracks had been laid deliberately.

*   *   *

The next morning, Violet and I walked through the quiet streets. There's nothing nicer than a morning after the rains have passed. The air is fresh and clean, the scent of rich, moist earth rises up, and flower petals and blades of grass sparkle with drops of pure clear water. This morning, I didn't let my mind wander but instead focused my attention on everything happening around us. I didn't expect to be followed, not in the light of day with so many people and cars around, and from what I could tell, we weren't. Except by Stanford, a bichon frise who lives the next street over and has a hopeless crush on Violet.

Stanford is frail and elderly, but although the body is weak, the spirit is still willing. He tries to follow us every morning, while Violet (heartless creature) ignores him. I try to shoo him back home while his equally elderly owner, Mr. Cruickshank, totters along after us, feebly calling Stanford to heel. I consider it unlikely that Stanford knows how to heel, even if he could hear, which doesn't appear to be the case. Every incident ends in the same way: I scoop up the protesting little dog, walk him and his owner to their yard, and deposit Stanford inside the dog fence. Mr. Cruickshank then invites me in for a cup of tea, saying, "I know you Englishwomen love your morning cuppa," and I decline on the grounds that I have to go to work.

I once asked Uncle Arthur if he thought it would be rude of me to offer to fix the hole in the dog fence myself.

Mr. Cruikshank's home and garden are so beautifully maintained, I thought it strange that he didn't have the fence repaired. He couldn't be that fond of his dog, could he, as to deliberately allow Stanford to pursue his unrequited love of Violet?

It wasn't the dog, Uncle Arthur said, who wanted company.

When I asked him what that meant, he just laughed and turned the page of the newspaper.

After returning Stanford to his owner and declining a cup of tea while Violet sniffed under bushes and checked out the news from the doggy neighborhood, I considered my options. Estrada couldn't arrest me, but she could make my life a misery. I wasn't a police officer, and I didn't have the resources to conduct a modern investigation on my own.

About all I could do was hope something (or someone) would break and the case would be solved.

The more I thought about it, the more convinced I was that someone—or two someones, either working together or separately—had been attempting to warn me off.

I could think of nothing else I needed to be warned away from than asking questions about the Elaine Kent and Mary Ellen Longton killings.

If anyone thought I'd stop thinking about the killings (even if I wanted to) because of being followed in the night, they didn't know me very well.

I took Violet home and got ready for a day at work.

A newspaper box for the distribution of the *West London Star* sits on the sidewalk outside the kitchenware store at 190 Baker Street. I get most of my news online, but I like to support the local paper, so I usually stop and drop seventy-five cents into the change slot. I opened the box, bent over, and took out the paper. Today's headline was large, bylined Irene Talbot. "Mayor Demands Answers in West London Brutal Murder."

As I straightened, paper in hand, a shadow moved behind me. By the time I turned around, it had melted into the alley.

The street was busy with storeowners opening up, business people fetching coffee, and tourists getting a start on their day. I might have imagined that someone was paying particular attention to me. But I didn't think so. Not after last night.

I went into the shop, performed my daily cat-owner (more like staff person) chores, and then spread the paper out on the counter to read. Moriarty jumped up and settled himself in the middle of page one. I picked him up and put him to one side. He returned. I moved him. He returned.

"Enough of this." I put him on the floor. "You touch that paper again, and it's a morning locked in the loo for you."

He hissed at me before stalking across the room to have a snooze on the reading nook chair.

Our intrepid reporter, I read, had overheard the mayor screaming at the police chief to get the murder of Mary Ellen Longton solved, and the chief screaming in return that he was doing the best he could. Words such as police incompetence and political interference had been bandied about.

Irene had later obtained a statement from the chief that they were "close to making an arrest," which I interpreted as "don't have a clue." The mayor replied that he had "full trust in the town's police service." Which I understood to mean that he wished he could "fire the lot of them."

I crumpled up the paper and tossed it into the trash can. This was not good news for me. If the chief was under pressure, he'd pass that pressure down the line. I didn't know enough about Louise Estrada to know how she'd react when the heat was on, but it was unlikely to be in my favor.

She came in around eleven, followed by minions carrying a box of papers and my computers. "We found nothing of interest," she said, with a considerable degree of ill grace.

I said, "Thank you," although I'd rather have said, "Told you so."

"Doesn't mean you didn't communicate with the dead woman or make plans to sell the magazine by other means."

"If you want to search my garage for carrier pigeons, go ahead."

"You'll trip up one day, Gemma Doyle. And I'll be waiting for you." Detective Estrada stalked out, and her people followed.

I watched them get into their cars and drive away. When I turned around, Ryan Ashburton was standing in the entrance to the tea room, his eyes focused on me.

A heartbeat passed, and then he crossed the room in a few strides. "You okay, Gemma?"

"I'm surprised you're allowed to talk to me," I said.

"You need to sit down."

"I do not. I'm fine."

"You don't look fine. You look shook up."

"Being hounded by the police tends to have that effect on me. What are you doing here? Are you their backup? Were you ordered to swoop down on me when I relax my guard and am vulnerable?"

"I came in for a coffee. I didn't know Louise was going to be here until I saw her car parked outside."

I took a breath. Moriarty had disappeared. About the only person, other than me, he didn't like was Ryan. "I don't care for the directions her questions are taking, that's all."

"You know she'll have questions, Gemma. Questions for Jayne as well."

"I understand that, but I don't like being the object of police interest. She's wasting her time focusing on me."

"I know," he said.

"Thanks, Ryan." I forced out a smile. "Sorry about what I said."

He smiled back.

I didn't tell him that I suspected someone was following me. Anyone else might think I was imagining things, but Ryan knew I didn't do that. He had, however, been ordered off the case, and I'd be compromising him by implying I needed help.

Estrada, on the other hand, would have said I was either imaging things or trying to divert attention from myself, which is why I hadn't told her either.

The idea that someone who had no connection to the Longton and Kent murders might be following me or hanging around my house under cover of darkness was one I'd dismissed as not worthy of consideration.

"Does she have any other suspects?" I asked. "What about the rest of the Kent family? Or Mary Ellen's son? Maybe he wanted the magazine—have you thought about that? And you can never rule out the random passing serial killer or attempted burglary gone horribly wrong."

"Gemma," Ryan said, "Louise is not forgetting any of those things. I have to go. Take care."

"You can't tell me anything?"

"You know I can't."

On the way out, he held the door open for two women coming in. I greeted them with a smile and told them to let me know if they needed anything.

Two minutes later, my phone vibrated with an incoming text.

Ryan: *Colin Kent is in town. Harbor Inn. He wants the magazine.*

Chapter 15

It was a profitable morning. The weather had cleared in time for the weekend and that brought more tourists flooding into the area. One woman bought a copy of every Mary Russell book, along with a hefty selection off the gaslight shelf. "My husband has gone on a golfing weekend with his incredibly dreary business partners and their even drearier wives," she said as I rang up the purchases. "I simply couldn't face it, so I persuaded my sister to surprise me with a girls' weekend in Cape Cod." Her sister—identical square jaw, thin lips, and cheerful hazel eyes—selected two mugs. "This," the first sister said, pointing a beautifully manicured finger at the books, "is a peace offering. He's a big Holmes fan, but I don't think he's read Laurie R. King yet."

"He's in for a treat," I said, handing her the heavy bag.

At ten after one, Ruby strolled in to begin her shift.

"You're supposed to start work on the hour," I said.

She shrugged. "Traffic was bad."

"Traffic! In West London? What, a school group on an outing to the ice-cream parlor?"

She looked around the store. A few customers browsed, but no one needed our attention. Her lip curled in disdain. I ground my teeth. She hadn't done anything to give me reason to dislike her. She was polite enough to the customers, efficient about handling money and goods, but her attitude toward me and my store sometimes grated on me.

A bird in the hand, I reminded myself. Some of my fellow shop owners put up with worse. "Try to be on time, will you?"

She shrugged. More gritting of teeth. *Young people these days*, thought thirty-two-year-old me, although Ruby wasn't much younger than I was.

"I'm going out now. If you need me, I have my phone."

"I won't," she said. I pretended not to hear.

I stepped outside my shop, turned the corner sharply, and almost collided with Roy Longton. He leapt back, mumbling apologies. A wave of tobacco residue hit me. He was still wearing the same shirt he'd had on when we'd met.

"Stop following me," I said.

"I can't walk down the street?" His eyes shifted to one side. He didn't do the innocent act very well.

"You can't walk down the street twenty paces behind me, no. You also can't be asking my fellow shop owners about me. People don't keep secrets in this town."

I hadn't asked Maureen why Roy had been in Beach Fine Arts. I hadn't needed to. I could tell by the devious expression on his face that I'd been right.

"You particularly can't follow my dog and me through dark streets at night."

"I didn't—"

"If you have any ambitions of becoming a private detective, you should give up smoking. The smell brands you with a personal signature."

"Look, I don't mean no harm."

"That sounds wise."

"I figured we have a common interest. You and me."

"We do?"

"That old man left my mom some of his stuff, fair and square. She looked after him. He provided for her. Nothin' wrong with that."

"All of which has absolutely nothing to do with me."

I might not have spoken for all the attention Roy paid. "I can't afford to go to court. She gave you the magazine . . ."

"She did not!"

". . . I'll let you keep it if you help me get the jewelry. You can tell them she told you she was going to give you the jewelry too and that's why you went to her hotel room that night."

"Mr. Longton, your mother gave me nothing, and I have absolutely no claim to the magazine or anything else. I've told the police I'd never spoken to your mother, and I'm certainly not going to perjure myself in court."

"But—"

"No buts. I'm sorry for your loss, but you'll have to fight this battle without me."

"I didn't mean to scare you," he said. "I was . . . out for a walk last night, and I saw you and your dog."

"You didn't scare me in the least, and you don't look like a nocturnal exercise junkie to me."

He studied the toe of his shoe. His feet were of a size to match his short stature. Roy might have followed me on our walk, but I didn't think he'd been my nighttime visitor. He wasn't the threatening sort, nor devious enough to try to disguise his footprints. If he had been at my house last night, he would have hammered on the door and demanded I talk to him.

His face was lined by pain and a hard life. I would have felt sorry for him, except that I thought he was more interested in finding out how his mother's death might benefit him than in mourning her passing. It wasn't public knowledge that I'd found her, but he seemed to know, and thus I assumed Irene told him. The only thing he wanted to talk to me about was the magazine. No questions about the manner of her death, how she'd looked, if she'd suffered, if I'd tried to help, if she'd given me any last words.

He hadn't asked because he didn't care.

"My advice, which I'll give you even though you're not asking for it, is to forget about it. You can't win against the man's children. If I catch you following me again, and I will if you try, I'll call the police."

I left him standing in the street next to a hanging basket of purple-and-white impatiens. He did not attempt to follow me.

I headed straight for the Harbor Inn. It's one of the nicest places in West London, with room rates to match. Not far from the center of town, it's a big old house perched on a small hill, looking east out to sea. Until a few years ago, it was a shoddy, crumbling two-star hotel with nothing going for it but the view through the salt-encrusted windows. New owners took over and poured a lot of money into it. Money and their own hard work. They reclaimed the historic formal gardens and thoroughly modernized the house with enough good taste to allow the original features of the building to shine through.

In the small lobby, huge tubs of lush ferns stood on either side of the French doors leading to the veranda. A comfortable brown leather sofa with overstuffed armchairs on either side faced the enormous fireplace, containing an arrangement of birch logs that wouldn't be lit until the autumn chill settled in. A glass vase full of red roses accented with sprigs of white baby's breath sat on the mantle. The floors were the original pine and oak, each plank a foot wide and polished to a high gloss, and the carpet in front of the reception desk was a deep red with gold trim.

My friend Andrea Morrison, co-owner of the inn with her husband, Brian, stood behind the desk, tapping on the computer. No one waited for her attention, and I approached her.

"Good afternoon, Gemma," she said, giving me a bright smile. Her smile was the same whether she was speaking to hotel guests or to good friends. Andrea genuinely liked people. Her husband is what's commonly called a curmudgeon. Brian was kept away from the public, busy enough running and maintaining the prosperous hotel from behind the scenes.

"I understand you have a guest by the name of Colin Kent," I said.

"We do. The very one who's involved in a legal dispute over some rare magazine, according to the papers. Which is, I assume, why you're here, Gemma."

Straight to the point, as she always was.

"Yup," I said. "Will you phone his room and tell him I'd like a word?"

"I don't have to. He walked past a few minutes ago, heading to the veranda. We're still serving lunch."

"Perfect, thanks." I crossed the room and went outside. I was a woman on a mission, but even so, I took a moment to admire the view. The sky was a soft robin's egg blue and sunlight sparked on the water while fluffy white sails and sleek blue hulls crisscrossed the horizon. In the warm months, the veranda's used as an extension of the hotel restaurant. Terracotta pots overflowing with mounds of red and pink geraniums or tall purple grasses lined the knee-high stone walls.

"Can I show you to a table?" The pretty young hostess plucked a menu from the top of the stack and gave me a smile full of blindingly white teeth.

"Thank you, but I'm joining someone." I'd spotted my quarry. Colin Kent was bent over a thick binder spread out on the wrought-iron table in front of him. A glass containing a couple of inches of a smoky liquid was at his elbow. Whisky, I guessed.

I crossed the old stone floor quickly. "Good afternoon, Mr. Kent."

Startled, he looked up. "Yes?"

"I'm Gemma Doyle. From the Sherlock Holmes Bookshop. We met the other day?"

He blinked. "Oh, yes, I remember."

"My condolences on your loss."

"Thanks. What can I do for you Ms. Doyle? I'm rather busy."

I pulled up a chair and dropped into it. I took a deep breath. Yup, whisky all right, and not the inexpensive kind. My ex-husband had been very fond of his Highland Single Malt, the more exclusive the better. We'd had quite the set-to one night. Business had been poor for the previous quarter, and I'd come home late after trying to balance the bookshop accounts, desperate to find the funds to pay the staff on time, to find him tucking into a fresh bottle of Laphroaig. I haven't been able to abide the smell of the stuff since.

It would appear Colin hadn't been told I was the one who'd discovered his wife's body, and that was definitely a good thing. A battle raged across his face. Good manners versus wanting to get rid of me. The latter won. "I'm sorry, Ms. Doyle, but I have a great deal of business to attend to."

"Business," I said, "is why I'm here."

A waiter put a plate on the table. A roast beef sandwich on a thick baguette. Leaves of bright-green arugula peeked out from beneath the bread and the scent of spicy mustard and caramelized onions overrode that of the whisky. A small pile of crisps—potato chips—sat on one side. "Can I get you something?" the waiter asked me.

"No," Colin said.

"Tea would be nice, thank you. Hot tea. With milk, not cream."

The corner of Colin's lip turned up, but seeing as how I didn't plan to leave, he put down his pen, reached for his glass, closed his eyes, and took a long drink. When someone closes their eyes to drink, it means they *really* need it. I leaned forward and quickly scanned the page open in front of him. It was a balance sheet, the print very small, and I was reading it upside down, but I got the gist. The company—Motortown Supplies—was deep, very deep, in the red. Expenses vastly exceeded income, a trend that had been accelerating over the past three years.

I changed my strategy on the spot. I'd come here planning to use the pretext of offering Mr. Kent something for sale. Judging by these books, he was not in the position to be buying anything. He might be drinking good whisky, but the collar of his golf shirt was slightly frayed on the left side. The tan line on his wrist indicated that he'd recently replaced a watch with a large face and heavy band with the smaller, lighter imitation he was now wearing. His shoes, I'd noted as I approached his table, were scuffed and slightly worn at the heels.

"Your late father was a noted Sherlock collector," I said.

He almost spat. "That stupid hobby was the ruin of my family."

If I'd known he'd be so blunt about it, I wouldn't have bothered reading the balance sheet upside down. It had given me a headache. "Be that as it may, he must have some good pieces."

He studied my face. The sandwich lay forgotten on its plate. "He might have."

"I'm interested in buying. If you're selling."

"You don't know what we have."

"*Beeton's Christmas Annual.*"

"The police have that."

"They can't keep it forever. In the meantime, I'm assuming additional items of similar value are in the collection."

"Maybe."

"May I examine them?"

"I've not had them properly evaluated yet, although I've already heard from some interested parties wanting to have a look. I don't like to be rude, Ms. Doyle, but judging by your little *store* and the sort of customers you have, you don't play in the big leagues." He was lying—he was perfectly happy to be rude to me. "I heard you're planning to make a claim for it on the highly nebulous grounds that Mary Ellen gave it to you before she died."

"I've heard that also, but it's simply not true. She didn't give it to me. She hid it, and I found it. If she'd hidden it under the bed in her hotel room, no one would think it was intended to go to the chambermaid."

"You're an honest person. A rarity."

I leaned back as the waiter placed a tray in front of me. I gave him a smile. The tray held a white cup with matching saucer, a small pitcher of milk, a bowl of sugar, and a tiny spoon. Plus a proper tea pot from which fragrant steam was rising. The water was hot, not lukewarm, and the tea bag had not been either dipped and immediately withdrawn, or left to stew for so long it stood up on its own.

"An honest transaction is all I'm interested in." I poured my tea, added a splash of milk and a half spoon of sugar. I stirred carefully. "As for being a small shop owner, that's true, but I have . . . contacts."

"Do you now?"

"My contacts are interested primarily in the *Beeton's* and would want it either alone or as part of a package. We know your father's will is in dispute, so I have to ask what your expectations are in that regard."

"The suit will be settled in my favor. I mean, in my family's favor. My father was taken advantage of by an unscrupulous, crafty woman, and I have no doubt the court will agree with me."

"You and your siblings are the rightful heirs?"

That was, of course, absolutely none of my business, whether I was interested in buying some of his property or not. But the sun was hot, birds were singing from the trees surrounding the property, and the whisky glass was almost empty.

He took a hefty swallow, and now it was empty. He glanced around for the waiter and pointed toward his glass. I sipped my tea.

"My father didn't even like her, that Mary Ellen Longton. She was a tyrant, and she bullied him relentlessly as his health declined. He wanted me to fire her. I would have liked to, of course, but it's not easy getting live-in nursing staff who'll put up with someone of my father's . . . temperament." I suspected Colin hadn't tried all that hard. "In retrospect, of course, I should have gotten rid of her, whether I had a replacement or not. But hindsight is twenty-twenty, isn't it?"

I took a crisp off the abandoned lunch plate and popped it into my mouth.

"I told the police they should check to make sure my father's death hadn't been hastened by that woman, but they said they found nothing. Frankly, I don't think they even bothered. A ninety-four-year-old, bed-ridden man—what do they care if he meets his maker a couple of months before natural causes would have had time to finish their work? Before the will was changed, a few pieces of my late mother's jewelry were to go to my daughter, Sapphire. My sister's daughter, Charmaine, was the only one in the family interested in Father's collection, so he left her some items from that."

"The *Beeton's*? I should be talking to her then."

"No," he snapped. "I speak for the family. My younger brother has never had any interest in the family's business affairs, and my sister is . . . a woman. My father had old-fashioned ideas about gender roles. He made a few bequests here and there, items of sentimental value, but our family has always believed in the importance of the family above all. Everything stays together."

The waiter brought a fresh drink, and Colin downed half of it in one go.

People, most people anyway, love to talk. And they love to talk most of all about themselves. Particularly if they have grievances and someone willing to listen to those grievances. I helped myself to another crisp.

"I *need* those jewels, and I *need* that magazine." Perhaps realizing he was talking too much, he took a deep breath and slowed down. "What I mean is, I don't trust items of that value in the hands of a bunch of small-town cops."

"Evidence has been known to disappear from custody," I said, stirring the pot a little. And I don't mean my teapot. Whether or not the officers of the West London Police had ever lost anything, I had no idea.

Might be worth investigating, though.

"I heard something recently," I said, "about a drug case being thrown out when it came to court and the evidence couldn't be found." I can lie if I need to, but I try not to. I'd heard of such a situation only last week. It happened on some TV show Jayne loves and persists in telling me all about despite my considerable lack of interest.

Colin Kent's face turned puce. He quickly took another drink. "That's why I'm here, Ms. Doyle. To make the police see reason and return my rightful property to me. Mary Ellen is dead, that's most unfortunate, but it does clear the air somewhat. The jewelry and the magazine belong to me. To my family. Good heavens; my wife died two days ago and here I am, stuck in this two-bit tourist town arguing with the cops."

I'd been wondering about that. Why he wasn't at home in the comfort of his close, grieving family. I hadn't been sure how I could ask the question with some degree of delicacy.

The hostess showed a couple to a table not far from ours. I watched Colin as he watched her. She was lovely, with long glossy black hair, sleekly muscled legs, a tiny waist, and small but perky breasts. She wore a short, tight skirt and a sleeveless, scoop-neck blouse. She bent over the table to arrange the cutlery, pointing her generously curved bum straight toward us. Colin's eyes practically leapt out of their sockets. Those same eyes then followed her back inside.

This was not a man grieving his wife. All men admire pretty young women—I know that, and I don't have a problem with it. But not two days after a beloved wife's death.

"Your sandwich is getting cold," I said.

"Not really hungry," He pushed it out of the way. "This has all been highly distressing. First my father, and then poor Elaine. That's . . . I mean she was . . . my wife."

Cry me a river, buddy.

"I'm sure the police'll protect your valuables. In the meantime, you must have plenty of other things to sell me. Your father's collection was legendary. One of the best and most comprehensive in the world, they say."

"You don't understand, do you?" His speech was starting to slur and his eyes were watering. He waved to the waiter and indicated he'd have another.

"This tea is excellent." I poured myself more. "They know how to do a proper English cup here."

He pounded the binder with such force, I jumped. "I'm ruined! It's all a sham. Every bit of it. I need that magazine, and I need it now!"

"Did you explain that to the police?" I said.

"Explain what? That I was forced to take out loans from less-than-respectable businessmen, and they don't care if my father's estate is locked up? That my brother bought himself a fancy vacation property in Florida only months before the market tanked, and now it's worth a fraction of what he paid? That my daughter doesn't know the meaning of restraint? That my witch of a wife was threatening to leave me over some stupid mindless affair, and her brother just happens to be the most ruthless divorce lawyer in the state of Massachusetts? That the stupid hick son of the useless private nurse is trying to shake me down? You tell me, Miss Fancy-Pants English Lady, how I'm going to explain all that to some small-town cop who can barely afford the down payment on a used Toyota Corolla." He pounded the binder again. Birds were flying out of the trees, and heads were turning. "Where's that blasted waiter!"

I pushed back my chair. "Thanks for seeing me. Do let's keep in touch."

I left him sucking on the edge of his empty glass and glaring at the people at nearby tables.

"A word to the wise," I said to Andrea as I passed the reception desk. "Keep a close eye on Colin Kent's credit card. I have a feeling it won't be good for too much longer."

"Thanks, Gemma."

"You might want to cut him off bar service too."

Chapter 16

That had been a highly informative conversation.

The question, however, was what to do with the information.

I should take it to Louise Estrada. But she was as likely to throw me into the slammer for interfering in a police investigation as thank me for being of service to the community.

That left Ryan. He told me where I could find Colin Kent because he knew I needed to do something to clear myself of Estrada's suspicions.

I walked back to the shop so deep in thought I almost forgot to admire my surroundings. The shopping district of West London is never lovelier than when it's freshly ready for the tourist season. The town had hung huge wicker baskets of flowers and greenery from the lampposts, and shop owners tended boxes in their window ledges or by their doors. Leafy trees hung heavily over the street, offering welcome shade on hot summer days. The neat rows of one- and two-story buildings housing the variety of stores sported deeply weathered gray siding or fresh paint with blue or pink accents and awnings. Alone on the street, 221 Baker Street didn't make any attempt to put out plants. Instead, or so street gossip said, one night after closing, Maureen crept over to the shops on either side of her and pulled their pots of flowers up to the property line. Thoughts of Maureen made me quicken my step, but I wasn't fast enough, and a flurry of righteous indignation burst out of Beach Fine Arts.

"Gemma Doyle," she called. I kept walking. When someone you know well calls you by both names, they don't mean you any good. I ran across the street, without waiting for a break in traffic. The cars were moving slowly, and I judged I could make it with inches to spare. A rude person—tourist judging by the Iowa license plates—honked at me, but I ignored him.

Behind me tires screeched, more horns honked, and drivers shouted, "Watch where you're going!" as Maureen attempted to follow me.

She made it across, pale faced and shaking. Knowing she'd just follow me into the Emporium, I waited for her on the sidewalk. "Gemma Doyle," she said. "Everyone in town is talking about you."

"Are they?"

"Police activity is never good in a tourist town. Cruisers parked outside your shop, detectives marching in and out. The police carrying away your computer. Unsavory men asking questions about you. People want to know what's going on, Gemma."

"Maureen, I'd think my willingness to help the police would be considered a good thing. As for unsavory characters, you don't have to talk to them. I would ask people not to spread idle gossip, but I can't think of anyone small-minded enough to do that." I smiled at her.

She shifted uncomfortably. "If the goings-on at your store interfere with business on this street over the summer, I'm going to have to speak to the business improvement association."

At that moment, a cluster of middle-aged women laden with shopping bags burst out of the tea room. One of them said, "I see an art gallery across the street. Let's see if they have anything nice." Being tourists of the polite sort, they headed to the corner to wait for the light before crossing. I smiled at Maureen. "You have customers. Imagine that, they didn't flee in fear of their lives after visiting Mrs. Hudson's and the Emporium."

"No doubt," she sniffed, "they didn't hear the latest news. You watch yourself, Gemma Doyle. You and your ridiculous store are a curse to this street." She marched off, head high, steps firm. She also crossed at the light. Only one of the tourists went into her shop; the others peeled off and headed for the adjacent accessories store. I suppose that will also turn out to be my fault.

I worked in the shop for the rest of the afternoon, but my attention wasn't on it. As I helped customers, rang up purchases, and chatted with browsers, my mind was on Colin Kent.

I had no doubt he'd killed first Mary Ellen Longton and then his own wife.

The motive for the death of Mary Ellen was obvious—she had the magazine, and he needed it. It seemed to me that the Kent family had an excellent claim to their father's bequests. The nurse had only worked for Mr. Kent for a few months. He was a frail, dying old man, and shortly before he died, he rewrote his will, leaving some precious items to her. It would help Colin's case if he'd told anyone his father accused Mary Ellen of bullying him, but I doubt he would have bothered. Regardless, any judge in the land would almost certainly decide in the family's favor.

Colin must have known that, but perhaps he'd decided he couldn't wait. Depending on the quality—and determination—of Mary Ellen's lawyers, the will could be tied up in court for months, years even. Colin needed to get that magazine sold to pay off some pretty substantial debts to what sounded like some pretty nasty people. He might have a buyer lined up already. No questions asked, no explanations given. Cash in hand.

The death of Elaine, his wife, might turn out not to be directly related to the magazine after all. Having taken the fateful step of killing one person, did Colin decide getting rid of Elaine would be an easy way of avoiding an expensive divorce? If the marriage was falling apart, it wouldn't be unreasonable for her to take a small vacation, get away from things for a few days. She wouldn't have needed to use a fake name, but she might have had her reasons. Perhaps her being in the Emporium when Mary Ellen came in really was a coincidence.

Although I still had trouble accepting that.

At 3:38, I headed into the tea room for my daily business-and-friends meeting with Jayne.

As we sat over our tea and today's selection of leftover sandwiches, Jayne expressed much the same thought I'd earlier heard from Maureen but in a far more reasonable way.

"What will happen, Gemma, if they never find out who did it?"

"Life will go on," I said.

"Will it? Or will they keep coming in here, asking questions, poking around? It makes the customers jittery."

"I thought the customers seemed to be enjoying the hint of high drama."

"They might at first, but when it starts to become a habit? People won't like that."

"*If* it starts to become a habit, and it won't."

"You're not concentrating on the business. I went in to talk to you a while ago, and Ruby said you'd gone out."

"I leave the store plenty of times, Jayne."

"Not in the middle of a Saturday afternoon at the start of the season."

She had a point there. I could tell the moment I walked into the shop after my tea and conversation with Colin Kent that we'd been busy. A good number of fiction books, a biography of Jeremy Brett, a DVD of *Murder by Decree* starring Christopher Plummer as Sherlock (my personal favorite of all the movies), two puzzles, three key rings, and six coffee mugs were gone.

"You can run the bookshop however you want." Her voice turned unusually sharp. "You can go on a Caribbean cruise in the middle of the season, if you feel like it, except that you also own half of *my* business. What have you done about finding me a new fruit farmer?"

"A what?"

"See what I mean? I told you that Ellie McNamara's daughter is taking over her farm, and I don't think she's going to be at all reliable. You said you'd look into it."

"Oh, right. I did say that. Sorry."

She let out a long sigh and touched the back of my hand. "I shouldn't have snapped at you like that. I know you're worried. I'm worried. Estrada likes you for the murders, Gemma."

"That's the only thing she likes me for."

"That means she thinks you did it."

"I know what it means, Jayne. Did she come right out and say it?"

"More implied it. Our interview yesterday was all 'just between us girls,' while that big lug from Boston tried to keep his hands off my strawberry tarts. 'You can tell me, Jayne. Gemma can be very persuasive, can't she? You didn't really know what was happening, did you?' She spoke to me like I was a first grader who'd been caught helping a bigger kid get to the cookie jar."

I glanced around the tea room. Two elderly ladies, Mrs. Hudson's Saturday afternoon regulars, had taken a table at the back. Jocelyn collected their used teacups and plates and asked after their grandchildren, whereupon photographs were instantly produced. A young couple put money on their table beside the check and left with a promise to return soon. Fiona wiped down the counters. I leaned closer to Jayne and lowered my voice. "I paid a call on Colin Kent this afternoon. He's staying at the Harbor Inn, and he's absolutely desperate, for reasons I don't need to go into right now, to get the magazine and the jewels back. I'm almost certain he killed both women."

Jayne's big blue eyes grew even bigger. "Wow! Are you going to tell the police?"

269

"I have to, but I've been thinking about the best way of going about it. Estrada is likely to dismiss me as trying to throw suspicion off myself. I'll have to talk to Ryan."

She studied my face. "Why haven't you?"

I hesitated. I couldn't answer that even to myself.

"Do you want me to be with you when you do?"

"I think that would be for the best."

She pulled out her phone. "What's his number? He can come down now and talk to us here. The tea room closes soon, and I can ask Fiona and Jocelyn to leave early. We can talk in private."

She placed the call. I held my breath, hoping he'd pick up. Now that I'd decided what to do, I wanted to get it done. Both accusing Colin Kent of being a double-murderer and facing Ryan Ashburton.

You can always tell when someone's talking to a person rather than a machine. For some reason, they go all formal and robotic when a machine's on the other end. In this case, Ryan had answered. Jayne told him where we were and that we had something important to discuss with him. "Great. Thanks." She hung up. "He'll be here in ten." She put her phone away and stood up. "Police questions go better with fresh baking. I'll see what we have left and tell Fiona not to dump the coffee yet."

The last of the customers left, and Jayne told Fiona and Jocelyn she'd finish the cleaning up so they could leave early. They gave us questioning glances but didn't exactly hang around to argue. Jayne was laying out a selection of fruit tarts when Ryan knocked on the door to the tea room.

I let him in, locking the door behind him, and then went to close the sliding door leading into the Emporium. Ruby gave us curious glances through the glass.

Jayne put the tarts on the table, along with a small plate and a paper napkin. "Coffee, Detective?"

"If I didn't know better, I'd think I'm being bribed," he replied.

"I have to get rid of the day's leftovers somehow. Consider it doing me a favor."

"In that case, I will. Black, no sugar." He gave her a smile. That warm, lovely smile. Then his expression turned serious, and he faced me. "What's up, Gemma?"

"Might as well get straight to the point," I said as Jayne served the coffee and sat down. "Your tip was exactly what I needed. I learned a lot."

"What tip? And what did you learn about what?"

"Why, Colin Kent, of course. I went to see him at the inn. Like you told me to."

"Good," he said. "I don't know how these things work, but I figured you would."

"You don't know how to question a suspect?"

"A suspect? What suspect?" He groaned and slapped his forehead. "Gemma! I told you Colin Kent's in town trying to get the magazine released because I thought you were interested in buying it."

"Buying it? I can't afford it."

"I know that, but don't you deal with book collectors and people like that? I thought you might be in line for a finder's fee or something if you can arrange the deal. You put me in touch with that guy, the one you were having dinner with the other night, so he could examine the magazine."

"You had dinner with Grant Thompson?" Jayne said. "You didn't tell me that."

"I don't tell you everything," I said.

"I thought you did," she said.

"It slipped my mind. It was just a business meeting."

"Didn't look like a business meeting to me," Ryan said. "But that's totally beside the point. Please tell me you didn't go around to the inn to interrogate Colin Kent."

"Hardly interrogate. I joined him for a cup of tea. It's extremely pleasant having tea at the inn on a lovely spring afternoon. We had a little chat. A highly informative chat."

"Might as well tell me," he sighed as he selected a tiny strawberry tart. It disappeared in one bite.

I explained what I'd learned about the state of the company's finances, Colin's debts, his family obligations, the pending— and potentially very expensive—divorce.

When I finished, I leaned back, feeling quite pleased with my reasoning, if I do say so myself.

"So there," Jayne said. "Means and motive, and probably opportunity too."

"Why didn't you take this information to Louise?" Ryan asked.

"I should, I know. But, well, I get the feeling she doesn't trust me. And to be honest, I don't trust her. She's likely to think I'm trying to throw suspicion off myself."

"It's a good thing you didn't," Ryan said.

"So you'll handle this?" Jayne said.

"If you had taken this to Louise, it would be entirely within reason for her to toss you in jail for a night for wasting police time."

"What?" Jayne and I chorused.

"Colin Kent was in a business meeting—a real business meeting—in downtown Boston from seven AM on the day of his wife's death until he got a call from the police in the afternoon. They didn't so much as take a break for lunch but had coffee and sandwiches brought in. It was a long meeting, very intense and very important because they're hoping for one last chance to restructure the entire group of Kent companies to save it from bankruptcy. At no time was Colin away from the meeting long enough to do anything but go to the restroom or make a quick phone call. Ten of Massachusetts's most prominent businessmen and women can testify to that."

"The Boston police got the time of death wrong," I said firmly. "He must have killed her before he left for work."

"The family has a part-time maid who comes in three times week. That's all, I've been given to understand, they can afford in the way of help. She arrived at six thirty, in time to wave good-bye to Colin as he headed for the office, and left at eleven thirty to get to her afternoon job. Mrs. Kent came downstairs at eight. Mrs. Kent took her coffee out to the pool, as is her habit when the weather is nice. The maid did not see her again, but she says that's not unusual. It's a big house, and Mrs. Kent, so the maid says, was not friendly. She often confined herself to her room or the pool deck when the maid was working."

"Oh," Jayne said.

"Did this maid see anyone come to the house?" I asked.

"She says not. As you yourself proved, Gemma, it's possible, easy even, to get access to the property and leave unseen. The maid said it was not window-washing day, so she doesn't think she so much as glanced outside all the time she was there."

"What about Mary Ellen Longton then? Colin was furious at the woman for trying to cheat him out of his inheritance. He suspects she might have helped hasten his father's death."

"He insisted the Boston PD investigate Kurt Kent's death, and they did, but they found no evidence of foul play. As for the time of Mrs. Longton's death, Colin Kent was in bed with a junior employee of his company."

"What?"

"A cast-iron alibi, Gemma."

"She's lying. Have you considered he paid her off to say that?"

"Gemma, we've checked. The couple was seen arriving at a not-exactly-family-friendly motel in Boston at the time in question. They are, apparently, not unknown there. The woman told Louise she was about to break the affair off anyway, because, reading between the lines, he wasn't giving her enough presents."

Didn't that take the wind out of my sails? I fell back against my chair.

"Oh," Jayne said.

Ryan helped himself to a raspberry tart. "I told you not to interfere, Gemma. I'm repeating that advice." He ate the treat and got to his feet. "Now, I'd better be going. Thanks for the coffee, Jayne."

I walked Ryan to the door and unlocked it. "I'm sorry," I said as we stepped out onto the sun-drenched sidewalk. "You once told me I'm too clever by half. Seems you were right. As usual."

He shook his head. "Gemma. Stay out of it. Murder is a nasty business."

"No more detecting," I said.

"My fault, I guess," he said. "For sending you after the magazine. Colin Kent is in the clear, so I probably figured you knew that." He walked away.

"Any developments?" said a voice behind me. I turned to see Grant Thompson.

"No. Nothing."

"Why was he here?"

"Ryan? He's a friend. We were having coffee with Jayne."

"I was coming to look for you. I had a great time the other night. Would you like to go for dinner again tonight?"

"I don't think so," I said. "I'm not feeling all that well."

I went into the shop, leaving Grant Thompson standing on the sidewalk.

Moriarty greeted me with a smirk.

Chapter 17

Staying out of it was exactly what I was going to do from now on. The police had resources I did not, and there was no point in me working on my own. I could be a help to them, if they'd ask, but as they—both Ryan and Louise Estrada—were too stubborn to ask, then I'd leave them to it. I put the entire case out of my mind and concentrated on my work.

Although it wasn't perhaps entirely out of mind, as I snapped at Ruby more than once. She simply rolled her eyes, curled her lip, and carried on with whatever she'd been doing. She left at eight with a grunt of "good-bye," and I stayed until closing at nine.

After I'd seen the last customer of the day out the door, I sent Uncle Arthur a text: *How U doing?*

He replied almost immediately: *Maude and I visited the Bodie Island Lighthouse today. Fascinating place.*

Who the heck was Maude?

Me: *When U coming home?*

Uncle Arthur: *When I'm ready. Am I needed?*

My fingers hesitated over the keys, but finally I said: *No.*

The streets and the boardwalk were busy as people enjoyed the warm spring evening. My mood didn't match theirs, and I hurried home, keeping my shoulders hunched and my head down in case someone I knew tried to engage me in conversation.

All the lights were off in our saltbox, and for the first time ever, the house didn't seem warm and welcoming. But I knew Violet was waiting, and that made me feel a little bit better. I let myself in through the back door and switched on the lights. While I was accepting the dog's enthusiastic greetings, and enthusiastically greeting her in return, my phone beeped.

"Hold on a minute, Violet," I said. "I'd better get this."

It was a text from Jayne: *Robbie and I going to a late movie. Want to come?*

This time I didn't hesitate before typing: *No.*

Aside from the fact that Robbie didn't like me any more than I liked him, I couldn't imagine myself sitting through anything he chose to watch. And Jayne's taste wasn't much better. Robbie liked action movies where no one said much of anything, leaving their fists and guns to do the talking, and Jayne liked European art flicks where all the characters did was talk to each other about their feelings.

I took Violet for an uneventful walk around the neighborhood. No one followed us and Stanford didn't hurry out to greet us, so we were soon home again. I pulled a container of beef stew Uncle Arthur had made out of the freezer and popped it into the microwave. While it was heating, I chopped vegetables and tossed together a salad. I arranged a single place setting on the kitchen table and sat down to eat, feeling about as low as I ever did. I have to confess that I do sometimes get a bit puffed up with my own cleverness. Things that are completely obvious to me seem to baffle everyone else. I know everything that's in my shop, and at the end of the day, if I've been working alone, I know the contents of the cash register and credit card receipts to the dollar without counting.

I'm so clever I chased away the man who loved me, and my best friend's starting to find me exasperating to be around. As I ate, I resolved to try to be more like a normal person. Whatever that meant. From now on I'd pretend not to notice things like dirty engagement rings, unraveling hems, watered-down drinks, or secret glances between two people who are married to others.

Thus resolved, once I'd finished my meal, I opened my iPad and checked for updates on the Longton/Kent case, as would any concerned citizen.

There were no new developments, at least nothing the police were sharing with the press. Tabloid and gossip blog reporters were staking out the hospital in which Sapphire Kent had been admitted, trying to get an update on her condition. Receiving nothing they could use, they churned up old stories about Sapphire's high-living ways, which they ran with file photos of her at various events. In one picture, she looked particularly unglamorous standing on the sidewalk on a dark rainy street. Her hair hung in wet strands, her makeup had run, her eyes were narrow with anger, and one corner of her lip curled up. According to the caption, she'd been caught having a "screaming match" with her boyfriend in the alley behind a night club.

I looked at the picture again. I looked closer. I expanded the view on the iPad and zoomed in on her face.

And I knew.

Chapter 18

Knowing who'd killed Mary Ellen Longton and Elaine Kent was one thing. Proving it was entirely another.

And getting the police to believe me was yet another.

I should have called Ryan, but after what happened that afternoon, I simply couldn't face him. It was likely he'd hang up without so much as hearing me out. I'd become the girl who cried wolf. I'd accused Colin Kent—fully confident of my facts, boastful of my reasoning—of a double murder when he'd had two cast-iron alibis the whole time.

An anonymous call to 9-1-1? That would work, but only if I could find a place to call anonymously from. Phone boxes were not exactly sitting on every corner as they'd been in the days of Superman, a.k.a. Clark Kent, and at this time of night, any teenagers hanging around street corners were probably not the sort to hand me their phones.

Even if I did place such a call, the cops might only get around to following it up in a week or two.

I groaned and shut the iPad. I couldn't sit on this. A killer was out there; I knew who it was and why it had been done.

I had to tell the police what I knew. If they laughed at me, so be it.

Violet leapt to her feet when I did.

"Okay," I said, "you can come. Car!"

She danced in excitement.

I grabbed my keys and headed for the back door, but the bell rang before I reached it. West London's a safe, low crime town. I never bother to check who's there before opening the door, and my mind was so occupied, I didn't even peek through the window next to it. I threw the door open. Violet dashed out, more excited about getting to the car and going for a ride than greeting a visitor.

"Sorry to bother you at home," Ruby said. "But I have to talk to you."

"I'm going out. Can this wait?"

"No, it can't." She pushed me aside and stepped into my house. "I quit."

"Fine. You needn't bother coming to work tomorrow. I'll put a check for payment owed in the mail."

"You don't want to know why I'm quitting?"

"Not particularly."

"Nice house." She kept her eyes fixed on my face. The motion light over the garage had come on, and she was a black shape surrounded by a circle of harsh light, standing firm in my doorway. Violet yipped at me to hurry up.

"We like it," I said.

"You live here alone?"

"With my uncle Arthur."

"Who's out of town, Fiona tells me."

"Who's out of town, yes. Now, if you'll excuse me, I have an appointment at the police station, Charmaine."

Her right eye twitched. She kicked back, and the door slammed shut behind her. "So you know."

"Yes, I do. You're Rebecca Charmaine Nichols, grand-daughter of the late Kurt Kent Jr. I assume you paid me a visit in the early hours of this morning."

She said nothing, but the edges of her mouth turned up ever so slightly. She didn't look much like her uncle Colin or her cousin Sapphire, but I'd seen the family resemblance in the curl of the lip: Colin when he first had a look at my shop, then again at lunch; Sapphire as she faced down a pack of nosy reporters; Ruby when she could scarcely contain how much she disliked working in my shop. In my initial study of the affairs of the Kent family, I'd read that Kurt's daughter, Judy, had a daughter of her own. I'd seen a photograph of Judy at a horse show, and I'd noticed that Judy kept the Kent surname after her marriage, but I hadn't bothered to try to find out her daughter's surname, nor had I tried to find a picture of the daughter. A serious oversight on my part. That Judy had no involvement or apparent interest in the Kent companies in no way meant that her daughter did not. Another bad mistake.

Ruby's application to work at the Emporium and her sup-porting documentation had given her name as Rebecca C. Nichols. She preferred, she told me, to be addressed by her childhood nickname, Ruby.

"I assume Ruby is a play on your cousin Sapphire's name."

"Stupid name. Stupid spoiled girl. What little money my family has left goes to keeping her in party clothes and deluxe

Caribbean vacations." Sheer, unbridled hatred for Sapphire shone deep in Ruby's eyes.

Violet finally realized that I wasn't coming, and she barked to be let back inside.

"I thought it'd be fun to let you call me Ruby. No one has, not since a kid at school did. She said a ruby was much less valuable than a sapphire. Too bad about what happened to her face." I couldn't suppress a shiver. Ruby noticed, and her lip turned up in a grin. "I read in the paper that my dear cousin's in the hospital. Poor Sapphire, she's all alone. No one to fuss over her or pay attention to her. She must be so unhappy. I might pay her a visit, bring flowers maybe. Accidents happen in hospitals, or so I've been told."

"What do you want with me?" I said. "I've no interest in your family's problems."

"The cops have been paying a lot of attention to you, Gemma. At first I thought that was good, so I hung around, figuring you'd let me know what they were thinking. But you don't talk much, do you?"

"I talk when I have something to say. And someone interesting to say it to. You could have pretended to be a Holmes fan. When I interviewed you for the job, you told me your dad had taught you all about Sherlock and the Holmes canon and that you loved it as much as he did. I'm assuming you meant your grandfather, and that although he might have tried to teach you, you didn't love it, did you?" I remembered the customer who assumed I had to be a Sherlockian since I owned a Holmes-themed bookstore. "He intended to leave you the *Beeton's*, thinking you'd appreciate it. But it was all a pretext to get close to him, wasn't it? Let him think you valued his collection, and you'd look after it once he was gone. You always intended to sell it the minute he was in his grave."

"Stupid old man. Up there in his stupid library, chuckling over a stack of old books. He talked about Sherlock Holmes as though he'd been a real person. What was the harm? I played along. I told him I loved all that stuff. I could quote lines from the books, and he liked that. He wrote me into his will, with a special bequest. And then that woman, that nurse, came along and tricked him. Tricked me out of what's mine." As she talked, Ruby's eyes widened and a light came into them. The light, I thought, of madness. Of jealously of the pretty, popular cousin, of plans thwarted, of years of pretending to care about her grandfather and his hobby coming to naught. Colin Kent had told me he suspected someone had caused Kurt's death. Had that been Mary Ellen, as he thought? Or Ruby, a.k.a. Rebecca Charmaine, trying to hurry her inheritance along?

She stood between me and the door. Violet had stopped barking. She'd probably gone off to sniff under the bushes. My phone was in my pocket. I felt for it. I pressed the power button and swiped the screen to bring up the password page. I knew the location of the emergency feature, but without looking, I'd never be able to find the right places to type 9-1-1. The moment I pulled the phone out, Ruby would be on me.

That she had come here to kill me, I had no doubt. I kept my face impassive, and my breathing under control.

"I saw you and Jayne having your private meeting with that cop this afternoon. I saw the way you looked at me when you came back into the shop after he left. I knew you knew, Gemma."

283

Ruby had interpreted my expression, but she'd gotten it totally wrong. I had been annoyed with her, but not for anything in particular. Most of all, I had been exasperated with myself.

I took a step backward. The kitchen counter was about six feet behind me. I hadn't washed the dishes yet, and the chef's knife I'd used to chop vegetables was resting on the cutting board. I could reach it in a few steps.

As if she'd read my mind, Ruby pulled a knife out of her pocket. It wasn't very big, but it was sharp. I swallowed a flash of panic. I have a lot of skills, but knife fighting isn't one of them.

"Give it up, Charmaine," I said. "You're right. I told Detective Ashburton who you really are. If you . . . hurt me, he'll know it was you."

"Then why hasn't he come to arrest me?"

"Because he's checking my story, of course. They don't act without evidence. He phoned a few minutes ago and said he's learned something important and is coming over."

"You said you had an appointment at the police station," she replied. Her voice was calm, and her hand did not shake.

I couldn't believe I'd made such a stupid mistake.

Her eyes narrowed, her hand moved, and I knew I'd run out of time.

I dodged to my right, moving forward as the knife swung. I lifted my left leg and kicked her, landing a solid blow in the center of her knee. She screamed and staggered, but she didn't fall. The knife swung at my leg, but I pulled it back in time. Off balance, I stumbled across the floor. I reached the counter and lunged for the chef's knife. My fingers closed around the handle, and I gripped it firmly. I whirled around in time to see Ruby's blade descending toward my neck. I pulled back and held up my own weapon.

"Drop it," I said. "You've lost. Get out of here."

"I can't let you tell them about me."

"Are you crazy?" The question, I knew, was redundant. "Killing me won't help you. Everything I know, the police will find out soon enough."

I screamed as loudly as I could, hoping one of the neighbors would hear and call 9-1-1. This wasn't the sort of neighborhood where people scurried away minding their own business at the first hint of trouble. We kept an eye out for each other. Unfortunately, these old houses were well built. Practically soundproof. Outside, Violet had started to bark, her tone getting increasingly hysterical. If someone heard her, they might come to see what was wrong . . . eventually. By which time it would be too late for me.

Ruby feigned a move to her left. I was watching her eyes and knew she planned to go right, and so I was ready for her and slipped out of the way.

We couldn't stand here all night. One of us would soon get tired, and judging by the fire in her eyes, it wasn't going to be Ruby. I had to make a run for it. I had the advantage of knowing the layout of the house. The loo had a lock on the door. If I could shut myself in, I could call for help. The question was, would I be able to reach it in time?

My back was pressed up against the counter; the knife was in my right hand. The top drawer held table linens. I might be able to throw a napkin over Ruby's knife hand and disable her that way, but it was a long shot. I mentally pulled up a diagram of the counter top behind me. The plastic cutting board, cucumber peelings, carrot tops, the tomato core, an unused tomato. The glass bottle of dressing would have been a good projectile, but I'd put it back in the fridge. The tomato. I'd taken two tomatoes out of the bowl but only used one.

I couldn't turn around, and I couldn't hesitate or I'd be done for. I reached behind me with my left hand, and my fingers closed on the tomato. "Catch!" I yelled as I threw it at her head. Instinctively, Ruby ducked. I broke for the hall.

I'd only taken a few steps when I heard a shout, a scream, a bark, glass breaking, and the solid thud of a body hitting the floor.

I spun around, still gripping my knife.

Jayne Wilson stood at the mudroom door. A bottle of wine had shattered at her feet and a tub of Ben & Jerry's ice cream rolled across the floor. She held her phone to her ear while Violet ran in circles around the kitchen, barking in a tone I'd never heard from her before.

Charmaine Nichols, a.k.a. Ruby, lay face down on the floor. Her arms were thrown out, and the knife was on the far side of the room. A man sat on her.

"Gosh, Gemma," Robbie said, "looks like we arrived just in time."

Chapter 19

I dropped into a kitchen chair. Violet licked my hand, and then she went to see what game Robbie and Ruby were playing. Jayne knelt in front of me. "Do you need an ambulance, Gemma?"

I shook my head.

"Why don't you give me that?" Her voice was very calm, as though she were talking to a fractious toddler.

At the moment, I rather liked being spoken to as though I were a fractious toddler. I nodded.

"Gemma?" She stretched out her hand. I was gripping the chef's knife so hard my knuckles were white. I handed it to her.

I gave myself a mental slap and took in the scene.

Ruby lay on the floor, face down and bellowing. Robbie sat on her while she buckled and screamed and her arms flailed. Violet ran forward and back, encouraging Ruby to get up and chase her.

"What brings you here?" I asked Jayne. "Not that I'm not pleased to see you."

"You were so despondent this afternoon when you left the tea room, and then you didn't want to come to the movies with us. I didn't think you should be alone, so I said to Robbie, 'Let's skip the movie and surprise Gemma.' We brought wine and ice cream."

I studied the mess on the floor. "So you did."

I leaned forward, and we wrapped our arms around each other.

Dear Jayne. I am an introvert. Jayne is an extrovert. When introverts are down, they need to be alone. When extroverts are down, they crave company.

Another aspect of extroverts is that they don't understand introverts. If not for the not-incidental bit about needing to be saved from a knife-wielding, Holmes-hating manic, the last thing I would have wanted tonight was a visit from Jayne and Robbie. Even bearing wine and ice cream.

Sirens sounded in the distance, getting closer. Jayne and I separated, and we both got to our feet. Robbie put his hand on the back of Ruby's head, and her screams were muffled by the kitchen floor.

"Help's coming," I said.

"It's okay," he said. "We're good here, aren't we, lady?"

I couldn't make out what Ruby said, but it was unlikely to have been polite.

"I'll go out and meet them," Jayne said.

*   *   *

I suspected that Ryan wouldn't let me sit in on the interview, but I figured it was worth a try.

No such luck.

"Why don't you go to bed, Gemma?" he said. "You can come down in the morning and make your statement. You need to rest."

"I'm hardly in the mood to sleep, Ryan. It's obvious that Ruby, whose real name is Rebecca Charmaine, killed Mary Ellen to get the magazine and searched my house looking for it. But . . ."

"It's not obvious to me," Ryan said. "Or to Louise. Thus we have to talk to her, without you present."

I ignored him, "What I don't know is where Elaine Kent comes into it, or why she had to die."

"Believe it or not, Gemma, we might get around to asking her that without you prompting us."

We were in my living room. In answer to Jayne's 9-1-1 call, uniformed officers had swarmed all over my kitchen, and a screaming Ruby was dragged away. I'd told the responding officers to call Estrada and Ashburton, as this was directly related to an active murder investigation. Jayne had taken a highly reluctant Violet to my office and shut her in to keep her out of the way of the police. I'd been offered medical attention but turned it down. A few deep breaths, and I'd been once again in control of myself.

Robbie puffed up his chest and explained to the police how he'd brought Ruby down with a tackle he'd learned on the high school football team while Jayne's blue eyes glowed with adoration. My plans to convince Jayne to dump the flakey Robbie in favor of solid, respectable Andy were clearly suffering a setback.

Jayne put the kettle on, but we didn't have to wait long before Louise Estrada arrived and ordered us out of my kitchen so the police could gather evidence. She was dressed in a black leather skirt that fell a couple of inches short of her knees and a frilly red blouse cinched at the waist by a thick black belt. The top two buttons on the blouse were done up, but they were in the wrong button holes, giving the collar a lopsided appearance. The third button had missed the hole all together. Her face was heavily made up, and her bright-red lipstick was smeared, indicating she'd tried to wipe it off without benefit of a mirror. Her hair had been pulled back into a rough ponytail and secured with a rubber band, but her bangs were so stiff with hairspray they didn't move as she strode into my house, shouting orders. Her bare feet were stuffed into slightly dusty trainers. The rubber band would have been in her purse, and the shoes in her car for just such an emergency.

She'd been on a date. A date she'd gone to a lot of trouble to dress up for but to which she'd taken her own car.

She caught me looking and gave me a ferocious glare. I smiled in return. She barked at Officer Johnson to get us out of the kitchen.

Ryan arrived a few minutes later and refused to allow me to go to the station with them. He and Estrada left Johnson to take photographs of the kitchen. Once they'd all gone, including Jayne and Robbie, I freed Violet and put the kettle on.

I looked at the fresh chaos of my kitchen. I still hadn't tidied up the house after Ruby had tossed the place on Tuesday night and then the police had stomped all through it. *No time like the present*, I thought as I gathered together cleaning equipment.

*   *   *

My phone rang at four AM. I answered right away.

"I figured you'd be still up," Ryan said.

I put down my book. The house was clean and tidy once again, and it was a good night to reread *The Moonstone* by Wilkie Collins, an old favorite of mine. "Tonight's events were not conducive to a proper night's sleep."

He laughed. "Gemma, I've forgotten how much I love the way you talk."

"What about the way I talk?"

"Never mind. We're done here, for now. If you put the coffee on, I'll come around."

"I can do better than coffee. Have you eaten?"

"No."

I was in the kitchen, cracking eggs, slicing green onions, and grating cheese when headlights lit up the driveway, the motion detector came on, and Ryan's firm steps crossed the courtyard. Violet and I met him at the mudroom door, and I handed him a mug of hot black coffee.

He patted the dog and accepted the drink with a smile.

"Have a seat," I said. "Scrambled eggs and toast is about the best I can do at this time of night."

He dropped into a chair. Stubble was thick on his jaw, and his eyes were rimmed red. I poured myself a cup of tea and joined him at the table. "Is Ruby talking?"

"Oh, yeah. She's talking so fast, we're having trouble keeping up. She's a pile of grievances looking for a sympathetic ear to unload all her troubles on. Louise is good at making suspects talk, particularly women. She can play the best-friends card like I've never seen."

Which is what Jayne had told me. *Just between us girls.* Interesting that she'd never tried it on me.

"Ruby, or Charmaine, as she's usually called," he said, "pretended to be interested in her grandfather's Sherlock Holmes collection with the sole intention of inheriting some of the stuff one day. No one else in the family had the slightest interest in it."

"What degree of involvement? Did she buy for him?"

"Nothing like that. She'd drop in now and again, and he'd show her what he had. Over the last several years, he hadn't bought anything new, and she says it was getting tiring pretending to be interested in the same dusty book or tattered magazine every time she visited. Some years ago, he told her he was leaving the most valuable piece in his collection to her in his will. It was a shock to her, and everyone else in the family, when the old man died and the will was read. By that time, Mary Ellen Longton had scampered off with her bequest."

The butter in the frying pan began to sizzle, and I jumped up to pour in the eggs. I added green onions and cheddar cheese and popped wheat bread into the toaster.

"Mary Ellen, in her capacity as Mr. Kent's private nurse, had a room next to his suite. After she left, Charmaine searched the room and found a card from the Sherlock Holmes Bookshop and Emporium."

"I was wondering how I got dragged into this."

"You don't deal in rare books, but I'm thinking that, as neither Mary Ellen nor Charmaine had any real interest in collecting, they wouldn't know that, and they both figured you'd be the place to buy the magazine."

"How convenient for Charmaine that I was advertising for a summer shop assistant."

"Exactly. How long did she work for you before all this began?"

"About two weeks. There was always something about her I didn't care for. I couldn't put my finger on it, and I know it seems like hindsight now."

"You have good instincts, Gemma. And I, for one, made a mistake expecting you not to follow them. I'm sorry about that."

I gave him a smile.

"Mary Ellen lay low for a while, but she must have decided she needed to sell the magazine while she still had it. The Kents were searching for her and wanted it and the jewelry back pending the result of the court decision on the validity of the will."

Bread popped out of the toaster, and I put it onto a plate and dished up the eggs. I placed in the food in front of Ryan.

"You not eating?" he said.

"Not hungry." I sat down and cradled my teacup. "Eventually, Mary Ellen did arrive at the Emporium, and who did she see but Charmaine, working under the name of Ruby."

"They recognized each other, and both knew what the other was doing there."

"Ruby offered Mary Ellen a deal," I said. "If she handed over the magazine, she'd see that Mary Ellen got a cut. Better to get something than risk losing everything if the court case went against her. Which it almost certainly would."

"You're right again."

"Ruby disappeared from the shop around the time Mary Ellen came in. We were busy, and I was annoyed at her for taking her break at such a bad time. They must have cut this deal, and then Mary Ellen left. Mary Ellen had no intention of giving up full ownership of the magazine, so she hid it where she thought it would be safe until she could come back and get it. In my shop, among the books and magazines we sell. A forest is the best place to hide a tree, isn't it? My staff and I don't wear name tags, so Mary Ellen might not have even realized Ruby worked for me. Unfortunately for both of them, I found it almost immediately. Ruby got a glimpse of it before I asked her to leave. She would have realized then and there that Mary Ellen had no intention of honoring their deal."

"So she went around to the hotel and killed her." Ryan mopped up the last of his eggs with the last of the toast.

"No honor among thieves."

"Ruby then came here, to your house, to search for the magazine but was interrupted when we arrived."

"And Elaine? Why kill Elaine Kent, her aunt?"

"According to Charmaine, Elaine and Mary Ellen were friendly when Mary Ellen was living at the house. Elaine and Colin's marriage was on the rocks . . ."

"As we know. In that case, it's likely Elaine and Mary Ellen arranged for Elaine to be in the Emporium at the same time as Mary Ellen. Mary Ellen must have been planning to offer the magazine to me, and Elaine was there to watch her back. The tour leader told me Elaine was late getting onto the bus and appeared to be flustered when she did. It's likely she and Mary Ellen talked, and they decided the plan had to change if Ruby was hanging around." The bus tour guide had said she didn't know why Elaine had come on that trip, as she was not friends with any of the other women and not much of a bridge player. Obviously, it was because she'd seen the visit to the Emporium listed as part of the tour schedule. "Trying to seem like one of the members of the tour group, Elaine bought a book. *How to Think like Sherlock*. You'd be surprised how many people I meet in the shop believe he was a real person. As if anyone could have a thought process like his. Why are you smiling?"

"Why not smile? A successful conclusion to a difficult and complex case." He lifted his mug in a toast. Violet barked her agreement.

"Anyway," I continued, "when Mary Ellen and Elaine saw, of all people, Charmaine, a.k.a. Ruby, in the store, the plan was canceled on the spot. I'm guessing they had a similar scheme for the jewelry, to try to sell it under the table. I wonder why Ruby didn't take the jewelry from the hotel room after killing Mary Ellen."

Ryan studied me. "How'd you know the jewels were in her hotel room?"

"A logical assumption. She brought the magazine to the Cape with her, thus I assume she brought the jewels also." I smiled at him.

He looked as though he didn't believe me, but he didn't press the point.

"Ruby must have killed Mary Ellen only moments before we called up. It's easy enough to get someone to open the door to their hotel room—just call out 'housekeeping' or something similar. She was interrupted before she could search the room, very likely when the receptionist rang the room for me. She slipped out in case someone followed up the phone call and came upstairs looking for Mary Ellen. Which, of course, is exactly what happened. When we got out of the elevator, we went in the wrong direction, and I called Jayne back. If Ruby hadn't already left the room, my voice would have alerted her. She didn't have a key, so she had to leave the door off the latch." I called up the image of the hotel corridor as Jayne and I arrived at room 245. "The room was at the end of the hallway, and I heard the door to the staircase squeak. Hotels are busy places, and I paid it no mind. Ruby had been standing there, watching us. She saw us go into the room, and we came out immediately. I told Jayne to run and call the police. Ruby would have realized I knew enough about the value of the magazine to want to secure it. Jayne and I both carried small purses that day, nothing nearly large enough to contain a bound magazine. Thus Ruby would have concluded we didn't have it on us. She knows I keep my car at home and walk to work every day. Therefore, as we drove to the hotel, I had to have gone home in the interim. Logically, that would be where the magazine was. Knowing we'd be tied up with the police for a long time, she headed for my house to search."

"You've got it all thought out."

"Unfortunately, not until it was almost too late. What did she tell you about Elaine?"

"Elaine, so Ruby told us, wanted revenge on the cheating Colin. What better way than to take his mother's jewelry? She was planning to divorce Colin, and she knew she'd

296

never get it in a settlement. Mary Ellen and Elaine came to an agreement. Elaine would argue in court that Mr. Kent had told her he was so grateful to his nurse that he wanted to leave her items of significance. In return, Mary Ellen would share the jewelry with Elaine. That's only Ruby's speculation, but it rings true to me. When Elaine heard of the murder of Mary Ellen, she leapt immediately to the correct conclusion and, instead of calling us, she foolishly blackmailed Ruby. We never released any information to the public about the jewelry, so Elaine must have assumed Ruby had taken it after killing Mary Ellen. She demanded the jewels in exchange for her silence. But Ruby didn't have the jewelry and wouldn't have handed it over in any case . . ."

"And so Elaine had to die." The day of Elaine's death, Ruby started work at noon. She would have had plenty of time to drive to Boston in the early morning, kill her aunt, and get back to West London.

Ryan pushed himself to his feet with a sigh. "I'd better get going. It's going to be another long day tomorrow. You might be interested to know that I contacted Grant Thompson and told him he can examine the magazine again. We've also got a jeweler coming to have a look at the gems. They're both coming at ten."

"I might just drop by," I said.

Violet and I walked with Ryan to the back door. He put his hands on my shoulders and looked into my eyes. If he'd kissed me, I would have kissed him back. But he did not. Instead he said, "What am I going to do with you, Gemma Doyle?" and walked away into the night.

Chapter 20

I continued reading *The Moonstone* after Ryan left. The tale of an enormous diamond stolen from mines in India leading to betrayal and murder on an English country estate seemed appropriate for the night. The rising sun had barely crossed the horizon when Donald Morris rang.

"Gemma, the most marvelous thing has happened. The Kent estate is opening their library for a viewing by the Speckled Band . . ."

"The what?"

"That's the Boston Chapter of the Baker Street Irregulars. I've been invited to join them. We have one hour only to examine the contents. I'm leaving now. I have to be there by ten. This is beyond my wildest dreams. I'll be in touch if I see anything you or Arthur might be interested in." He hung up before I'd had time to tell him to have fun.

I arrived at the West London police station promptly at ten o'clock. I met Grant Thompson as he was coming up the steps, and we walked into the building together.

"Excited, Gemma?" he asked me.

"Not particularly."

"Why not? This is a big deal. It might well be the real thing."

"I already know the value of the magazine, Grant."

"You do not."

"I do. It's elementary."

Ryan opened the inner doors for us.

"Okay," Grant said. "Let's have a bet. We'll both write down what we suspect to be the estimated value of the magazine at auction and ask Detective Ashburton here to hold the guesses until we've seen it. Person who's closest wins and the other one has to take him . . . or her . . . to dinner at the Blue Water Café tonight. Deal?"

"Deal," I said.

He took a pad of paper out of his brief case and ripped off two sheets. He handed me one. I jotted down the dollar amount, folded the paper, and gave it to Ryan. Grant did the same.

"Mr. Conrad, the jeweler, is in an interview room with Detective Estrada," Ryan said. "I'll take you two to the magazine."

Uniformed officers and civilian staff stopped what they were doing to watch us pass. I suppose the unveiling of a magazine with the potential value of half-a-million dollars isn't something they see every day.

Ryan unlocked the door, and we went in. The unadorned room was painted industrial beige. A single table sat in the center of the room, bolted to the floor. Three chairs were arranged around it.

The magazine, still wrapped in plastic, was the only item on the table.

Grant put his briefcase down and opened it to reveal the tools of his trade arranged within. He slipped on a pair of white gloves and took a deep breath. Ryan leaned closer. I was the only one who took a seat.

Very gently, Grant slipped his hand into the plastic and took out the bound magazine. The golden gilt script glimmered in the harsh overhead light. He opened it slowly and carefully, revealing the magazine cover. *Beeton's Christmas Annual*. December 1887. The man rising from a desk chair to switch on a lamp. *"A Study in Scarlet* by A. Conan Doyle."

Grant held a magnifying glass to his eyes and bent close. For a moment, in profile with his strong nose and chiseled cheekbones, he looked very much like a modern Sherlock Holmes. His look of delighted anticipation faded. He quickly flipped the page.

He groaned, threw the magnifying glass onto the table, and stepped back.

"What's the matter?" Ryan said.

I didn't bother to put on white gloves to feel the pages. "Computer paper. The contents have been printed by a computer. The cover is moderately well done, good enough to fool an expert without close examination, but the interior wouldn't deceive anyone who bothered to so much as glance at it."

"So it's fake?"

"Completely and totally." Grant ripped off his gloves in disgust. "Literally not worth the paper it's printed on."

Ryan unfolded the two pieces of paper we'd handed him. "Grant, you guessed five hundred thousand. Let's see what Gemma said. Five dollars and seventy five cents."

"How did you know?" Grant said. "You told me you never opened it."

"I didn't have to. By all accounts, Kurt Frederick Kent Jr. hated Mary Ellen Longton. He described her as a tyrant. He wanted his family to fire her, but Colin couldn't be bothered. Kurt was an old man, his health rapidly failing. He lived alone in his private suite, attended only by his nurse, Mary Ellen. Even his granddaughter Charmaine, who we know as Ruby, had abandoned any pretext of being fond of him or interested in his hobby. He was frail and dying, but he was still far sharper than anyone realized. He let Mary Ellen persuade him to change his will to leave something to her. His Holmes collection had been extremely important to him for a good part of his life, never mind his late wife's jewels. What better way to get back at Mary Ellen than to pretend he was leaving her items of value? I briefly considered that Ruby might have hastened his death, but Ruby didn't pay sufficient attention to him in his last months to slowly administer poison. Mr. Kent knew he was close to death, but he had one last joke to play on the people who'd made his final days a misery."

"Wow!" Ryan said.

The interview door flew open. Louise Estrada stood there, her face like a thundercloud. "You'll never guess."

"The jewels are fake," I said. "Two people died for nothing."

My phone rang. "Let me take this call, please. I'm expecting another update."

"Gemma!" Donald screamed. "There's nothing here! You might get ten dollars a pound for the books on the shelves. There's not a first edition to be seen, not even any seconds! The letters between Sir Arthur and his publisher are photocopies.

Photocopies! Someone's drawn a mustache onto his face in the reproduction photograph." I had to strain to hear him over the noise in the background. I might have heard someone weeping uncontrollably.

"Jayne's always looking for tea sets to use in Mrs. Hudson's. Is there anything like that?"

"Tea sets! How can you talk about tea sets at a time like this?" he wailed.

"Drive carefully, Donald." I put the phone away. Grant and the two detectives were staring at me. "Mr. Kent's businesses have been in decline for a long time. When he became ill and his son Colin took charge, the decline only accelerated. Kurt might not have liked his offspring much, but I'm guessing he did what he had to do to try to save the companies. He's been selling off his collection for a long time. All the items sold at auction to unnamed collectors that Donald was so excited about? They were coming *out* of the Kent collection, not *into* it. He didn't want anyone to know he was desperate, so the sales would have been conditional on the seller's identity being kept secret."

"Poor guy," Grant said.

"His *Beeton's* was probably sold a long time ago. It might even be the one that went up for auction in 2010. He didn't get the price he wanted, and Sotheby's withdrew it, but he could have sold it directly to an individual. Same, of course, for the jewelry."

"Why have the fakes made?" Estrada asked.

"He didn't get on with his family, as we have seen. He probably thought this was the best way of doing what he had to do without them being any the wiser. In fairness, the children might have objected to the selling of their mother's jewels for sentimental reasons. Maybe he wanted a copy of the *Beeton's* so he could remember what he once had."

Silence fell over the room.

"I think," I said. "I would have gotten on with Kurt Frederick Kent Jr. extremely well."

Chapter 21

Colin Kent came into the Emporium in the afternoon. He did not look happy, and I assumed he'd been told the bad news about his inheritance. He carried a plastic bag, and I didn't have to be Sherlock Holmes to guess at the contents.

"I've been told you were there when the book expert examined the magazine," he said.

"Yes."

He took it out of the bag. "Do you want it? I'll sell it to you."

"Sure," I said. "Five dollars and seventy-five cents?"

"Done."

When he'd left, I tore the cover page out of the binding, found a cheap frame in the storage room, and framed the cover. I hung it behind the counter and thought it looked very nice there indeed.

* * *

As promised, Grant took me to dinner at the Blue Water Café that night. Not entirely sure I wanted the evening to turn into a date, I suggested Ryan and Jayne join us. After leaving the police station, I'd gone straight to the Emporium where, not having an assistant anymore, I'd remained all day. In a momentary lull, I made a couple of phone calls and found a local berry farmer more than eager to supply the tea room. We'd been busy at three forty, when Jayne and I normally met for our daily business chat, so I hadn't had a chance to tell her about the events of the morning.

I was the first to arrive at the restaurant, and I asked the hostess to let Andy know we were here and to ask him to join us for a drink if he could get away.

I had not invited Robbie, but he came with Jayne anyway. He dropped into a seat, snapped his fingers at the waitress, demanded a beer, and then spent more time than I thought proper regaling Grant and Andy with the story of how he'd overpowered Ruby and saved my life. He was thinking, he told us, of abandoning his current art project and painting the darker side of Cape Cod. Ryan stared out over the calm waters of the harbor, and Grant attempted to surreptitiously check his phone.

Andy had one drink and then stood up. "I have to get back to the kitchen. Nice seeing you all. Uh, good night Jayne."

"Night," she called, wiggling her fingers.

"Can you get me another beer on your way, buddy?" Robbie said. "Thanks. Hey, there's Irene." He called and waved. "Why don't you join us? Did you hear what happened last night?"

Irene was on her own, and she didn't have to be asked twice to sit down. She pulled up a chair. "Exciting stuff. The chief gave a press conference this afternoon. It was long on facts but short on juicy details. I've been looking for you,

Gemma, and I thought you might be here. You going to give me the scoop?"

"It's before the courts," Ryan said.

"The chief didn't say where the arrest took place or under what circumstances, but I heard there was lots of police activity outside your house last night, Gemma."

I sipped my drink.

"You can talk to me," Robbie said. "I was the one who brought her down. And let me tell you, it was touch and go for a while there."

"Not now," Ryan said. "If you're going to give a statement to the press against my advice, don't do it in my presence."

"When it's over," I said to Irene. "I'll tell you all about it, like I promised. But not until then."

"Fair enough. In the meantime, maybe you can clarify one thing for me. The chief said the items believed to be the motive for Mrs. Longton's murder were of no monetary value. Is that true?"

I nodded. "Drop in tomorrow and you can see the new addition I've added to the walls of the Emporium. It will remind me not to take things at face value."

Ryan and Jayne both laughed. "As if you ever do," Ryan said.

"I feel sorry for Roy Longton," I said. "Although I probably shouldn't. Despite what he said to create public sympathy, he and his mother weren't at all close. Has he been told that his so-called inheritance won't get him a cup of coffee at Starbucks?"

"He's been told, but he doesn't believe it. It's a plot cooked up by the Kents and their high-priced lawyer to cheat him."

Irene attempted to hail a passing waitress. The waitress pretended not to see.

"It's time art faced up to the darker side of life," Robbie said. "Don't you think, Ryan? You must see some things you don't talk about."

"Never," Ryan said flatly.

Jayne shifted in her seat, and I realized she was embarrassed. At last, the appeal of Robbie was beginning to wane.

I leaned over and whispered in her ear. "I forgot to ask Andy what the special is tonight. Why don't you go into the kitchen and find out for us."

"Good idea." Jayne pushed her chair back.

"I'm thinking morgue shots mixed with the standard tourist stuff," Robbie said. "Shock people out of their complacency."

* * *

When Jayne came back from the kitchen, Robbie was still talking, Irene was trying to attract a waiter's attention, and Grant and Ryan were holding their phones under the table. Jayne slid her chair closer to me.

"I made a couple of calls this afternoon," I said. "I found you a local berry farmer who's more than delighted to start supplying the tea room."

"Great."

Robbie paused for breath, and Ryan put away his phone. He gave me a big smile. Heat rushed into my face, and I smiled back.

Jayne looked at Ryan. She looked at me. She looked back at Ryan and then abruptly downed the rest of her drink. "Wasn't that fun? Come on, Robbie, let's go."

"What? We haven't eaten yet."

"I'm cold. There're plenty of tables inside."

I eyed her sleeveless sundress. It was so warm out, I'd taken off my sweater earlier and draped it over the back of my chair. "I can give you my cardigan."

"No. That won't be enough. Irene, you'll get better service inside, you know. Grant, I've been wanting to talk to you about book collecting. That must be so fascinating. I want to hear all about it."

"You haven't been interested before," I said.

"Sure I have. I just haven't met the right person to ask. Now I have."

"But Uncle Arthur . . ."

Robbie lumbered to his feet. "I guess you better come With us then, buddy. Gemma said you're paying."

"Andrew warned me that they're almost out of the flounder. Better hurry and order," Jayne said.

I glanced at Ryan. He gave me a shrug and picked up his beer bottle. I began to collect my handbag and cardigan.

"The only table inside by the windows is for four. Sorry," Jayne said. She dragged Robbie away. Irene followed. Grant looked at Ryan and touched the first two fingers of his right hand to his forehead in a salute. And then he walked away.

"Did that seem odd to you?" I asked Ryan.

He laughed. "No odder than anything else that happened this week."

Acknowledgments

I came up with the concept for this series while relaxing on the dock at Barbara Fradkin's cottage during our annual writers' "retreat" (much retreating, not so much writing) where Barbara and Robin Harlick helped me toss ideas around. The best part of being a writer, as I have said many times, is the friends I have made and the people I have met. People such as Cheryl Freedman, who provided helpful comments and suggestions on the manuscript that turned into this book.

I'd like to thank my agent, Kim Lionetti, for believing in this series, and for the good people at Crooked Lane, particularly Matt Martz and Sarah Poppe, for making it a reality.

I wrote this book during my time as the board chair of the Crime Writers of Canada, where Cathy Ace, Melodie Campbell, Vicki Blechta, and Alison Bruce made the job easy, giving me the time to write.